MORE THAN LOVE

STONE RIVER
BOOK 3

KAY LYONS

KINDRED SPIRITS PUBLISHING

Kay Lyons, Author (Pinterest)

SIGN UP FOR KAY'S NEWSLETTER AND RECEIVE FREE BOOKS, UPDATES ON NEW RELEASES, CONTESTS, PRE-RELEASE BOOK INFORMATION, EXCLUSIVES AND MORE!

MORE THAN LOVE
A STONE RIVER NOVEL

SIGN UP FOR KAY'S NEWSLETTER TO RECEIVE UPDATES ON NEW RELEASES, CONTESTS, PRE-RELEASE BOOK INFORMATION, EXCLUSIVES AND MORE!

1

The rich smell of coffee and decadently sweet baked goodies filled the air inside of Cuppa Jo's, and despite her early morning breakfast, Jolie Carter found herself fighting the tempting aroma of the pumpkin spice bread drizzled abundantly in shiny vanilla icing.

Such a weak will, Jo-Jo.

As it always did, the overly critical sound of her mother's voice filled Jolie's head, souring her mood but ending her desire to snag one of the pumpkin slices from the display case.

Jolie grabbed her water bottle from the counter and took a long sip as she walked into the rear storage section to get a new supply of coffee cups. She shoved the plastic-wrapped cups under her arm and took another long sip, wishing someone would create a calorie-free substitute for all the pound-adding goodies that went so well with her gourmet coffee business.

She reentered the area behind the counter and stooped to stow the cups in their proper place only to find herself face-to-glass with a sealed container of replacement pumpkin bread, waiting for its turn to go on display. Shaking her head, she took another large swig of water as she stood.

"Smells good."

Startled by the sudden appearance of Nathan Quinn—how had he entered without her hearing the chime on the door?—she choked and coughed and struggled to catch her breath.

Quinn leaned over the counter separating them and pounded gently on her back with one hand while grabbing a napkin with the other, handing it to her so she could wipe her watery eyes. "Th-thanks," she gasped, still coughing.

"Didn't mean to startle you."

But he does it so well, she thought.

She wiped her eyes and her now-running nose and fought for composure. A mere month ago, one of her best friends had married Quinn's best friend and business partner, officially making her and Quinn acquaintances. But no matter how many times she found herself in the same room as the tall, imposing man with his raspy, damaged voice and intimidating physique, she couldn't get used to it —to him. He was too...much. "It's fine," she said, clearing her throat as she moved away from the counter and out of reach. "What can I get you?"

She tried, as she always did, not to look at the half-circle scar on his throat, but her gaze fell to the thin, jagged line crossing the front of his otherwise tanned skin. Obviously the cut hadn't been fatal, though she imagined he'd spent quite a long time fighting for his life as a result. How had it happened? Why? She wanted to ask but wouldn't let herself.

"Large coffee, black." Quinn's expression darkened to an even more imposing frown, and she wondered if he'd caught her staring.

Coffee, she reminded herself.

His order didn't surprise her. By all accounts, Quinn appeared to be a basic kind of man. He wore jeans and T-shirts, well-worn shoes that looked surprisingly expensive but aged with use.

No, a surprise would have been Quinn asking for one of her chocolate-whipped-and-dairy-laden drinks that rivaled the big-name coffeehouse chains. But then, given his physique, he would burn the calories off in no time. No man obtained those kinds of muscles from sitting in a chair.

But if Quinn wasn't prone to a sweet tooth, what were his vices?

Yet another question you aren't going to ask.

She filled his request, aware of Quinn's gaze following her the entire time. "What brings you to, um, town?"

Making idle chitchat with customers was one of her strengths. Something she'd forced her painfully shy self to learn to do.

But with Quinn... chitchat didn't come easy.

She peeked at him over her shoulder, taking in his six-foot-plus height, broad shoulders and chest, arms barely contained by the sleeves of the black T-shirt he wore. A baseball cap covered short hair the color of her most decadent mocha grind, and he had several days' worth of shadow lining his jaw and cheeks.

She let her gaze drift, noting the scrolling tattoo trailing down his left arm from beneath the shirt sleeve and over his thick bicep.

"Careful."

"Huh?" Hot coffee poured over her fingers and scorched. "Ow!"

She set the cup down with a bang, spilling even more of the expensive brew, and waved her fingers in the air in a poor effort to cool them.

She turned and startled again, coming nose-to-chest with Quinn, who had apparently jumped the counter to get to her so quickly.

"Give me your hand."

He didn't give her a chance to respond. He simply took hold of her wrist and tugged her to the sink, flipping the tap to full blast before shoving her hand beneath the cool water. If it hadn't felt so good, she would've taken him to task for moving behind the counter, but she found herself lacking when it came to words.

Get a grip, Jo. He's just a man.

A big, unsettling, disturbing man who always watched her, seemingly as aware of her as she was of him whenever he was near.

"Better?"

Did Quinn ever use more than five words in a sentence? Better yet, could *she* ever use more than a handful of words in talking to him? "Yes."

She pulled her hand from his and grabbed a nearby towel, ignoring the painful sting in her fingers. "Thanks for the, um, save."

"No problem."

"Let me get your order," she said. "And the— the ten dollars in change you left last time."

"Just trying to help a new business."

No one in this economy had ten dollars to waste. And if he did, she couldn't accept it when there were other businesses in Stone River and the college community around Zailer University struggling a lot more than she was. The coffee business was brisk. It was amazing how hard people would dig for spare change to fund their habit. Not that she was complaining.

Ignoring him as best she could, she grabbed the cup she'd poured for him and dumped a bit of it down the sink before wiping the cup thoroughly to remove the mess. Finally she added a lid, grateful the simple task was complete. "Here. On the house. For the rescue."

Quinn accepted the cup but didn't move.

"You seem distracted. Everything okay?"

Other than seemingly hallucinating on her way into work and making a fool of herself just now, she was peachy.

Jolie ignored his query and slid along the edge of the counter to avoid further contact. She made her way to the moveable section, waiting for him to follow her and go back to the proper side. "I'm fine."

"Sure about that?"

Would he drop it already? Surely she wasn't the only woman who got... *tongue tied* when he was around. "Positive."

If the *Besties* could see her now, she'd never hear the end of it. They'd tease her about her clumsiness and encourage her to flirt with Quinn. To *smile,* at the very least. But Quinn wasn't her type, not that she really had one.

All she knew was that Quinn was former military turned private contractor/mercenary before he left that life to stay stateside.

Based on the few things Emma had said, Quinn's past was secretive and dangerous and something he never discussed. "Have a good day," she said, quickly lowering the divider. "If you talk to the honeymooners, tell Em I hope she's having fun."

Emma had tutored Ian MacGregor, a blinded former soldier, in ways to come to terms with his blindness before falling head over heels for the man.

Emma and Ian had tied the knot the first week of September but had waited another month to take their honeymoon, just so Emma, who had recently regained her sight after fourteen years of blindness, could see the glorious colors of fall on the drive to board a plane to St. Lucia. Quinn had driven them to the coast since Emma hadn't mastered driving just yet, put them on a plane, and a military buddy of Ian's on R&R had met them on the island to do double duty as tour guide and guard.

Due to his inability to see, Ian had issues with making sure Emma stayed safe, especially after what had happened to her recently when one of Emma's students had stalked her.

"Will do."

Quinn turned away just as the chime on the door sounded, announcing a customer's arrival. Jolie exhaled in relief and focused her attention on the patron walking in, but her smile of welcome froze on her face. She choked again, unable to catch her breath or move. "*Quinn*," she said before he could walk out the door. "Y-you forgot something."

Quinn froze with his hand on the push-bar of the door, his gaze zeroing in on her before sliding to the man who'd just entered.

"Give me a minute," she said to Quinn, trying to keep the unease out of her voice. "Have a seat?"

Her heart pounded in her chest, and for a brief few seconds, she actually felt the room whirling a bit. *Please don't leave me.*

"Yeah, no problem," Quinn said, idly moving toward the tables and chairs and displays she had featuring coffees, teas, books by local authors, and other odds and ends the university town seemed to favor.

She stared at the man now standing across from her, gazing at her with a quizzical expression, as if he knew her but couldn't place her.

Was it possible? Could he *not* know her? Recognize her?

"I'd like a large coffee, three creams, two sugars. And one of those," he said, pointing to one of the brownies in the glass case. "But you can finish with him first."

"No hurry," Quinn quickly said, countering the offer.

Her hands trembled when she grabbed the brownie and shoved it into a bag. The coffee was next, and as she placed the items on the counter, she realized it was the fastest she'd ever completed an order.

"What do I owe you?" the man asked.

Money. He needed to pay. She kept her head low so that her hair slid forward and hid her face from view. "Four fifty-three."

"Keep it," he said, handing her a five. "Have a good day."

She stared at the five-dollar bill, vaguely hearing the chime on the door sound as Blake Parker left her business and went on with his life even though his sudden appearance had just shattered hers.

Hot yet numb, she placed the bill in the cash drawer and counted out the difference, adding it to the empty tip jar by the side of the register.

Each drop of the coins pierced her ears and mocked her.

Forty-seven cents. Was that really all she was worth?

"What was that about?" Quinn asked.

Quinn's raspy, injured voice pulled her out of her dazed state, and now that Blake was gone, she realized because of her haste to not be alone with him, she owed Quinn an explanation. Her mind scrambled and finally hit on her earlier comment about returning Quinn's too-generous tip. She had forgotten about it after getting burned, but it was the perfect excuse now.

She hit the button on the cash register once more and retrieved a ten-dollar bill, holding it out to him.

"I don't want it, Jolie."

"Please," she said, only then noticing how badly the bill trembled in her grasp. She lowered it to the counter and shoved it toward him. "Take it."

A long moment passed with Quinn staring at her face. Her cheeks were flushed, and sweat beaded on her forehead and at her temples. She felt it gathering and hoped Quinn didn't notice.

"Did you know that guy?"

She wet her dry lips and tried to shrug casually. "Don't laugh, but I-I thought for a second there he was one of the fugitives from the news this morning." She forced a laugh that emerged shrill and off-key, and winced. "Silly, huh? I-I mean, why would a fugitive stop for coffee, right? Sorry to keep you." Jolie wrapped her arms around her waist and squeezed, her nails digging into her skin through her loose blouse. Harder, until pain cleared the fog from her mind. *Please, God.* "Guess I'm jumpier than normal. You know, after what happened with Emma."

Quinn's dark green eyes narrowed on hers. He didn't believe her. And why would he when she was a horrible liar? But it wasn't like she could tell him the truth.

"You're sure?" he asked, his gaze shifting over her face.

She squared her shoulders and managed a nod. She'd been taken by surprise and shocked by Blake's sudden appearance but— She was smarter and stronger now, not a stupid, naive little girl. "Yes. I'm fine. Take the money. Use it to buy more coffee later," she said.

"I'll do that— If you promise to call if you need me."

She nodded again and kept a smile pinned to her cheeks until Quinn finally turned and left the coffeehouse.

All too quickly, she realized she couldn't move. Her feet were planted on the beautifully stained wood floor as though glued there by the varnish, her legs locked, body frozen. She gazed at the sidewalk on the other side of her store window as passersby stopped to chat with one another, inserted coins into the parking meters, and window-shopped the main street closest to Zailer University. As life moved on at its regular pace while she...

The pain in her sides finally registered, and she looked down, realized she stood there hugging herself, her nails clenched into her body, releasing the scream she couldn't voice because, inside, she fought the urge to do something she hadn't done in a very long time.

Ten years, six months, five days...

The accomplishment was there, a number tallied in her journal every morning. But the overwhelming urge was too strong to ignore, and she moved along the counter, thankful that her normally bustling business was presently empty. The glass tip jar drew her like a beacon, and she stared at the forty-seven cents lining the bottom.

She glanced up long enough to see if anyone was near the entrance before taking the jar with her into the back and hurtling it as hard as she could onto the floor. It shattered with a sharp explosion that did nothing to soothe her pain.

She stared at the pieces, at the mess, anger and bitterness welling up inside her because, like her life, it was another mess she now had to clean up.

Moaning, she dropped down and quickly gathered them up, scrambling across the floor on her knees paying no attention to the tiny, prickling pieces jabbing into them.

Blake's face appeared in her mind, and she whimpered as she sat back, a long glass shard in her hand.

Forty-seven cents.

That was the price of her virginity. Her dignity. Her reputation. Family.

Every ounce of pain she'd felt flooded her. A tear slid down her cheek, and humiliation and fury took hold. A minute or two in her store and Blake Parker had reduced her to this. To pain, sharp and biting, then a few dark seconds of oblivion.

I'm sorry.

The bell chimed on the storefront entry, and Jolie slowly blinked her eyes open, stared at the blood now trickling down her thigh. Regret filled her, clashing with the numbness that never lasted long enough.

"Jolie?" one of her regular customers called out. Mrs. Patel. The woman came in every day after her trip to the library.

"B-be right there!" She reached for a roll of paper towels on the shelf and slapped a few of them on her leg, grabbing a towel next and tying it in a makeshift bandage. The pain left her teary-eyed, but the shame was worse.

She couldn't change what she'd just done; all she could do was start the count again. Try to do better. Always better.

Such a weak will, Jo-Jo.

Her wound momentarily cared for, Jolie straightened her skirt, washed her hands, and composed herself as best she could before shoving through the door to the front where her customer waited. "Hi, Mrs. Patel," she said to the smiling woman. "Your usual?"

2

———

Quinn left the coffee shop, disturbed by Jolie's unusual behavior and request for him to stick around. She'd tried to pass the incident off as a case of mistaken identity and nerves, but the expression she'd worn when he'd turned to face her... He'd seen that look too many times in his life. Terror. Horror. Fear. Jolie had been blown away by the man standing on the opposite side of the counter.

Thank God she felt comfortable enough with him to trust he'd keep her safe or die trying. Few people mattered to him in this world, but those in Emma and Ian's inner circle of friends topped the list.

Jolie especially.

Of all of Emma's friends, Jolie was the one who intrigued him most. Jolie held her emotions in check, more of an observer than a participant. It was a quality he identified with, but also one that made him ponder her reasons for holding back.

Quinn walked to his truck, taking his time and searching the street for any sign of the other man. The street was full of small businesses, all of them currently open, so the guy could've ducked inside any one of them.

Maybe he would just sit in his truck and enjoy his coffee, see if the guy reappeared.

Tucker, Emma's yellow Lab, spotted Quinn. The large dog shoved his head through the opening left by the lowered passenger window, and the big baby whined and licked his chops. Quinn shook his head. "No treat until you work."

And work the dog would. They had a big day of training ahead of them, which meant he didn't have time to spare. But the thought of something happening to Jolie cooled the need to hurry back up the mountain.

Quinn climbed into the truck and tossed the ten-dollar bill into the open console for future use. The money meant nothing to him. His needs were simple, and he had more stashes and offshore accounts than he'd need in two lifetimes.

He didn't like watching Jolie run herself ragged working nonstop, and if filling her jar with tens and twenties or whatever amount he managed to sneak in without her being aware helped her, it was worth it. She'd noticed last time because he'd been in too much of a hurry to be discreet, but she wouldn't catch him in the future.

The cool October morning breeze carried hints of warmth and the promise of another hot afternoon. This was his favorite time of year, when leaves changed and looked so pretty because of the fresh coat of color.

Quinn drank his coffee and surveyed the street, hoping the guy from Cuppa Jo's reappeared so he could get a better look.

Tucker butted his large head against Quinn's shoulder, demanding attention as only a drama-mutt could. The moment Quinn's hand landed on the dog's head, the big lug plopped down on the bench seat and shoved his head between Quinn and the steering wheel before performing an awkward roll so Quinn would rub the dog's belly. "You're pathetic, you know that?" he said to the animal, never taking his gaze from the sidewalk and busy street, even though he shifted his hand and rubbed Tucker's underside as expected.

Who was the master here?

He'd never had a pet. Up until Emma's arrival at the MacGregor house, when her kenneled dogs and service dogs-in-training had moved with her, he'd never spent much time with any animal. Foster families usually had enough mouths to feed without adding a chowhound.

But since partnering with Ian MacGregor, creating a security company situating normal, typically overlooked dogs into the lives of very important people as protection had quickly become a mission. As Ian's eyes, Quinn found himself looking forward to the time he spent in training, working with multiple dogs on a daily basis. The tasks soothed the sights and sounds of his past and all he'd done.

Coffee consumed, Quinn replayed the scene in his head as he placed the cup in the truck's holder to be dealt with later and started the engine. He could sit there all day and not see the guy again.

The man hadn't acted strangely, hadn't responded to Jolie's nervousness. She'd laughed at herself thinking she'd come face-to-face with a fugitive bent on getting his coffee fix, but there was nothing going on here other than Jolie's normal skittishness.

Despite her asking him to stay, he'd felt the way she'd flinched when he'd moved behind the counter and touched her. Jolie's small hand was red but not blistered, fragile; her flinching reaction was a reminder of the differences in their lives. Hardened soldiers gave him a wide berth on sight, but he didn't like it that Jolie was skittish around him. She couldn't take her eyes off his scar whenever she was near, her horror apparent in her expression.

Muttering under his breath at his thoughts, he backed the truck out of the spot and shifted gears. The partnership with Ian was an opportunity to stay in one place for a while, for however long he felt like staying. But settling down? Not his style.

Besides, Jolie was all flowing skirts and picket fences, books and coffee, while he had way too much blood on his hands. Buying a few cups of coffee to check on Jolie until Emma and Ian returned was as far as things could go.

Thirty minutes later, Quinn rounded the outside of the MacGregors' mountaintop home. He drove the truck around the house to the kennel behind and parked beside the newer-model motorcycle already there. Zack Dupré, Emma's half brother, appeared in the entrance of the stable-turned-kennel, covered in dog hair and soapsuds, soaking wet and visibly irritated. "The dogs get the bath. Not you," Quinn told the teen.

Zack planted his hands on his hips and shot Quinn a humorless glare about the same time that Goli, Emma's Great Dane, appeared. The large dog loved to be chased, especially at bath time, and bounded around the corner of the kennel before skidding to a halt at the sight of Quinn. She took a long look, tongue hanging out of her mouth as she panted. Goli glanced at Zack, and Quinn believed the dog actually grinned before she crouched down and sprang away, inviting Zack to chase her again.

"Ha," Zack said, his tone dry. "You're just in time. You can hold Goli."

Quinn shut the truck door before lifting Tucker's leash and waving it like a flag. No way was he getting in on that battle. "Can't. Behind on training."

The kid cursed and shook his head when Goli reappeared around the other side of the kennel, moving back and forth like a boxer waiting for the bell. The sight made Quinn wish he could pull up a chair with a cold drink and watch the show. Goli was in top form today.

"Do I at least get to help with the training when I'm done?" Zack lifted an arm and wiped at the suds, spreading even more in the act.

Since Zack was another person Emma expected Quinn to keep an eye on, he nodded. The kid needed something to look forward to after all the hassle. "We'll be in the yard."

The younger man let out a loud whoop and pivoted toward Goli, who immediately hunched down and waited for Zack's approach before leaping to the side out of reach. Quinn watched their antics for several seconds before tightening his hand on Tucker's leash, knowing the dog would like to join in on the game of tag. "Not now, Tuck. Not unless you want a bath."

Hearing the B word, Tucker put his head down and took off toward the side yard where they trained, the leash pulling taut until

Quinn put his feet in motion to keep from being dragged along for the ride.

In short order, Quinn had the training area set up with props and the necessary tools and treats and got to work.

To be used as a secret guard and protection for his future owner, Tucker had to obey every command without hesitation. Which meant practicing the hand signals and commands repeatedly until they became second nature.

Quinn put Tucker through a series of basic commands, treating and petting in praise when the dog successfully performed. By the time they were done with the easy stuff, Zack would be finished bathing Goli.

A thought formed, and Quinn chuckled, well able to imagine the younger man's indignity when he showed up and was asked to don the protective attack suit. "What do you say, Tuck?" Quinn murmured, rubbing Tucker's head. "Wanna get in on the fun?"

3

ny word from the honeymooners?" Morgan Ashley asked as she entered Cuppa Jo's later that morning.

Jolie turned and smiled at her friend, wondering how it was possible for someone to look so miserable and happy at the same time. Morgan always looked beautiful, and today was no exception. She wore khaki slacks, cuffed at the ankle, with cute, strappy wedges, a billowy, cream silk top, and enough bling and bangles and chunky jewelry to supply a store. With her salon-perfect hair and makeup, the former pageant and beauty queen looked ready to hit the stage. Or the local singles scene.

Morgan had initiated divorce proceedings after discovering her husband had a bad habit of cheating and lying. The divorce decree was due to arrive any day, and as soon as it did, the *Besties* planned to throw a divorce get-together to celebrate Morgan's freedom from a man who didn't yet know the treasure he'd lost. Jolie didn't know why Rory had found it necessary to cheat, but in doing so, he'd done major damage to Morgan's self-confidence. "Not according to Quinn," Jolie said without thinking.

Jolie wished she'd kept her mouth shut when Morgan's eyebrows shot up beneath her fringed bangs.

"When did you talk to him?" Morgan asked as she strolled toward the cash register.

Jolie placed another plastic-wrapped sandwich into the case in preparation for the lunch crowd. "He came in for coffee this morning."

"Did he leave another big tip?"

"No, and I returned that one, thank you." Jolie shook her head and turned away from her friend's inquisitive gaze.

She really had to monitor what she said to Morgan and Tasha about Quinn because they were making too much of Quinn's visits. Thankfully as soon as Emma returned, things would go back to normal, and Quinn wouldn't be driving down the mountain for a cup of coffee he could make at home. "What are you into today?" she asked, desperate to get Morgan's mind off the topic of Quinn. "Where's my little Camilla?" she asked, referring to Morgan's fourteen-month-old daughter.

"My mom has her today."

"Oh? Something going on?" Jolie asked.

When Morgan didn't answer, Jolie looked up to see her friend squirming and at a loss for words— something that *never* happened. "Morgan?"

"I'm doing it."

Jolie wasn't sure what that meant. "Pardon me?"

"Do you remember the contest I told you guys about at the beginning of the summer? Rory said I couldn't sign up because of taking care of the kids, right? I kinda forgot about it. But a few weeks ago, I talked to my mom, and even though she's not thrilled about the divorce—"

"She *still* thinks you need to get Rory back even though he's living with that woman?" Jolie asked, unable to believe Morgan's parents would want such a thing after seeing how the news had devastated Morgan.

"She's going to watch the kids for me so I can enter the bake-off and, *hopefully*, final in the cake design contest. And, yes, she does. At least until the kids are out of school."

"That's twenty years from now!"

"I told her no," Morgan said, sounding defensive.

"Good. I'm glad you did. And how wonderful that you entered the contest." Jolie forced a smile when another problem crept into her head and dimmed her enthusiasm.

"I know! I'm so excited," Morgan said, taking a seat at the narrow bar closest to where Jolie stood. "And I refuse to let Mom's other comments and doubts bring me down."

Jolie didn't ask what other things had been said. Truthfully, she wasn't sure she wanted to know. Because while Morgan's mom was usually great, Morgan's parents were very upset about Morgan's divorce, mostly because, to them, staying with Rory was better than Morgan's lack of a plan for the future.

Rory had agreed to pay child support, but being the jerk he was, Jolie highly doubted the man would pay up without a court-ordered wage garnishment. In the meantime, grocery bills, utilities, and the like were paid courtesy of sporadic payments from Rory, along with Morgan's savings and money she made from baking.

Jolie and the other *Besties* had chipped in and anonymously paid an electric bill, just so Morgan wouldn't lose her power or have to acquiesce to Rory's demands that Morgan take him back. Rory didn't want the divorce, but only because it meant disrupting his cushy life wherein Morgan cooked, cleaned, and took care of his every need while he kept a girlfriend on the side. One he refused to give up. "Good. I'm glad to hear it."

"I have so many ideas and designs in my head. And the grand prize. Did I tell you it's a cash prize? I could open my own bakery! Plus, the winner gets a magazine spread, and another write-up in a year's time to showcase how things are going."

"That's great." It was a lot of cash and great advertising, but Jolie had a hard time believing either would be enough to cover the cost of a start-up bakery that required special ovens and equipment and experienced employees, along with childcare, health benefits, and the like. And she hated to be a downer but— What if Morgan didn't win? What if, in the time she spent practicing and designing, she missed a job opportunity that was a sure thing?

"You're not happy for me," Morgan said, her gaze narrowing, mood instantly darkening in the face of Jolie's hesitation. "I can tell by your expression. Jolie... Seriously?"

"It's not that." Jolie backpedaled fast and tried to neutralize the situation. "*Of course* I'm happy for you. I'm thrilled! I just worry about you and the kids."

"We're fine," Morgan said. "It will all work out. If all else fails, maybe I can get a loan from my parents."

Jolie winced at the news. "Are you sure you want to do that? Maybe... you should still be job hunting. *Just in case.*"

Morgan's multiple bracelets banged together when she lifted her hands and ran her manicured fingers through her long, blond hair. "You don't think I can do this, do you? You don't think I'll win."

The chime on the door saved Jolie from having to answer. Jolie turned to see Tasha, Stone River's vet, crossing the threshold. "Please tell Morgan I do believe in her."

Morgan went off on a mini-rant to Tasha, and not for the first time, Jolie realized Emma was the glue that really held their foursome together. Emma was the peacemaker, the one who could always turn the tide so that they were laughing instead of bickering.

Tasha listened to Morgan for all of two minutes before cutting her off.

"Stop. We believe in you. You're stressing yourself out and taking it out on us. Jolie, make hers a decaf," Tasha ordered.

Morgan glared at Tasha before taking a deep breath and sighing in obvious temper.

"Fine. Maybe I am a little nervous, but job hunting? I can't even think of that right now," Morgan told them.

Morgan's expression revealed just how big a chore that posed for her, and Jolie's heart sank. "Morgan, I know it's hard to consider taking on a job with everything else you're going through, but you're going to be a single mom. You're going to have to work."

"*I know that*. But, guys, come on. It's different for you. You went to college. Both of you. I graduated high school. Big deal."

"Don't put yourself down," Tasha stated firmly. "You're smart. You can do anything."

"Yeah? Well, if that's the case— I want to win this contest," Morgan said, her gaze sliding from Tasha to Jolie and back again. "No offense to anyone, but I don't want to wait tables or shampoo dogs," she said, referring to the part-time work Jolie and Tasha had both already offered Morgan. "I'm really, really good at baking and designing. And maybe I don't have a concrete plan just yet, but I'll figure something out. I have to have faith, right? I'm just... still trying to figure out how single moms do it because I can't imagine leaving my babies at daycare so I can put food on the table. All because I was stupid enough to marry a cheating loser."

"We get that. But if you win," Jolie said softly, "you won't *be* home, Morgan. What then?"

"I'll still be able to spend time with them," Morgan argued. "If I own my own business, I'll make the rules. The kids can be in the store with me sometimes, and when they can't, maybe my mom and dad can."

"I think she's saying they've raised their kids, Mo," Tasha interjected softly. "And they're not young, much less in good health. Which means, before you get to the backup plan, you're going to need a backup for your backup."

Morgan pressed her palms to her forehead.

"Guys, I'm doing the best I can, okay? If I do well in the contest, instead of daycare or my parents, I could at least afford a babysitter. A good one," Morgan told them. "I hoped, of all people, you would support me. Guess I was fooling myself, huh?" she said, grabbing her bag.

"Morgan..." Jolie said.

"Stop," Tasha said. "Put that down right now. Look, we love you, Mo. But honestly? You've been a little off the rails since the whole Rory thing. We're just worried about you because we know you've got to start thinking long term. That's all Jolie meant."

Tasha snagged a cushioned barstool near the pastry case by Morgan and effectively blocked Morgan's exit short of Morgan knocking her over and making a run for it.

"That *is* what I meant." Jolie inserted Tasha's regular order into her hands. "And I guess you are thinking ahead if you've thought about hiring a babysitter to take the load off your parents," she said in an attempt to make peace.

"Oh, wow. You have no idea how much I need this today," Tasha said as she inhaled the fresh-brewed coffee smell.

"Bad day?" Jolie asked.

Tasha shrugged and glanced at Morgan. "Just busy. And for the record, you wouldn't *only* be washing dogs if you decided to take the job I mentioned."

Morgan was silent a long moment before she sighed.

"Thanks but... I'm still not interested. And enough about me. Have you heard from Owen since he went to see his sister?" Morgan asked in a deliberate bid to change the topic of conversation.

Tasha stared down at her cup, and Jolie noticed her friend biting her lower lip.

"Last night. He called to let me know he's investigating his sister's ex-boyfriend's death, and won't be available for a while," Tasha said, lifting her gaze and locking it on Jolie's. "Tell me again why I started a relationship with him?"

The quietly worded question left a wealth of silence in its wake.

Jolie's heart broke for Tasha. Having already buried her police officer fiancé who had died in the line of duty, Tasha had fallen into a complicated situation with one of the men who worked for Emma's brother-in-law in his personal security business. Being "unavailable" meant Owen Redd could be doing anything from acting as a bodyguard and personal shield to... whatever was required in investigating a death that required investigation. "Because you care for him?"

"And because he's nice," Morgan countered.

"Or because I'm a glutton for punishment," Tasha murmured, running her hands through her hair and shoving it back from her face. "If not for the fact I have a practice to run, I think I'd lose my mind. There's definitely something to that saying about idle minds being the devil's playground."

Morgan fiddled with one of her bracelets, her mouth pinched into a frown.

"Guys, I can *do* this. I know I can. But I need you to believe in me. I know I'm a little flighty and I can get scattered, but if you don't believe in me... I won't be able to believe in myself." Morgan sniffed and blinked hard, battling tears. "All I've ever heard from Rory is that I'm an airhead who can't do anything but have babies and keep house. I have no education, no formal training. But this is my God-given passion, and I need to— I *have* to make this work."

Jolie exchanged a glance with Tasha before they both nodded, a silent promise to set their doubting thoughts aside in the face of Morgan's despair. She needed their support, so she would have it. Period. That's what *Besties* were for, after all. "You can totally do it," Jolie said. "Nothing sells as well as the muffins and cakes you make for me."

"Yeah," Tasha added. "Ignore me, okay? I've taken a few hits over the years so I'm a little cynical. That's all."

"Maybe we're all cynical because of the men we're around," Morgan muttered. "Heaven knows Rory could make any woman cynical."

Tasha patted Morgan on the back, her tough love from earlier forgotten in the face of Morgan's plea.

"Might work for you and me, but what about her?" Tasha asked, indicating Jolie with the point of a single finger.

Morgan stared at Jolie but ignored Jolie's slight head-shake of warning.

"Quinn came to see her again," Morgan said with a sudden smile, her childcare and divorce woes forgotten in the face of that tasty bit of news.

"*Again*?" Tasha grinned from ear to ear. "He's become quite the gourmet coffee drinker. Who would've thunk it?"

"Don't." Jolie winced. "Quinn is... Ian and Emma's friend. He's only checking on me because of what happened between Emma and her crazy student. There is absolutely nothing going on between us, and there never will be."

"Uh-oh. Famous last words if I ever heard them," Morgan said. "She's doomed."

"Mmmhmm," Tasha added with more than a little attitude in the sound. "Totally."

"Will you two stop?" Jolie glared at them. "I'm not in the market for a man, and I don't know if I ever will be. Look at you two. Men are obviously more trouble than they're worth."

Tasha blinked at Jolie before turning to look at Morgan, then both of them shifted their attention back to Jolie once more. "What?" Jolie demanded, battling the urge to shift and squirm, or better yet, hide.

Tasha grinned. "Nothing. It's just nice to see some attitude coming out of Miss Prim and Proper."

"Yeah," Morgan quickly agreed. "After all these years of thinking you were pretty much a mouse, we just saw a glimpse of a lion."

For some reason, Jolie couldn't accept that as a compliment. Especially not when her thigh throbbed. "You think I'm a mouse?"

Tasha finished off her coffee and stood. "Can't come as much of a surprise, Jo." She pulled some bills from her wallet and frowned. "Where's the tip jar?"

Her heart thumped against her ribs, and heat crawled up her chest and neck. "It broke," Jolie told them, lifting her shoulder in a shrug. "I haven't replaced it."

"Yeah, well, grab a coffee can and get it out here," Tasha said as she tossed the ones onto the bar despite Jolie's protests. "I've gotta run. Bye!"

Jolie scrambled to retrieve the scattered bills off the counter to give back to Tasha, but she was long gone.

"Hey, now you're the one who needs to lighten up. We're teasing you," Morgan said as she grabbed her purse and stood. "We love you the way you are. You're just quiet, you know? But it's all good. Now, I'm gonna go buy some supplies to practice. See you later maybe?"

Maybe. Maybe not. Who wanted to be referred to as a *mouse*?

"Wait," she said, motioning for Morgan to step closer. The moment she did, Jolie tucked Tasha's tip into Morgan's tiny designer shirt pocket.

"What's that for?" Morgan asked, her expression revealing her surprise that Jolie would do such a thing.

"I'm proving to you that I believe in you. Put that toward your supplies," Jolie ordered. "And don't you dare try to give it back. I'm with you in this, okay?"

Once again, Morgan's eyes filled with tears, and she quickly blinked them away.

"Jo…"

"I mean it. Put it to good use," Jolie said.

Morgan nodded and waved a hand in front of her face to cool the tears brightening her dazzling blue eyes.

"Thanks."

"You're welcome."

"Jolie?" Morgan called over her shoulder once she had made her way to the door. "Maybe we've both got something to prove. I mean, it's not like a mouse would go and open her own coffeehouse, right?"

Jolie got the point. Not that it was subtle. "Right," she said, watching as Morgan flashed her infamous Miss Stone River smile and left the building.

Jolie watched Morgan through the window, saw Morgan's wave of good-bye and how more than one man turned to watch Morgan as she walked down the street. Morgan seemed oblivious to the attention she received from the opposite sex, her heart and head still mending from Rory's betrayal.

Jolie grabbed a nearly empty napkin dispenser and began to fill it, ignoring the cut on her thigh.

She wanted to be confident, self-assured. She had opened her own business, but she still had things to prove. Especially to herself.

And the first step to making that happen was to find out if that really was Blake Parker who had darkened her door.

4

Jolie spent the rest of the day serving coffee, making sandwiches, and keeping an eye out for Blake Parker or whoever the man was who'd sent her into such a tailspin. She never spotted the man again, and by the end of the evening, she had all but convinced herself the long days and late nights were to blame for believing her past had come to Stone River for a coffee fix.

The stress and fatigue were taking a toll, as if she needed proof she needed to hire more help. She didn't require professional counseling to tell her that with her history of self-harm, downtime was a necessary expense.

Soon, she promised herself. *You can hire someone else very soon.*

Putting it off only extended the problem, but interviewing candidates was one of her least favorite duties, yet it wasn't one she was comfortable delegating to Tommy or Elaine, her current employees.

Her gaze was drawn to Tommy, who bussed the corner table. He was a great help but more concerned with his schooling and future career than finding her a new barista.

Jolie busied herself with the details of running Cuppa Jo's and forced her mind to focus on facts. This past July marked fifteen years since she'd moved to Stone River to live with her grandmother. The anniversary of that momentous date had been swirling around in her mind, unearthing memories best forgotten.

July also marked the ten-year anniversary of her grandmother's passing. Combine the two, and the emotions tied to those traumatic events had to be the reason she'd thought her customer resembled Blake Parker. Begging the question— Would she live her entire life unable to move on and regretting that summer of extreme stupidity? Would it ever really go away? How many prayers had she said, wanting it to happen? Why hadn't it?

She gripped the coffeepot handle tight and stared into the dark brew.

Was it Blake? Or merely her worn-out body and mind playing tricks on her? How could she go about finding out? Where would she begin? Maybe the man had merely stopped on his drive through town. Maybe he had business here. Anything was possible— including the fact she might never set eyes on him again. She could drive herself truly insane with all of the what-ifs. So maybe, for her sanity's sake, she should put the incident behind her, unless she saw him again?

"Time for me to go," Tommy said. "You going to be okay?"

Jolie looked up in surprise. The busy afternoon and evening had flown by. "Yeah, yeah. Go. I'm good."

Her legs ached, her back throbbed, and she was exhausted, but that wasn't Tommy's fault. She couldn't continue to open and close on her own every day. But it wasn't like she had a family to go home to, or even pets. And she knew herself well enough to know she couldn't turn over the running of things to just anyone. Better to work. It helped keep her mind busy, focused on something other than the past.

Tasha was right. Idle hands did no one any good.

Waving good-bye to Tommy, Jolie left the counter with a rag and disinfectant in hand. All but two of the tables were empty because the more popular place to sit was in the comfy chairs and couch in the corner near the empty fireplace, or around on the other side. It was quieter there, and between the fireplace and the wall, and a person could sit undistracted by customers coming and going in a rush.

She wiped down one table, arranging chairs back to their proper positions, then moved around the fireplace and set things to rights.

Back in front, a sharp movement outside the coffeehouse window caught her attention, and she spied a couple of teenagers outside. The couple argued, and the guy attempted to grab hold of the girl's arm. The girl moved away and managed to sidestep the guy, but the larger boy quickly trapped the girl against the brick beside the window.

Jolie gripped the rag and spray bottle in her hands, unable to look away from the scene playing out. The guy snagged the girl's upper arms and lowered his head until they were nearly nose-to-nose. He said something to the girl Jolie couldn't hear, but the boy's expression... There was no mistaking that.

Images flooded her mind, and for the second time that day, she was rocked by a massive surge of fear and anger so great she staggered.

The way she'd been held down. Hands trapped. The awful, horrible words spewed into her face when she'd begun fighting in earnest.

The girl's yelp of pain broke the cycle of memories and snapped Jolie out of her trance. She ran for the door and out onto the sidewalk, not stopping until she stood with them, the bottle of disinfectant aimed at the boy's face. "Back off!"

The guy smirked and told her mind her own business.

"I said, *back off!*" Jolie lowered the squirt bottle to hit the teen in the chest and pulled the trigger.

"What the—!" the teen said, finally letting go of the girl.

When he faced Jolie, she lifted the bottle higher and aimed at his face once more. "There's bleach in it. Let her go and leave her alone, or you'll be making a trip to the emergency room."

A long, tense moment followed her words as the teen stood there cursing her, nostrils flaring. But finally he did as ordered, sneering as he took several steps away from the girl.

"Are you all right?" Jolie asked the young woman.

The girl was about sixteen, with long straight hair that showed no sign of curling even in the cooling dampness of the October evening. She had one arm crossed over her front, rubbing the spot where the boy had grabbed her.

Unlike most girls her age, she wasn't caked in makeup. She had on jean shorts and flip-flops, a chunky belt with bling on the buckle, and a white, ruffled top that dipped low in the front, revealing teasing glimpses of cleavage. The girl looked shaken and ill at ease, like she was embarrassed and wanted to run away but wasn't sure what to do.

"This is none of your business, lady," the boy said. "You didn't have the right to spray me." He cursed. "Look at my shirt. You're going to pay for it."

"You were *manhandling* her," Jolie argued.

"Damien, just go," the girl said. "I'm walking home."

"No way," Damien growled. "Come on. Let's get out of here."

"*No*," the girl said. "And you know this isn't about her."

"Kaylee, babe, we had a fight. Everybody does," Damien said.

"Just *go*," Kaylee said, not looking at Damien or Jolie now.

The teenage boy glared at Jolie before uttering another string of obscenities and stomping away.

Jolie waited, watching as the boy hopped over the closed driver's door of a new-model convertible Camaro and gunned the engine, squealing out of the street-side parking and into the night. "Come inside," Jolie said to the girl. "I'll get you some ice for that arm, and you can call your parents for a ride."

"No, I'm good," Kaylee insisted.

"I know it's none of my business, but I don't think you should be walking home alone... Kaylee, that's your name, right?" Jolie asked.

"Yeah."

"Well, Kaylee, either you come inside with me and call someone to pick you up, or you hang out until I can drive you home myself.

Or... I call the police and tell them what I saw, and then you can explain it all to the cop and to your parents."

"It was nothing," the girl insisted. "Why are you making such a big deal out of it?"

"Because it didn't look like nothing. And when he hurt you, it didn't *sound* like nothing," Jolie argued. "Who is he?"

The girl lifted and lowered her shoulder in a shrug.

"My boyfriend. He's harmless."

"Kaylee, harmless doesn't cause pain— or bruises. Boyfriends shouldn't grab you like that," Jolie said, trying to get through to the girl but seeing a shield cover Kaylee's face with every word.

"We had a fight. It's no big deal. I'm sure it won't happen again," Kaylee said. "So, is this your coffee place?"

Jolie recognized a dodge when she heard one, but she nodded, willing to chat up the girl if it meant she stuck around. "Yes. Come inside, and I'll make you a frappe, on the house."

"No, that's okay. I should probably get going. Thanks, though."

Kaylee began walking backwards at a rapid pace.

"Kaylee, stop." Jolie took several steps after the girl. "Let me drive you home."

"Thank you. Really. I'll be fine, though."

Short of following the girl and leaving Cuppa Jo's open with no one around to keep watch, there wasn't much Jolie could do but stare as the girl turned and raced up the street as fast as her flip-flops could take her.

"I'll follow her and make sure she gets home okay," Quinn said, appearing out of nowhere.

Jolie gaped at him. "Where did you—"

"Later."

Quinn took off on foot up the street with one of Emma and Ian's dogs on a leash. If she didn't know any better, Jolie would think he was merely walking the dog because, rather than pursue Kaylee directly, Quinn made a point of crossing the street up ahead yet keeping the girl in his sight.

Jolie watched as they faded into the night, then turned to look around the quiet street before going back into the coffeehouse.

She was on edge from the incident, so she used her adrenaline-born energy to finish wiping down the tables. Her customers slowly began to pack up textbooks and laptops and called it a night. At 8:58, she closed up and dimmed the lights, using the time until Quinn's return to prepare for her early morning tomorrow.

What would Tasha and Morgan have to say about him showing up twice in one day?

They should probably be upset that he was taking Emma's request to watch over the *Besties* so seriously when they were grown women perfectly capable of handling themselves. But she'd be lying if she denied that the entire time she'd stood there confronting Kaylee's boyfriend, in the back of her mind, she'd known Quinn was there. She'd... *felt him*.

Was that possible? She pondered her mixed emotions as time passed, but when Quinn didn't return, she let herself out of the building and locked up, searching the sidewalks for any sign of Quinn or the teens. Where were they? Had the boy waited for Kaylee up the street? Had something happened?

Jolie cruised through the quiet streets, looking for them on her way home, but gave up when she saw nothing except college kids and dog walkers making a final trip outside for the night.

A full, nerve-racking hour later, Jolie heard a soft knock on her front door. She hurried to the window and peeked outside, recognizing Quinn's broad frame. "What took so long?" she said without greeting, then winced at her rudeness. "Sorry. Is everything all right?"

"It took longer than expected because her boyfriend was waiting for her," Quinn said as he stepped into her home without an invitation.

Jolie backed up a step, uneasy with his entry but desperate enough for answers that she overlooked his intrusion. "What happened?" she demanded. "Is she okay?"

"Yeah. She refused to get into the car with him, so he rolled along beside her until they got to her house. They stayed outside on the porch, and he put the moves on her, but she was ticked enough to shut him down. He finally got the hint and left."

"But he left? For sure?" she asked, needing the reassurance.

Quinn frowned, and she forced herself to take a breath and calm the frantic beat of her heart. Quinn studied her much too closely, his gaze seeking answers.

"She's fine. I knew you'd worry, so I hung around until her father got home. I would have called, but I don't have your number," he added. "It's not listed."

"Oh. I— Yeah." Jolie sagged against the door, her thoughts on things best left in the past where they belonged. "I've never listed my number." She was a private person. The people who needed her number had it. Period.

"Who was he?" Quinn asked.

She blinked up at him. "Who was who?"

Quinn narrowed his gaze, and she squirmed beneath the intensity. Quinn unnerved her on a good day, but when he looked at her like that?

"The guy in the coffeehouse earlier today," he said patiently. "The one who made you ask me to stay."

The blood drained from her head, leaving her woozy. She opened her mouth to speak but couldn't find the right words. The cut on her leg throbbed, a reminder of the worst kind. "I told you," she said, finally finding her voice, "I thought I'd seen him on television. And I needed to return your tip."

"Sweetheart, don't ever play poker. You'd suck at it," he said, using more words than she'd ever heard him use at one time. "Now tell me —who was he?"

Sweetheart?

The air left her lungs at the endearment. She hugged her arms around her front and frowned up at him, wondering if she would ever get used to being around Emma's husband or his friends without feeling... uneasy. They were all so big and tall and brawny. Intimidating.

Caring and kind and willing to help at a moment's notice.

And let's not forget deadly.

Quinn's use of *sweetheart* in reference to her was unusual, but she knew not to take it seriously. All of Ian MacGregor's buddies used some sort of endearments when speaking to certain women, namely Emma and Tasha. It was something Jolie had noticed from the beginning. Sweetheart. Love. Honey. Maybe it was an extension of their southern upbringing, but the words weren't used in a sexist sense. More to convey tenderness— which was quite a concept considering the men were by no means guys who wore their hearts on their muscle-bulked sleeves. "Thanks for walking Kaylee home and making sure she was okay."

Quinn didn't move. Not even a blink.

"Quinn… It's late."

"You were terrified of that kid," he said in response to her pointed statement.

"He was *hurting* her."

"It was more than that," Quinn murmured. "You looked like you'd seen a ghost."

"Am I not supposed to care?" she asked, growing exasperated. "I didn't know if he'd listen to me or not. I didn't know if he'd back down, and *then* what would I have done?"

Quinn moved closer to where she stood and lowered his head to better see her face. "It was more than that," he repeated softly. "Your expression… It was like you'd lived it. Like it was happening *to* you."

She recoiled from his words and quickly worked to arrange her expression into a cool smile. "You're wrong. Thank you for helping her. I appreciate it, but it's late and I have things to do." It took a huge effort to breathe. To get enough air. Because when she did, all she could smell was Quinn's clean, masculine scent.

She didn't doubt he'd worked with the dogs all day, but before coming back to town, he'd obviously showered, shaved. Then there was the question of why he'd come. Again. Surely he had better things to do than follow her and the other *Besties* around, but she couldn't even be upset when she was so grateful.

Quinn speared her with a long stare before he turned away from her to look around her home. The muscles in his back and arms flexed with the motion, and she was drawn to the beauty of him, despite her unease.

She didn't mind his quietness. His raspy, damaged voice. She admired his strength and protectiveness of Emma and Ian and... herself. Not that she would ever admit that to him or anyone else. But it was sort of like having her own guardian angel in the flesh. A very dangerous one— which wasn't always a bad thing? "Thank you again, but I have another long day ahead of me tomorrow." She opened the door for him to go, the intensity of his stare too much to bear. To think of after such an exhausting day. She wanted her bed. Her pillow. The locks fastened on the door and her quiet, secured haven.

Quinn retraced his steps toward her, out the open door. But he paused on the top step of her porch.

"Jolie... I'd never hurt you. You don't ever have to fear me."

She opened her mouth to say she didn't fear him, but the lie froze on her lips. She did fear men, no matter how hard she tried not to. Oh, she could put on a brave front, but having had a man's dark, brutal nature turned against her, she knew fear. Because everyone had a dark side. Even her. And most definitely Quinn. The scar circling his neck stated that point loud and clear. "Good night."

Jolie closed the door the moment he descended the steps, but she still listened to his footsteps crunch across the gravel. Seconds later, the truck door slammed shut, and the engine roared to life. She remained by the door, holding on to the knob with a tight grip.

You don't ever have to fear me.

She closed her eyes and rolled her body along the door as she turned to flip the deadbolt.

In fifteen years, no one had ever seen through her acting skills, never zeroed in on her reactions enough to question them. Not the *Besties*, no one. Except Quinn.

Because of his past?

As strange as it seemed, it was also fitting. They both had scars.

And his made him the only man who'd ever tempted her to want to bare her soul and share the burden she carried.

5

5

───────

Quinn sat in his truck outside of Jolie's house, gazing at her quiet street.

He'd picked up enough of Jolie's history from Emma to know that Jolie now owned her deceased grandmother's home, the same one she'd lived in since moving to Stone River.

What would it be like to grow up here? Go to school here? Every town had its problems and issues, but Stone River reminded him of old television reruns he'd watched as a kid. Picturesque town. Quiet neighbors.

Kids' bikes lay on their sides in some of the yards, and nearly every house on her street had a basketball hoop either above the garage doors or positioned off to one side. There were high school football signs cheering on certain numbers in two of the yards near the mailboxes, the homes' front doors decorated in the local school colors.

Freaking Mayberry. No wonder he stuck out like a sore thumb. Everywhere he went, people had a tendency to stare if his scar was visible, but here...

Absentmindedly, he scratched Tucker's ears, drawing more comfort from the dog than the dog drew from him, no doubt.

It *was* getting late, but Jolie's words, her expression, and the way she'd flinched— just slightly— when he'd needled her about her reaction to the teenage bully crawled deep beneath his skin and itched, keeping him there in the dark.

Taking on the angry kid had frightened Jolie. In and of itself, that wasn't such a surprise. He'd been around her enough to know she wasn't a confrontational person. When with her friends, Jolie was the quiet one. The one who listened and observed and rarely spoke. She was shy smiles and hair over her face, soft-spoken. Maybe she was different around her friends when they were alone, but when he was present, Jolie kept her thoughts to herself.

Still, he couldn't shake the feeling that there was something tangible to her pale-faced and trembling response to the teenage idiot from earlier. Something deep-seated and ugly that made the back of his neck prickle in unease.

Maybe if his instincts hadn't kicked in, he might be able to pass off the incident, but his gut never led him astray. Something told him Jolie's reaction wasn't due to her being a non-confrontational introvert.

A light on the second floor of her home clicked on, and he stared at the window as her shadow passed.

He shut his thoughts down before they had a chance to drift into dangerous territory and shook his head. He couldn't go there. Ever. Not with her. Jolie Carter was off-limits for a multitude of reasons. She was one of Emma's *Besties*, which meant he couldn't hint at interest without consequences.

He spent a lot of time with Ian and Emma, lived on their property. He couldn't allow things to get awkward and uncomfortable. "Only a stupid dog messes where he sleeps," Quinn murmured to Tucker.

The next day, Jolie replaced the tip jar with one of the gourmet coffee containers that couldn't be shattered.

Avoid temptation.

That was one of the tips she'd picked up from the many self-help books she'd read on cutting and emotional healing. Simple in theory but not so much in practice. Especially not since she'd learned the hard way that she could cut with just about anything. Broken glass. Razor blades. Her fingernails. Press anything hard enough or sharp enough against your skin and it would bleed.

This morning, after she'd showered and gotten ready for the day, she'd applied cream to the angry red cut on her thigh to speed healing and hopefully prevent infection, saying a prayer for forgiveness and strength. She'd also marked the lapse in her journal and documented her emotions after spotting Blake Parker or his look-alike, and what she'd felt as a result. She was disappointed in herself for self-harming, but she knew not to beat herself up too much. She had done it, had to accept it, had to move on. It was all she could do to help herself, and for now, it had to be enough.

She'd never gone to counseling. In small towns, nothing ever remained secret, and the few times Gram had mentioned it, Jolie had flat-out refused, knowing someone would find out. Besides, Emma's uncle was the only shrink in the area when Jolie had first moved to Stone River, and she certainly couldn't tell him. As a compromise, she'd promised to read every book Gram could find on the subject of cutting and rape, but nearly twenty years ago, the subjects were still somewhat taboo, and there wasn't much information to be found.

Jolie had discovered on her own that journaling helped. At least sometimes. Sometimes writing about her desire to cut just made her wonder if she was one step closer to crazy.

Exercise garnered the best results for offsetting the need, but since opening Cuppa Jo's, she hadn't made time to exorcise her demons properly. Yet another thing that was catching up to her as the stresses and fatigue of owning and running a new business shredded her worn nerves.

Since seeing Blake or whoever the man was, she'd spent a lot of time staring out at the street. Watchful. Wary. But she hadn't seen the man again. Hopefully she wouldn't. Considering she'd only seen him once in the last fifteen years, what were the odds? Maybe he *was* just passing through town. Cuppa Jo's was the only coffee shop on the main road through Stone River, with signage along the highway, so that theory was a possibility.

Jolie's morning flew by with customers making a nonstop stream through the doors. They kept her from focusing on anything but coffee and service with a smile. She and Elaine, a single mom who worked day hours while her kids were in school, poured coffee into the afternoon, skipping out on lunch in an effort to keep up.

By three, Elaine left, and Tommy came in, allowing Jolie to stand in the back room long enough to eat a fast lunch. When Jolie emerged, she immediately spotted Kaylee sitting in one of the chairs in the far corners. The girl's backpack was on the floor by her feet, her books spread out on the table. And despite the cup of coffee in front of her and all of Kaylee's bluster and confidence from their previous meeting, Jolie noted the girl used a pink Hello Kitty pencil to scribble in a notebook.

Jolie went back to work alongside Tommy, keeping an eye on Kaylee and thankful Kaylee's boyfriend was nowhere to be seen.

"Jolie? I hate to do this to you seeing as how slammed we've been, but I've got to take off, or I won't make it to class," Tommy said. "I can come back afterward to help you close if you want me to, though."

It was time for him to leave already? Jolie glanced at the clock and sighed. Wow. It was nearing six. Her late lunch had totally skewed her inner time clock. "Yeah, that would be great. I appreciate it."

"No problem. See you later." Tommy carried his messenger bag with him as he hurried out the door.

Jolie cleaned off tables and performed general cleanup when time allowed between customers but still found herself behind on several occasions. She couldn't get the tables cleaned fast enough because she was stuck behind the counter.

The next time she looked up, she blinked in befuddlement. The tables were clear?

"Um... hey," a feminine voice said from the left. "I didn't know what to do with them."

Kaylee stood on the other side of the counter, her hands gripping a plastic bin of dessert plates and coffee mugs. "You bussed the tables?"

"I... Yeah. I hope that's okay? I mean, you're busy, and I wanted to say thanks so— Do you need some help until that other guy gets back?" the girl asked in a rush. "I mean, I'm here, and I'm finished with my homework so... I wouldn't mind."

She needed the help. And the girl was going above and beyond to show her appreciation for something anyone would've done. Maybe Kaylee hadn't appreciated the interference last night, but it took courage and humility to speak up now. "Do you mean that?"

"Yeah, if you want. Look, last night I was embarrassed and mad because Damien was acting like such a jerk. But you were only trying to help me," Kaylee said ruefully, her expression one of apology. "I'm sorry for snapping at you and taking off like that."

Jolie finished measuring the grounds for a fresh pot and reached beneath the counter for an apron to hand to the girl. "I understand. And I appreciate you doing that." She waved her hand to indicate the bin of dishes. "I'd love the help, but I'm hoping the offer means you might be interested in a job? Say yes and you're hired. I've been needing to get an extra pair of hands for a while and have been putting it off."

"For real?"

Jolie laughed at the girl's excitement. "For real. Have you ever worked before?"

"No, but I've been thinking about getting a job for extra money. I'd like to save up for a car so I don't have to borrow my dad's old, ugly one."

Jolie nodded her understanding. "Bring those dishes back here, and I'll show you what to do. Will your parents will be okay with you working?"

"Oh, yeah," Kaylee said. "And it's just me and my dad. My mom died a few years ago."

"Oh, I'm sorry."

"Me, too. But my dad won't mind. He works at the college, and he has night classes so..."

So working here was better than being at home alone? Dealing with a boyfriend who didn't appreciate her? Give the girl an excuse as well as a safe place?

Those were questions Jolie wanted to ask but didn't, knowing from experience that no teen wanted to admit she might be dealing with things well beyond her comfort level. "I'm glad. And I don't know about your dad, but I don't want you putting on an apron until your homework is finished. No exceptions. I'll happily take the help when you're done, though. If you don't do anything after school, you can come here and eat while you finish your homework, then grab an apron and clock in."

"Awesome," Kaylee said softly, smiling. She looked down at her shorts and T-shirt and back at Jolie. "Am I dressed okay?"

"I know the high school has dress codes, so if you can wear it there, you're fine for here."

"Cool. I thought maybe I'd have to wear skirts all the time like you do."

Kaylee's comment made Jolie pause, and the cut on her leg pulsed a bit in discomfort. The soothing balm she'd applied this morning had worn off around noon, and when she'd bent to retrieve a bag of coffee beans earlier, she'd felt the cut tear and reopen. She'd had to make a quick trip to the back for a bandage to keep it from bleeding through her skirt. "No, you're good. I wear skirts because they're comfortable and professional. It's not really that I have to dress up, but as the owner, I do want to look nice." It also helped that the long, maxi-style skirts she preferred covered her legs completely, and she didn't have to worry that the thin, white scars there from years of cutting would be revealed.

The next hour was spent showing Kaylee the basics until Tommy returned from his class. Jolie introduced the two of them and noticed Tommy looked a little relieved to have another person there to pitch in. Hiring Kaylee brought Jolie's total number of part-time employees to three, when, truthfully they could use two to three more people manning the workload in shifts.

Patience, she mused. She'd taken business courses in college, and she knew one of the worst things a small business could do was expand too fast. It took time to build a financial buffer to make payroll and expenses, and since this was her livelihood and her future, she didn't want to do anything to screw it up.

At 8:55, Jolie walked to the door and flipped the sign to CLOSED. On weekends, Cuppa Jo's stayed open until ten p.m. and served as a hangout for the hipsters, so weeknights she tried to get everyone home at a decent time, including herself.

The three of them left Cuppa Jo's as a group, but when Jolie realized Kaylee planned to walk home alone in the dark, Jolie refused to let the girl go. "I'm taking you home. I insist."

"It's only a few blocks," Kaylee argued.

"It doesn't matter. No woman should be walking alone in the dark these days. Get in," she said, rounding the front of her black Maxima.

Kaylee rolled her eyes at the order but did as she was told, fastening her seat belt while balancing her backpack on her thighs.

"Where to?" Jolie asked.

The address Kaylee gave was indeed only a few blocks away on the university's main campus. But it was on the far side, meaning Kaylee would've had to walk through the student housing section and a large part of the campus alone. Safe enough in the daytime to walk after school, but Zailer had its share of parties and mischief. A girl alone could draw unwanted attention. "I'll drop you off after work," Jolie told her, rounding the curve to the nicer, older homes where a lot of the university staff lived. "Until you save up enough for that car you want," she added so Kaylee wouldn't argue. "Is your dad home?"

"No, doesn't look like it," Kaylee said, gathering her things. "But it's okay. I've been a latchkey kid since my mom died. It's fine. Thanks again for the job. It's kinda fun."

"You're welcome. I'm glad you like it. You did fantastic for your first day."

Kaylee flashed a bright smile and got out, crossing the street in front of Jolie's car. Jolie remained in the idling Maxima, wanting to make sure Kaylee made it into the house okay.

Jolie scanned their surroundings, noting an older woman framed in a window across the street. It looked as though she was washing dishes given her movements.

The house next to Kaylee's was dark, but the one on the other side of that was lit up from top to bottom. Apparently the owners weren't worried about their electric bill.

A door slammed, the sound echoing down the quiet street. A shadow emerged from the brightly lit house, moving quickly down the steps and across the yards between that house and Kaylee's. The moment the shadow stepped into the light, Jolie recognized Damien, Kaylee's boyfriend. He lived that close?

Apparently so.

Jolie gripped the steering wheel so tightly her fingers hurt, watching as Damien bent and kissed Kaylee on the mouth.

With a weak wave in Jolie's direction, Kaylee then led the way up the steps and onto her porch. Damien followed, but Jolie saw him glance over his shoulder to where she sat in the car, a deep scowl on his too-handsome face.

Jolie didn't want to leave. She wanted to tell Kaylee to get away from that boy, because he'd already proven himself abusive. Maybe the couple had only been having a spat, but things had been escalating toward violence, and that couldn't be ignored.

A car turned onto the street behind her, ending Jolie's mental debate of stay or go. The side-street parking was bumper-to-bumper, so she had no choice but to let her foot off the brake and move on.

She rolled forward slowly, noting the car behind her had slowed. The vehicle turned into Kaylee's driveway, and Jolie let out a sigh of relief.

Kaylee's father had arrived in a timely manner, but what if he hadn't? Would Kaylee have remained on the porch or let Damien inside?

Questions flickered through her head as Jolie made a loop around the cul-de-sac. Facing the home once more, she saw Kaylee's father talking to the teens as she drove by. She slowed for the stop at the end of the street, watching via her rearview mirror until lights turned on across from her, making her blink. A truck sat in the first parking space from the corner, but it wasn't until she drove slowly by that she realized it was Quinn's truck.

He'd followed them there?

The question was pointless. Of course he had. Emma had made Quinn *promise* to look after the *Besties,* but why did it seem all his attention was focused on her?

Are you really surprised after what happened last night?

Tasha rarely left her clinic and her home right next door, and besides, she checked in with Owen Redd whenever possible. Morgan had her parents looking after her and spent her evenings home with her children.

Like it or not, she was the only one entirely on her own— if not for the man now following her home.

6

The next morning Jolie still wasn't sure what to think. Quinn had followed her to her house, waited until she'd made it inside safely, and then left as though he'd performed the chore every night since Emma's honeymoon departure.

But why hadn't she noticed before?

Thankfully the morning rush kept Jolie from focusing too much on Quinn and required her to pay attention to her customers' orders. Elaine helped open, agreeing to take on the morning shifts once her kids boarded the bus. Kaylee would work the evening shifts after school, and Tommy would work a flexible schedule around his classes at Zailer to get his hours.

When Kaylee showed up after school, she looked a little tired and very young, but her energy and excitement over her new position made Jolie smile. The girl was eager to learn and quick to pick up how things were done. Kaylee didn't get flustered when things backed up due to her inexperience. Instead, she concentrated on her tasks and tried to go faster.

By the end of the night, Kaylee was filling orders nearly as quickly as Jolie, which meant later, when things slowed down again, Jolie was free to count out the cash register and begin the process of closing up.

At 8:50, the chime on the door sounded, and Jolie looked up to see the boy— Damien— enter with a searching glance of the interior. The moment he spotted Kaylee bussing a table in the corner, he headed her way, a dark glower on his model-pretty face.

"May I help you?" Jolie called out, making sure the boy knew he was being watched.

The teen sent her a silencing, narrow-eyed glare and kept going, not stopping until he stood towering over the girl.

"What are you doing?" he demanded of Kaylee, making no attempt to keep his voice down.

"Damien, hi. What are you doing here? I thought you had plans after practice," Kaylee said, sliding a glance toward Jolie before focusing on Damien once more.

"I asked you a question."

Damien's voice carried enough threat across the coffee shop to have Jolie reaching for her bottle of bleach.

"I'm *working*. I told you I got a job."

Damien muttered a raw curse, something that would've gotten him kicked off the field had he said it to a ref.

"And I told you to forget it," he said, his words emerging with such force that Kaylee blinked.

"Damien, please. Don't mess this up for me. I want to save up for a car."

Kaylee shot another nervous glance to where Jolie stood.

"I'll drive you wherever you want to go, but you're not working here. Not with her," Damien said.

He grabbed Kaylee's arm and dragged her two steps toward the door before Kaylee dug her heels into the floor and stopped their progress, yanking her elbow out of her boyfriend's grip and wincing at the pain Damien caused.

Jolie slammed the cash drawer closed and was in the process of flipping the counter bar up to intercede yet again, bleach bottle in hand, when she noticed Zack Dupré, Emma's half brother, walking around the hearth to make his presence known.

Jolie stared at Emma's sibling, guessing Elaine or Kaylee had filled his order when he'd come in, because Jolie hadn't even known he was there. *You're getting sloppy, Jo-Jo. You have to pay more attention. What if it had been Blake sitting back there?*

"Is there a problem?" Zack asked.

"Damien, go home. I'll be there soon, and we can talk," the girl said.

Damien puffed up like a blowfish, fists clenching at his sides. Zack was bulkier than the high schooler, and the two stared at one another a long moment before Damien sneered.

"I get it now," Damien said, glaring at Kaylee. "You're here because of that loser."

Kaylee's head swung back and forth between Zack and Damien before she shook it in denial.

"I don't even know him. Damien," Kaylee said, lowering her voice, "stop this. Please. You're worrying for nothing."

"Am I? Then why are you here with the guy who assaulted me?" Damien demanded.

"I was protecting my little sister," Zack said in a surprisingly calm voice.

"And I'm not here *with him,*" Kaylee argued. "What is with you?"

Damien stared at Zack for another long moment before he turned and shoved the door of Cuppa Jo's open so hard it snapped back. Jolie worried the glass would shatter. Thankfully it didn't, and once it caught on the automatic thingie above the door that controlled the speed, it closed quietly, leaving a deafening silence in the wake of Damien's temper.

"I'm sorry," Kaylee whispered, her face a bright, hot red. "He's not that bad, really. He's just... Things are messed up at his house, and he's having a hard time right now. That's why he's being a jerk."

Jolie exchanged a glance with Zack, who muttered another kind of name for Damien before Zack went back to his spot behind the hearth. Jolie crossed the floor to where Kaylee stood trembling by her container of dirty dishes and wrapped an arm around the girl's shoulders. "Hard time at home or not, he shouldn't be taking his anger and upset out on you."

"I know," Kaylee agreed with a sigh, blinking rapidly to rid herself of the tears flooding her pretty hazel eyes. "It's just, I know he doesn't mean it. You're seeing him at his worst, but he isn't always so... He just needs some time for things to settle at home."

"And if they don't settle down? If he continues to behave like that?" Jolie squeezed the girl's shoulder gently. "Promise me you won't let him bully and abuse you."

"I won't. I promise."

Kaylee glanced at the wall Zack had disappeared behind, and Jolie could see questions lingering in the girl's gaze. Maybe what had just happened would instill enough doubt in Damien's behavior to bring Kaylee around to seeing her so-called boyfriend without rose-colored glasses.

The remainder of the evening went as well as could be expected given Damien's angry appearance. Once the door was locked and the morning prep completed, Jolie and Kaylee left the building together. They talked about an upcoming movie release as they walked toward the Maxima, but Kaylee's smile dimmed when she spotted Damien waiting for her.

"Kaylee, let me take you home," Jolie murmured. "Don't go with him."

Kaylee shook her head and murmured an apology, sliding one last look over her shoulder before taking off with her angry boyfriend. Jolie watched from beside her car, wanting more than anything to snatch the girl back before Damien could do real damage. Didn't Kaylee see Damien was trying to control her? Keep her from living her own life? Having her own things?

Not your responsibility, her mind whispered. Kaylee had a father to look after her, to protect her.

Unless he's like yours.

The thought slammed through Jolie, stealing her breath and leaving her weak-kneed and shaken as she moved to the driver's door of her car. Images flickered through her head, each of them as horrible as the one before it. Once upon a time, she had been the apple of her father's eye, but with one horrible mistake on one horrible night, she had ruined everything. Permanently. The gaping distance between her and her parents had grown over the years, and Jolie had given up on ever making amends. They exchanged Christmas and birthday cards, but Jolie didn't go home to spend time with them— nor did they ever ask her to. She felt some things were simply best left alone.

That was the thing about bad things happening to a person... Sometimes, when people found out, they never looked at you the same way again. People who were supposed to love you no matter what. People who were supposed to be there for you.

Love was supposed to be unconditional but... it often wasn't.

In her distraction, Jolie stumbled over a rough patch of concrete. Her purse and keys slipped from her hand and hit the asphalt with dull thumps.

She made a frustrated sound, fed up with herself because every time Damien appeared, she thought of that horrible night fifteen years ago. Damien's anger, his rage. The bitterness on his face as he spoke to Kaylee. All of it was too raw and real and familiar. And there wasn't a thing she could do about it except be there for Kaylee and hope the girl came to her senses before it was too late.

Jolie squatted down to retrieve the purse and keys and felt the cut on her thigh rip open again. A gasp left her at the sharp jab of pain, unwelcome tears stinging her eyes. "Stupid, stupid, stupid," she muttered, hating that she'd lapsed back into that mindset, all over a man who hadn't recognized her and probably wasn't even the person she'd believed him to be.

She grabbed the items and unlocked her car, climbing inside and slamming the door in her frustration. Bed. Sleep. That's what she needed. She'd been burning the candle at both ends for months now. The fatigue was wearing her down. The cut was proof.

She drove home on autopilot, using the distance as quiet time to de-stress. In her driveway, she gathered her things but was so tired she sat there for a long moment, too exhausted to climb out of the vehicle. Something had to give soon, and it couldn't be her sanity, she mused.

"Jolie," Quinn said from outside her car window.

She jumped in the seat, her nerves so on edge she'd forgotten all about his new routine of following her home. She hadn't even noticed his lights behind her. "I seriously doubt Emma wanted you to take the whole safety thing to such extremes," she said after she opened her car door.

"Doesn't matter. I wouldn't be able to face Emma if something happened to you."

The way he said it gave her pause. "Did Zack call you?"

"He said Kaylee's boyfriend had showed up again," Quinn said, confirming her words. "And that things got heated."

Which made it seem as though she needed Quinn's presence and protection all the more. "It was fine," she said, sighing. "Damien took off when Zack made it clear Kaylee had backup. Is Damien really the reason Zack is on probation?"

"Yeah," Quinn said. "Zack swears he slugged the guy because he'd made a pass at his little sister, a fourteen-year-old girl. The school is too small for Damien not to know Zack's sister was too young for him."

She grimaced at the news and climbed out, aware of Quinn's gaze on her even though she wasn't looking at him.

What was it about Quinn? Why was she so aware of him?

A raw mutter slipped from Quinn's lips before his hands descended on her. She yelped in surprise when he lifted her up like a child and cradled her against his chest. "What are you doing? Put me down!"

"You're hurt," he said, carrying her toward her house.

"What? No, I'm not."

"You're bleeding."

The cut. She'd worn a light gray skirt today. Oh, no. It must have bled through. "It's fine. I'm okay."

He lowered her to the cushioned swing at the end of her well-lit porch and shoved at her skirt.

"Quinn! No!"

But his hands were already there, baring her skin—with all the tiny, silvery scars marring her upper thighs.

She tried to push his hands away, to cover her legs, but Quinn's hands wouldn't budge. He knelt there in front of her, stared down at her legs, his expression unreadable at first and then... She knew the exact moment he realized what he was looking at.

"*Why*?" he asked in his rough, damaged voice.

She released her breath in a rush and shoved him away, aware that she was able to do so because of the shock he experienced at the sight of her scars. "Mind your own business."

Jolie jumped up from the swing and hurried toward the door, but Quinn was right behind her. Faster and stronger, his hand and the strength behind it not allowing her to shut him out.

He knows, he knows, he knows. Now what?

She gave up her feeble attempt to keep Quinn out and turned to dump her stuff on the first flat surface she came to inside her home. Quinn's broad shoulders filled her doorway, his expression dark and full of anger.

"Why?" he demanded again, firmly closing the front door behind him before he moved toward her.

She wasn't afraid of him. Emma would kill Quinn herself if he did anything to hurt her. But that didn't mean he wasn't big and intimidating and scary as all get out because of the expression on his face...

She backed away, every step matched by a forward step of his until she found herself by her downstairs bath. "It's fine."

"It's not fine," he growled. "You *cut* yourself."

Her back hit the wall by the bathroom door, and she ducked her head, lowered her lashes. Her body burned with shame. Embarrassment. Humility. Some people drank; some people did drugs. Some people's bed resembled a revolving door of salacious acts of whoever, whatever, whenever. Who was he to judge her? She hurt no one. No one but herself.

"Jolie, say something. Talk to me."

The growled demand sent a shiver through her, and she squeezed her eyes shut to block out his hulking presence in front of her. What was there to say?

"Tell me why."

She shook her head, at a loss. Until Quinn grabbed one of her hands and lifted it to the scar on his neck, placed her fingers against the thick ridge and held them there.

"I didn't choose this," he told her softly. "I had no say in it, but you — *You* make the *choice*. Jolie..." He muttered a curse. "How can you do that to yourself? *Why* do you do it?"

People who didn't cut didn't understand. It wasn't about the act, but... expression. Cutting was about releasing pain so great there were no words to describe it. He was right. She made the choice to cut. It was a coping mechanism, albeit not a good one. She knew it was failing, that she failed each time she lapsed. But it was her struggle and vice and a way to feel better without hurting anyone else. The pain took her away and brought her back, both at the same time.

"Look at me," Quinn ordered.

She couldn't. She didn't want to see what he thought of her now. See his pity or disgust. Whatever.

But she lifted her gaze to where he held her fingers and noted the dark purple line circling his throat.

Awareness dawned, horror. Jagged and raised, Quinn's scar was brutal and ugly compared to her pale skin. Someone had done that to him. *Slit his throat* with the intent to kill him.

That act in comparison to her own self-harming rocked her to her soul. His choice had been taken away, whereas she used cutting to escape. It was wrong on too many levels to comprehend them all. *Perspective.* "I'm sorry," she whispered, tracing her fingers lightly over the raised, thick scar. "I'm sorry they hurt you."

He muttered a raw curse she'd never said in her life. Good girls like her didn't say words like that.

Maybe if you did, you wouldn't cut.

A huff escaped her instead of the laugh that formed. She'd always been such a good girl. That's why her parents had been so shocked and horrified by her behavior. She was the epitome of good girl gone bad. One who'd then learned her lesson the hard way.

"This isn't about me. Tell me *why*, Jolie."

She wouldn't explain herself or the emotions involved in cutting. Much less her reasons. Honestly, she wasn't even sure of them half of the time. The devil just appeared, overwhelming her, until she *had* to do it.

But now that he knew... A man like Quinn... maybe he'd understand? "It's habit. I haven't done it for a long time," she said. "I... lapsed."

She stared at his scar, raised and ridged. The rough-soft prickle of stubble above and below the area.

Quinn pressed a palm flat against the wall by her head, moving to stand close but not touching her except for the way he held her fingers to his throat. She was surrounded by his warmth, his strength. In that moment, she understood why Emma trusted Quinn.

Strange as it seemed, she felt... safe.

"Why?" he demanded in his raspy voice.

Her muscles clenched at his persistence. "I got upset. It's... I reacted to something, but I'm fine. It's fine."

But then a horrible thought registered.

She yanked her fingers from his skin and finally forced eye contact. "You can't— Quinn, you can't tell Emma. You can't tell *anyone*. Promise me."

Quinn's stare burned into hers. Emotions she didn't have a hope of identifying flickered through his eyes as he stared down at her.

"No one knows you do this?" he said, more than a bit incredulous. "How is that possible? Your friends—"

"They don't know. They don't *need* to know. Quinn, please, this is none of your business!"

"You're hurting yourself. What kind of person would I be if I didn't care?" he demanded, staring into her eyes until she couldn't look away.

Coming from a man who rarely showed any emotion at all, his

comment made her falter. "Because I'm Emma's friend? You're off the hook. I'm telling you, it's okay."

He lowered his lashes over his smoldering gaze, but it only served to increase the tension in the way he looked at her.

"It's not just because you're Emma's friend."

Meaning what? He considered her *his* friend?

A tingle shot through her at the thought before she squelched it and focused on repairing the damage done by his discovering her secret. "You had no right to touch me. No right to look at my legs. It's my body. And it's my choice."

His expression darkened, and she knew saying he'd overstepped boundaries wasn't the way to go with him. Not when he was loyal to Ian and Emma, and not when he'd just told her he cared.

"You expect me to walk away and forget you do that to yourself?"

She nodded, because it would be better for both of them if he did. "Quinn... I appreciate your concern. I do. But you don't understand, and I doubt you ever will. I expect and-and *demand* that you keep this secret between us. Please," she added, choosing to ignore the pleading quality of her tone.

He drew back and paced away from her, his broad shoulders tight and lined with tension. She watched him move through her house, taking in her furniture, decorations. She wanted to scream at him to stop but managed to suppress the urge, only because there was one thing he *had* to promise and that had to remain the focus of their discussion.

Waiting for him to speak, she tried to see her home through his eyes. She liked neatness and order. Some might even call her a neat freak. Everything had a purpose, a place. After her grandmother had died, Jolie had gone through the house and removed every item that wasn't used. Every memory of the family she no longer knew because they had turned their back on her when she'd most needed their support and love. She'd painted and cleaned and redecorated to her taste, getting rid of all the clutter. She had made the house her home and her safe haven in a chaotic world.

"I can't promise that. Not until I see for myself how bad it is. Here, in the light."

Quinn's request broke into her thoughts, and everything skidded to a halt. "No."

Bad enough he'd seen the scars on the porch, but in the bright light, he'd see just how awful, just how many there were, with no shadows to disguise the number.

"You let me see. Or I call your friends right here, right now, and you deal with them."

She flinched at the thought. If the *Besties* had any idea... If they discovered what she was capable of, not only the cutting but the violence she'd inflicted...

She'd lost everyone in her life in one way or another. She couldn't lose the *Besties,* too.

"What's your answer?"

Quinn's compelling gaze captured hers and wouldn't let her look away. She swallowed hard, her entire body flushing hot with unease and fear. Let him see or face her friends. As horrible of a choice as it was, Quinn seemed the lesser of two evils.

Maybe it was the scar he bore or her awareness of his past as a soldier and then a mercenary. But he'd seen things. Worse things than marks on her legs. Which meant showing him was better than traumatizing her friends and changing the way they thought of her. "Fine," she whispered. "I'll show you," she said, wetting her dry lips with a flick of her tongue. "But I don't want you to touch me."

7

———————

But I don't want you to touch me.

Jolie's words repeated themselves in Quinn's mind, darkening his mood even more. She *hurt* herself. Yet she couldn't stand the thought of him touching her.

The fury and all-out rage he felt made him want to punch his fist into a wall. The awareness of her...*condition*, or whatever it might be called, made it hard for him to think straight. Because he couldn't understand why she did it. Jolie was smart. Beautiful. Gentle and kind. She had everything. A home. A business. Friends. What could possibly cause a woman like her to do such a thing?

He paced down the hall once more, unable to stand still, taking in the details of her house.

Jolie's home looked like something out of a showroom, as beautiful as its owner. The walls were either white or beige or some sort of neutral, mostly bare, with only a mirror and a couple framed images for decoration.

The large pictures... There were two. One was of a woman, her face concealed by a black umbrella. She was dressed in red and stood in the rain. Making no effort to seek cover in the dark shadows of buildings around her. The other image was of a girl, long hair flowing down her back, alone in the woods.

He frowned at the similarities. Both were dark, the women alone. Isolated.

But still standing.

Quinn inhaled a ragged breath and moved on down the hallway, stopping when he saw a line of six photographs hanging in black frames. The *Besties*. There was a photo of each of Jolie's friends. Emma with her first canine companion, Roxy. Tasha in her smock at her vet clinic. Morgan holding one of her cakes. The other three photos were of them all together. Smiling. Seemingly happy.

But how happy could a person be if she cut herself in secret? Where was the disconnect? How was it possible that Jolie's friends didn't know?

As much as he wanted to walk out the door, pretend he hadn't learned such a disturbing thing about her, he couldn't. No one should carry a secret like that alone. And if she wouldn't tell her friends...

He turned and saw the way she watched him. Wary and on edge. "Where's the kitchen?" he asked, figuring it would have the best light. He didn't want to scare her by crowding her too much.

"This way," she said, tilting her head toward a darkened area farther down the hallway.

She turned on more lights inside the kitchen before making her way to the table and pulling out a chair to sit down.

To keep himself from paying too much attention to the seductive sight of her slowly inching up her skirt, he focused on the kitchen like he had the living room and hall.

The kitchen cabinets were newer, with an old-fashioned whitewashed look to them. The granite countertop had hues of black, brown, gray, white, and more, with a pitcher of flowers set in a deep corner beneath an open glass cabinet. A dark blue candle decorated the window ledge above the sink, where black-and-white-patterned curtains framed the window. A giant wood butcher-block table served as an island, and it held a smaller pitcher filled with knives and utensils.

Had she purposely positioned her chair near the butcher block to be close to the knives? What did she think he would do, throw her to the floor and... Was that why she cut? Had something like that happened to her?

He inhaled a calming breath and saw that Jolie had draped the material of her skirt just above the cut and tucked the hem in beneath her thigh, like a pair of shorts.

Her pale skin was smooth and toned and covered with a gut-wrenching amount of long, thin, silvery scars below the fresh cut. There were so many....

Curses came to mind, but he bit them back, not wanting to scare her or make her more uncomfortable.

If those were beneath, how many were above it?

His hands fisted as his uselessness took over. He didn't know what to do. Didn't know how to handle a situation like this. He wasn't a shrink. Some people might consider him more animal than human due to his previous occupation as a paid mercenary. Ian or his brother, Duncan, would've been better at finding the right words to say to her. Anyone but him.

He continued to struggle with his fury while grabbing a chair. He hefted it over in front of her and saw how Jolie tensed, her grip on her skirt and the chair seat so tight her knuckles nearly matched her white cabinets.

But one glance told him what he needed to know. Deep cuts left scars. And apparently Jolie liked to cut deep. "You need stitches."

She'd sliced into her skin a good five inches or so in length. But why? What could have set her off so much that she'd done that to herself? He wanted answers to questions. Questions that would take him to a place in her life he didn't want to go, much less know about.

"It will heal. I don't need to go to the hospital."

Probably not. But deep as it was, that cut would leave scar tissue like that on his neck. "I've sewn up more than my share of wounds. I'll do it."

"No."

"You would rather it get infected than to let me touch you?" he demanded, not going to let her push him away now that they'd come this far.

She squeezed her eyes shut and shook her head.

"It's not you. Quinn..."

His elbows dug into his knees as he leaned forward, his previous thoughts returning with a rush. Someone had hurt her; that was why she hurt herself. And if he ever found out who... "It needs stitches."

"It's fine."

"It's deep, and the edges are red and inflamed," he said, growling the words due to his anger. "How many times has it ripped open?"

Silence followed his words, but after a moment or two, she inhaled and sighed.

"Fine. Do it. Just don't—"

"Touch you," he bit out, angrier than he could remember being in a long, long time. "I'll see what I can do."

"*Quinn.*"

He ignored the way she said his name and stood, desperate for some time and fresh air to process things. "Don't lock me out, or I will break your door down."

He left the house and walked to his truck to retrieve his first-aid kit from the backseat. Some habits were hard to break, and he never went anywhere without a backpack filled with the basics: medical supplies, some MREs or Meals Ready to Eat, rope, knife. Odds and ends of things he might need at a moment's notice or in an emergency.

Jolie bleeding because she'd cut herself definitely qualified.

He fisted his hand around the bag, but instead of lifting it from the truck, he reared back and punched the cushioned seat in frustration.

How had watching over Emma's friends turned into this? How did her friends not know she did that to herself? What was he supposed to do about it now that he knew?

A low whine sounded from the front seat, and he looked up to see Tucker staring at him from the passenger side. Emma's friends. Ian and Emma's dogs. Maybe going into business with Ian— and therefore Ian's wife— wasn't such a good idea.

He was a loner for a reason. He *liked* it.

So was this his hint to leave? Staying in Stone River meant dealing with all the things left in his care, but were they what he wanted?

Tucker placed his front paws on the console between the seats, his tail hitting the truck's interior as it wagged. With every thump of Tucker's tail, Quinn battled the urge to climb into the cab and drive without looking back. "You need to learn how to talk," he told the dog. "Then you can tell Emma what her friend is up to and save me the grief."

He'd made a promise to Jolie he didn't want to keep. She needed help. If not from Emma and her friends, then from a professional. But instead, he wasn't allowed to talk about her slice-and-dice routine, which to him was the same as cutting her up himself.

He punched the seat one more time for good measure before he dragged the backpack out of the truck and slammed the door with enough force to rattle the lowered windows.

Thankfully Jolie had known better than to lock him out while he'd gone to get the gear. She'd stayed put, still sitting in the chair where she'd been when he'd walked out.

He unloaded the backpack atop the kitchen table to get to the medical supplies on the bottom. "This is going to sting," he told her, eyeing the wound. "I need to clean it before I stitch it."

Jolie lifted her shoulder in a shrug but didn't comment.

Quinn bit back the words he wanted to say and grabbed a packet of gauze and the peroxide. He doused it thoroughly, wincing in empathy even though Jolie barely flinched. "Sorry."

"It's fine."

Working quickly, he mopped up the cut, then grabbed a jar of topical numbing cream. "You want me to use this?" he asked, the words sounding more than a little bitter.

"Afraid if you don't, I'll like the pain?"

Quinn lifted his head in surprise at her verbal bite and found Jolie merely staring at him.

"I'm not a masochist."

He slid a finger over the scars below the cut. "Could've fooled me."

Jolie tried to stand, but he crowded her back into her seat by leaning forward. She wasn't going anywhere until he took care of her wound.

They had a short, silent battle of wills in the stare they exchanged, but finally, she gave in with a blink and a deep frown.

Quinn opened the small jar and dabbed a sterile swab inside, then carefully moved it over the outside edges of the cut. He knew the moment the medicine began to kick in because her grip loosened on the chair seat.

He remained silent while he prepared to sew up the cut, determined to do the job right.

By comparison, this cut was much worse than the others. Longer, deeper. Like she'd done it in a hurry to punish whatever made her do it in the first place. "I still want to know why."

"What, am I too wholesome for you?" she said, her tone holding more than a bit of sarcasm. "Everyone has secrets. I'm betting you have plenty."

He glanced up to make eye contact and realized he'd underestimated her. Jolie possessed attitude and spirit beneath her soft exterior.

Intrigued, he paused in his task. She lived life one way, but perhaps she wanted to live another? "Is this your way of being a bad girl?" he questioned. "Because I can think of much better ways to do it."

He regretted his words when he saw her expression alter. She closed herself off, but her eyes relayed her fury at his choice of words. Normally a beautiful mix of green and blue and even a bit of golden-yellow, her eyes were stark and hard and angry.

"How much longer?"

He would take however long he needed to get the answers he sought. If he was going to be forced to keep his word about not telling her friends, he wasn't going to let the moment pass without doing some digging. Besides, he hadn't even started yet. "You don't like the phrase *bad girl*. Any particular reason why?"

She didn't respond.

"Just going to keep asking questions, sweetheart. Might as well answer a few."

"And if I don't want to?"

He took great pleasure in sliding his hands around her lower thigh, lifting so that her calf rested atop his knee. Jolie stiffened in response, but the move allowed him to scoot closer. Not touching her wasn't an option now. "One way or another, you'll answer to someone. I know your secret, so it might as well be me. Why do you do it?"

Jolie shifted in the chair as though trying to establish some space between them, but when he didn't let that happen, she inhaled a shaky breath and settled, her back pressed hard against the wood slats. Quinn shoved her skirt a bit higher above the cut and got an eyeful that left his gut in knots. Her upper thigh was riddled with scars.

He ground his teeth together to combat his anger and opened a sterilized suturing kit. The cut was too deep to glue because it could cause a contained abscess, so suturing it was best. "This is going to sting despite the cream. You probably shouldn't watch while I do it."

He took the first stitch and glanced up, noting she didn't so much as bat an eye. But having cut herself so many times, he doubted sewing her up caused as much pain as the cutting itself. "You were about to tell me why you do it," he reminded her.

"Look it up," she murmured. "There's plenty of information on the Internet."

"I don't want to read about it. I want you to tell me why *you* do it."

"Different reasons. There's nothing else to say."

He stopped stitching long enough to wrap his hands around her thigh and smooth his thumbs over the scars, careful to avoid the fresh cut. "Lots of people get angry and upset, but they don't do this."

Silence.

He stared her down, then got back to work, shifting to make another stitch and forcing his attention off the feel of her lightly muscled legs. It took an effort to keep his hands steady, but whether it was from his upset or her proximity, he wasn't sure. Angry as he was, he still noticed she smelled like perfume and coffee and the sweets she sold in her shop.

Jolie was such a mix of strength and vulnerability, sexiness. Dysfunction. All of which he found attractive. Scarred as she was, the thought struck that maybe she wasn't as put off by the scar he couldn't hide.

Over the years, the semicircle lash around his neck had sent more than a few women, as well as some men, in the opposite direction to avoid him. And the women who hung around... They usually turned his stomach with the things they suggested he do to them, as though the scar were a rope burn left by rough play. "You can tell me," he said, keeping his eyes on his task. "I know you do it, so it's not a secret anymore."

"Quinn, drop it. Please. Sew it up if you must, but once it's done—We never had this conversation."

"You and I both know that's not going to happen." He remembered every conversation they'd shared, not that there had been many. But he remembered them, because from the moment he'd set eyes on her, he'd wanted to know her despite his better judgment.

She made a frustrated sound.

"Because of Emma? Do you really think she needs something else to worry about?"

"Tell me, and maybe she doesn't have to know."

"That's blackmail."

He pierced her skin with the needle again, not commenting, but hated it that she flinched.

"Fine. I'll tell you—after you tell me how you got that scar around your throat."

He should've been surprised by her challenge, but he wasn't, not now that he'd seen how strong she was. His instincts told him weak people didn't cut, only those strong enough to handle the pain of the emotions they couldn't voice.

His scar was a topic few had the courage to ask about and one he didn't discuss. Emma had asked upon meeting him how his voice had been damaged, but she'd been blind at the time, and he'd cut her some slack on the intrusion. He'd refused to answer, and Emma had dropped the subject, accepting his denial at face value.

But once Emma had begun working with Ian, Quinn didn't doubt the subject had come up with her friends. Or that the topic had been discussed, the cause speculated. In fact, he'd bet cold, hard cash that Emma had told her friends to leave the matter alone.

"See? Some things are private. You want me to answer? Tell me what happened to you first," Jolie challenged.

A stalemate. One there was no getting around without talking about things dead and buried six feet under. But if it meant she would talk... "My mother's junkie boyfriend did it," he heard himself say, concentrating on keeping the sutures neat and tight so that the scar wouldn't be as visible. "I ticked him off. He tried to kill me."

This time when he looked up and caught her staring at him, she didn't look away when their eyes met.

"I-I'm sorry. I thought— I don't know, I guess I thought it was something like a bike ride into a clothesline, o-or something while you were imprisoned with Ian overseas."

"Would that make it more acceptable?" He watched her expression, wondering at her thoughts.

"No. Of course not. It's just— How old were you when it happened?"

Watching her, he saw the Jolie he'd come to know. Soft, concerned. Fierce to protect. He'd seen this Jolie in action with Emma and her friends and, most recently, with Kaylee. "Thirteen."

"Thir— Quinn, *seriously?*"

So fierce. She was angry on his behalf. Maybe he could use that to his advantage.

This answer wasn't any easier to reveal than the first. "I came home from school and walked in to see him shooting up. There was another guy there with my mom. She was naked. Her boyfriend had pimped her out for a fix."

Jolie's shock was evident, her eyes wide, mouth open.

"I lost it," he said, continuing the story because now that he'd started telling it, the words were easier to say. "I charged the guy with my mom, shouting and making a ruckus. They didn't want someone calling the cops, so to shut me up..." He shrugged, knowing she was able to fill in the rest.

There were a few people who knew the story. The police, doctors, social workers. But it was the first time he'd shared his past voluntarily. Not even Ian knew the story.

"Please tell me they were punished."

He ground his teeth together and shook his head. "A neighbor had heard and called 911. But both the guy and the boyfriend took off. Far as I know, they were never caught." He focused on her wound to keep the mental images of that event from taking over. It wasn't easy, but after watching his mother self-destruct, he'd vowed to follow a different path, to turn the anger and fury into motivation. Whatever it took to get out, away. So that he never had to go back.

"What happened to your mother?" Jolie whispered after a bit.

Ah, now that was more complicated. "Child Services took over," he said. "Deanna was an addict, and I'd screwed things up with her sugar daddy. She wanted nothing to do with me after that, didn't try to get me back. I haven't seen her since. If I had to guess, I'd say she's dead. She wasn't far from it then."

The next time he glanced up, it was to see Jolie sitting there on the kitchen chair with her eyes closed, her lashes wet with tears, hands fisted on her lap. He reached out and placed his hand over hers, smoothed his thumb over her tight, white knuckles. "I'm sorry it hurts," he said, wishing he could have used the glue and not caused pain with the needle.

"It's not that," she whispered. "It's *you*. I can't believe anyone would do that to a child."

"It was a long time ago. I made it. And so have you."

He hoped something about his story sank in. That she realized she had a lot going for her and needed to find another outlet for her frustration. Exercise, cleaning. Anything but this. "Why do you cut yourself?"

A long silence followed his query, but she stared into his gaze the entire time, searching for something he hoped she found.

He'd always thought her attractive, always wanted to connect with her more than he should, but he'd never have believed they'd share scars as a commonality.

Jolie tilted her head sideways and inhaled a shuddering breath, lowering her gaze. He missed the connection immediately.

"I got upset and reacted," she said finally. "It's the first time I've done it in years. It just... happened."

It might have been her first time to cut in years, but she'd gone at it with a vengeance. "What set you off? This is deep. You really must have been angry."

"I was."

"About?"

She slowly shook her head back and forth.

"I can't."

"Yes, you can. You're going to tell me because I'm not leaving until you do."

"Quinn, please..."

The pleading tone in her voice killed him, wormed beneath his skin and clawed at his insides. She'd been through enough, and he didn't want to hurt her any more, but he had to know. Had to find a way to help. "No. You'll get no sympathy from me. I just told you I had a crack whore for a mother. That her boyfriend and one of her Johns tried to kill me. What can be so bad that you can't tell me? Sweetheart," he continued, lowering his voice even more, reaching out to her and lifting her chin gently so that she'd look at him, "whatever it is, you can trust me."

He watched as Jolie closed her eyes and inhaled a shuddering breath. Her mouth quivered until she bit down on her lip to still it, her hands fisted. Quinn stayed quiet, waiting, willing her to confide in him.

Finally she opened her mouth, the words a bare, hoarse whisper as she said, "I started cutting after... I was raped."

8

———————

Quinn's silence deafened her.

That look. The one he wore right now... *That* was the look she didn't want to see on Quinn's face or anyone else's.

She shoved his hand off of hers and tried to pull her leg off his knee, but Quinn quickly stopped her. "Let go."

"No."

"Quinn—"

"Who was it?"

She shook her head back and forth. What did it matter?

"You told me the hard part, love. Now tell me the rest," he ordered. "Who was it? What happened?"

At one point in time, she'd dreamed of confiding in the *Besties,* but over the years, she'd decided not to. She didn't want to relive the past. Didn't want anyone to know. Moving to Stone River was supposed to have been a new start, and it had been— until she'd seen Blake. But telling Quinn... "You can't tell Emma. You can't tell anyone," she said in a gush. "I don't even know why I told you."

"You need to talk to someone."

"Quinn, *please.*"

Without warning, Quinn leaned toward her and gently folded her against him. She stiffened at the embrace, but when he did nothing but hold her, she took a breath, barely able to force the air into her lungs.

"You're okay," he whispered next to her ear. "You're safe now."

That was the moment it sank in that she wasn't alone anymore. She'd told someone, and the world hadn't come to an end, the sky hadn't fallen.

She buried her nose into his shoulder.

Quinn smelled so good. He didn't wear cologne, and she couldn't smell fabric softener on his shirt, but still... He had a natural masculine scent that was oddly comforting. Or was it simply that *he* was comforting?

"You're safe," he said again. "There's no need to hurt yourself. It's over."

"It will never be over." Not as long as there was a chance of Blake walking through her door.

Quinn brushed his lips over her temple.

"Tell me what happened."

How had her evening turned into this? She'd just wanted to come home, go to bed. Not spill her darkest secrets to a man who— understood? "I was...stupid. I-I was homeschooled, so I didn't interact with kids. Especially boys."

It was easier to talk to Quinn now that she wasn't looking at him. She closed her eyes and leaned into his strength, relishing the contact in her moment of weakness. "But we went to church, and I-I had a crush on an older boy, a neighbor's son. I flirted with him shamelessly when my parents weren't around, but he didn't notice me. And one day, I made a plan to change that."

She took another deep breath, fighting the mortification she felt at the images and memories flickering through her mind. How childish and naive she'd been. So, so stupid. She'd had a woman's body but no clue of the significance of it. No hint of how horribly wrong things could go.

"Tell me," Quinn pressed.

She sat back in her seat when her back began to protest the

awkward position, but she kept her head down, unable to look at him. She stared at her hands, at her chipped nail polish. "I cut off a pair of jeans into the shortest shorts ever, took one of my dad's white, sleeveless undershirts and wore it so it showed my bra." A bitter laugh huffed out of her chest. "I'd gone up a size and talked my mom into buying me matching underwear. They were bright orange."

"How old were you?"

"I'd just turned fourteen."

Quinn muttered a raw, explicit curse. "You were still a *child*."

"So were you." It was getting easier to say the words. Quinn was right. Given his childhood and what he'd told her, how his throat had been slit and he'd been abandoned soon after, her story didn't seem as... violent? No, that wasn't the right word. Because it had been violent. But it wasn't as... Oh, who knew?

"Go on," he urged with a gentle squeeze of her hands.

She blinked down at their hands, making note that his were twice the size of hers. Saying she'd been raped was hard enough. Telling the details of it... "I knew where he'd be. Every weekend, h-he and some friends would go to the pond between his house and mine to party. I-I snuck out and went there, wearing my outfit."

She imagined herself there now. Hiding behind the trees, too embarrassed to come out while his friends were there, and the long wait for them to leave. Watching him, thinking all the romantic thoughts girls did at that age. His too-loud laughter and drunken staggering had seemed... fun. Adventurous. "When his friends finally left, I walked out of hiding and— We wound up swimming. I-I wore my orange underwear, and he wore his trunks. We were just playing at first. I felt safe because his little brother was there, by the fire. We drank, and swam some more. Splashed... kissed. Then I was on the bank and... I remember looking up at the moon and crying because he'd— he'd torn my new underwear." Her voice broke with a strangled laugh, but she cleared her throat and kept going, rushing now to get the words out. "I knew what was h-happening, and I wanted to at first, but then I got scared. I told him no, but he grabbed at my hands and held me down, pinned my arms. I couldn't make him stop. And all I could worry about was how he'd torn my new panties," she said. "How was I going to explain that to my mom? Funny, huh?"

"You are not to blame. Don't ever think you're to blame," Quinn said, his damaged voice gruffer than usual. "Jolie, look at me, love."

It took more courage than she ever thought possible to follow the order. She wet her desert-dry lips, lifted her lashes, waited for the words she knew would come out of his mouth eventually. *Stupid, disgusting, whore.* Whatever the word, she'd heard it from them— his parents, hers. She'd *asked for it. What did she think was going to happen when she went there that night*? Dressed as she had been? Behaving as she had been?

"That's what bad girls get, Jolene," she whispered, repeating her mother's words. She shut her eyes and squeezed them tight, wrapped her arms protectively around her front.

"Stop, *Jolie.*"

Quinn fastened his hands over hers and yanked them away from her body. She'd hadn't noticed the pain she inflicted on herself by digging her nails into her skin, but Quinn had noticed, and the rush of him grabbing her hands, holding them so that she couldn't do it again, set something off deep, deep inside.

She ripped her hands away with a cry, then flattened her palms against his chest and pushed, shoved. He didn't move, which angered her more.

Quinn let her hit him. Hurt him. Turn on him because he'd made her feel safe. Made her trust him. Enough to tell him things she wanted no one to know.

"Shhh," he crooned softly. "Jolie, please. *Stop.*"

"Stop. Please, stop! Please! I don't want to!"

Memories overwhelmed her, flooding her mind and body now that she'd opened the vault.

Exhaustion was her downfall. She tired of trying to push Quinn away and slowed, gasping for air.

She lowered her gaze, her burning eyes taking a moment to

adjust. She saw the dark hairs on Quinn's forearms— and the scratches she'd inflicted. "I'm *sorry*."

"It's fine."

"It's not *fine*," she whispered, hating herself for hurting him. "You were trying to help me."

"I scared you by grabbing your hands like that. It's fine."

He would say that. Think that the scratches were nothing given the scar he carried, but he was the only one who would.

"Tell me his name," Quinn demanded. "Who hurt you?"

She stared at Quinn but didn't respond.

"Jolie, what was his name?"

Emma had told the *Besties* all she knew about Ian and his brother, Duncan. Quinn. They were men trained to protect at any price. Deadly, if needed and the task required.

What would he do if she told him? She had enough on her conscience without adding Quinn going to jail for seeking revenge on her behalf. "It doesn't matter now. You asked why I cut. That's why."

I *was raped.*

Late the next morning, Quinn rolled over in his bed, located in the apartment above Emma's kennel, and tried to get the sound of Jolie's voice out of his head. It didn't work. The three words repeated themselves for the millionth time, making sleep impossible.

After bandaging her up and growing angrier every time she denied his request for a name, he'd left her house and raced up the mountain. He'd spent hours searching the web for information about her, only to come up empty, and had fallen into bed just before dawn. But now the sun burned across the sky, and he reached for his cell, quickly finding the number he sought.

"What's wrong?" Duncan MacGregor said the moment the call connected. "Something happen with Ian and Emma?"

"No. They're good," Quinn said to Ian's brother. "Last time I talked to Jagger, he said Ian was doing great. Seemed to be enjoying himself." Ian hadn't been thrilled about a honeymoon on which he'd have to be led around due to his blindness, but Emma's desire to see the water in the Caribbean had overcome Ian's hesitation. "I'm calling about someone else."

"I've got five minutes. What's going on?"

"I need information about a rape that took place about fourteen years ago," Quinn said to Duncan. "The girl was underage."

"Name?"

He inhaled and winced. Once he did this, there was no going back. "I can't tell you."

Silence filled the air for a long moment.

"So it's one of Emma's friends," Duncan deduced quickly. "Tasha's seeing Owen, so he would be calling me or doing his own digging if it were her. Morgan... She was married too long for this to be coming out now. That leaves... Jolie?"

Quinn faltered, but only for a moment. Jolie needed help, and if anyone in this town was discreet, it was Ian— with Duncan coming in a close second. A man couldn't work the security business and not be able to keep his mouth shut. "Yeah."

Duncan's sigh held all of the frustration boiling inside Quinn.

"Tell me the guy is in prison."

"I don't know for sure, but I don't think so. I got what information I could, but it wasn't the time to press for more." Jolie's face appeared in his mind, and his anger bubbled like a volcano.

"Understood. I'll call you when I know something," Duncan said.

"Thanks."

There was another moment of silence before Duncan sighed.

"I know I don't have to say this, but I'm going to— You hurt Jolie and you hurt Emma. And if you hurt Emma—"

"I'll have to deal with Ian and you," Quinn stated. "Understood."

Quinn rolled to his feet and carried the cell with him to the kitchenette. Tucker left his cushy dog bed on the floor and joined Quinn in the kitchen, greeting him with a grunt and a wide yawn. "Me, too, Tuck."

Quinn opened the miniature fridge, frowning at the lack of

contents. It was amazing how quickly he'd grown used to going to the house for meals. So much so he added anything he purchased to that fridge instead of the one in his apartment. He and Emma both enjoyed cooking, so between the two of them, breakfast and dinner were always covered, with lunch usually consisting of lunchmeat sandwiches or something else as simple.

Quinn grabbed a pair of shorts and a T-shirt, deciding he'd hit the gym in town and then grab some coffee and a sandwich at Cuppa Jo's, maybe hang out and get a feel for Jolie's mood now that she'd confided in him. Last night, after he'd finished suturing her leg and returned the supplies to the backpack, she'd wanted him gone. Not surprising given the hour and the day she'd had, much less needing time to come to terms with him now knowing her secret.

The cutting, her wariness and skittishness. It all made sense. But it also left him with more questions than answers.

9

J olie squatted down to retrieve the batch of chocolate chunk brownies from beneath the counter and stood without pain in her thigh. The stitches pulled a bit, but she'd noticed the cut wasn't as red and seemed to be healing nicely. Thanks to Quinn's suturing skills last night.

Given the little she knew about his life before he'd settled in Stone River to help Ian after the man was blinded, she could only imagine the types of wounds Quinn had stitched in his work as a hired gun in war-torn countries. Then again, who was to say he hadn't begun sewing himself or his mother up during his childhood?

Quinn hadn't said he was physically abused, but with that lifestyle, the odds were high that he had been. One day, maybe she'd be brave enough to ask. That was... if she ever saw him again after her dysfunctional show-and-tell.

She'd shot down Quinn's requests for more information and urged him on his way, but there was a part of her that wished he'd stayed. Wished he had... what? Comforted her? And then what?

He'd hugged her once and offered her a shoulder to lean on, but his willingness to leave as soon as his task was finished told her that her past was too much. Most men steered clear of emotions, and what was more emotional than cutting to express pain?

But who was she to condemn Quinn for leaving so quickly when her past scared *her*? Rape messed with a person's psyche. And if that wasn't enough, other people's inability to handle what had happened to her messed with it more. Maybe combined with his past, Quinn felt it best to keep his distance. That worked for her— so long as he kept her secrets *secret*.

A niggle of freedom pierced her because now that he knew... a very small part of her felt lighter, free from the entire weight of the burden.

But she struggled with unease. If a man like Quinn couldn't handle her past, what hope was there that *any* man would be able to cope with it?

Jolie frowned at her chaotic thoughts and unwrapped the brownies. The delicious scent of chocolaty goodness filled her nose, and she set the container down for a moment to don plastic gloves, then refilled the glass display case, stacking the brownies one by one.

The chime on the door sounded, and she looked up with a smile, spotting Elaine as she walked through the entry. But the man holding the door for the woman sent Jolie's mind spiraling down that dark, terrifying hole into her past. Only this time it was so much worse... because Blake Parker— or his look-alike— wore a deputy sheriff's uniform.

What kind of a sick and twisted joke was *that*?

Unable to face him, she turned and hurried into the back room out of sight.

"Gimme just a second, and I'll get your order," Elaine told the man.

"I have time. No hurry," he called back.

Jolie busied herself with straightening the supply shelf and tried to get a grip on her panic. It couldn't be him. It couldn't be! It wasn't possible. Was it?

Ask his name. Ask him, Jolie mentally urged the other woman.

The chime sounded again as more customers entered, and she

blessed them for making the need for a name on the order all the more pressing.

Jolie heard a few thuds as Elaine stowed her purse beneath the bar and found an apron. She then made small talk about how pretty it was outside since the temperature had dropped to the mid-eighties as she washed her hands.

"Okay, what can I get you?" Elaine asked.

The man requested coffee with sugar and cream and added a sandwich to go.

"It'll be a few minutes for the food," Elaine told him.

"Not a problem. I'll wait," he said.

"Name?"

Jolie wrapped her arms around her waist and waited for his response. *Please, no. God, no. Please, no. Let me be mistaken.*

"Parker."

Jolie's head spun so fast she slid sideways against the shelving and barely managed to catch herself with one hand. *Why is this happening? Haven't I hurt enough?*

She had to get out of there. Had to leave. Get away. She couldn't bear to be in the same building as him.

Because it *was* him. In the flesh.

Bile rose in her throat, and she shoved through the backroom pantry to the employee bathroom, barely making it in time to hurl her breakfast into the toilet.

Weak and dizzy, she stayed there a long time, unable to move or care that she should be out on the floor giving Elaine a hand.

The moment the other woman got a chance, Elaine came into the back to find her.

"Hello? Jolie? Oh my goodness, are you all right?" Elaine asked, rushing to Jolie's side.

"Fine," Jolie managed to whisper, ignoring her raw throat.

"No offense, but you don't look it. Can I get you anything?"

"None taken." Jolie forced herself to her feet. "How's the front? Busy?"

"Yeah, but it's fine. I can cover it. Can you drive yourself home? Want me to call someone to come get you?"

Jolie shook her head at Elaine's question. As long as Blake Parker wasn't anywhere near her, she should be fine. It was just such a shock. Suspecting his identity was one thing, but to find out it really was him— and then to discover he was a *deputy*? "I'm going to sit in the office for a bit. I don't want to leave you completely alone."

"Come on. I'll help you," Elaine said, reaching out to steady Jolie.

Jolie felt foolish and wobbly but thankful for the woman's assistance when her knees threatened to give out and her head spun.

"Are you sure you don't need to go home?" Elaine pressed.

"No. I'm fine now. I think it was just... I'm fine." Jolie managed a smile and focused on putting one foot in front of the other to get to her office. She collapsed into the cool, faux-leather seat with a grateful sigh. "It will help knowing you're out there with the customers," she said, hoping Elaine got the point.

"I've got it covered, don't worry. Sit still and take your time," Elaine told Jolie with a worried frown.

"Shut the door please?" Jolie asked.

"Oh, sure. I'll come back to check on you when I can."

Jolie impatiently waited for Elaine to close the door, the urgency inside her growing rapidly. Finally alone, Jolie opened her desk drawer and pulled out the scissors.

She stared at the blades, sick with the urge, the extreme *want*, to cut.

Never taking her eyes off the sharp edges, she held them against her fingertips as she inched the material of her skirt up her long legs. The moment the metal touched her skin with a cool rasp, she bit her lip, preparing for the pain. For the blessed sting it would bring. For the shame and regret she knew she'd feel once it was over.

Don't do it. Don't let him win. Leave! Go do something else! You're stronger than this.

Her hand fisted in the material of her long skirt, and before she could let herself contemplate it further, she threw the scissors back inside the drawer, slamming it shut with a bang.

But the need persisted. It scraped at her insides, teased and taunted her, refused to leave her mind. *Just one cut.*

"Jolie?" Elaine called, knocking softly on the door before opening it. "You okay?"

Desperate, Jolie fisted her hands in her lap beneath the desk. She had to get out of there. "I'm going to leave for a bit. Can you handle things here? Just for an hour?"

"Yeah, sure. Seriously, I can. Go; get some fresh air. I'll be fine. Tommy will be here in twenty, anyway."

Yes. She'd forgotten today was one of Tommy's days to come in. Kaylee was still learning, but Tommy and Elaine could handle things with no problem.

Alone once again, Jolie grabbed the workout bag she'd brought with her two weeks ago and never used. *Hang in there. Just a little longer. You can do this.*

She didn't remember leaving Cuppa Jo's. Didn't remember the drive. Only getting to the gym and being surprised she'd made it so quickly.

"Welcome," the attendant said. "Just sign in."

She blinked dazedly at the reminder and scribbled her name across the paper before turning toward the equipment area and running face-into-chest with Quinn.

"What's wrong?" His hot gaze swept over her.

She stared up at him, the fear of relapse and cutting herself, the need to, leaving her raw and exposed.

That desire must have shown on her face because Quinn's expression changed, seemingly softening in empathy and hardening in anger at the same time.

"You want to do it again, don't you?"

"I'm sorry," she said, looking all around them, anxious and desperate and on edge. "I have to go."

"No. Come with me." He grasped her arm lightly in his hand. "This way."

Quinn wouldn't take no for an answer and led her the opposite way she normally went, into an area of the gym she'd toured once but never used. There were separate areas for racquetball, yoga, and karate classes, but Quinn took her into the room at the end of the building. Inside, there was a heavyweight bag, jump ropes, and other equipment. "Why are we here?"

Quinn moved to the adjacent wall and dug through some bins, finding wraps and— boxing gloves? In short order, he had her hands covered and ready, which was when he picked up the blocking mitts. "You want me to hit you?"

A small smile curled his firm lips.

"You did it last night, and it seemed to help."

"I'm *sorry*," she whispered, mortified at the reminder of her behavior.

"I'm not, which is why I want you to do it again. You won't hurt me, sweetheart."

There it was again. Sweetheart. Love. "But…"

"Jolie, you're not hitting me. You're hitting the monster who makes you want to hurt yourself. He's right here." He whacked the blocking mitts together, the sound exploding inside the high-ceilinged room. "Come and get him."

She blinked, torn between the desire to start pounding and the embarrassment that she was so easy to read now that Quinn knew the truth.

"He's in your way, Jolie. He's screwing with your life."

At that, she nodded. Yes. Yes, to both of Quinn's statements. She'd moved to a different part of the state to live with her grandmother. To get away from her parents and the Parker family. Why on earth would Blake show up here?

"Pretend it's him. Take back your power, Jolie. And don't stop until the urge to hurt yourself is gone."

Hit him. Hurt him. Make him *go away*.

A rush of adrenaline filled her, stronger than the urge to cut.

She raised her gloved hands and focused only on Parker's face in front of her.

She made a few jabs that connected but had no force. Still, the blows felt good.

"That's it," Quinn urged with a grin. "But you can do better. Gimme all you got."

Yeah, she could do better. Just ask Rick Parker.

Quinn showed her some basic kickboxing moves to get her entire body involved, murmuring suggestions when she needed them. Then she let him have it. Every hit and kick, every breath-stealing punch bringing back another memory so that the next strike was harder.

She'd punched and kicked when Rick Parker had pinned her to the muddy bank. Not that it had helped.

"Yeah, baby, that's it. Come on, you can do this," Quinn said, encouraging her. "You're strong. Hit it harder," he ordered, his raspy voice growling the words.

Harder. Faster. Left and right and left again. Her hands. Her legs. Her feet. She pounded the mitts, losing herself in the process. She zeroed in on the pads but imagined that night. Releasing her anger and pain with every blow until she hurt the monsters in her head and reclaimed some of the power taken from her.

Time passed, but she didn't care. She kept going. Until her arms ached and her back and shoulders burned. Until her thighs quivered with fatigue. Hitting, hitting, *hitting*.

Until her eyes stung from the sweat dripping into them.

Until she forgot everything but the battle raging in her head and her movements became wild and desperate and clumsy, accompanied by broken, chugging sobs that ripped from her lungs.

She stumbled forward in complete exhaustion, but Quinn caught her as she went down, cradling her against his chest as he lowered them both to their knees on the matted floor.

"It's okay," he said into her bound hair. "Shh, baby. I've got you. You're okay."

Baby. Love. Sweetheart. Maybe he could call her those things, but he couldn't call her "okay."

She pressed her face into his shirt long enough to hide her tears, then shoved Quinn away, unable to look him in the eyes as she rejected his comforting shoulder.

"Jolie…"

She wasn't okay. She never would be. But the need to cut was gone, and that had been the goal. "I'm good."

"You want to talk about it?"

"No. No, I don't but— thanks." She lifted and lowered her shoulder in a shrug, still too embarrassed to meet his gaze.

"I do it, too."

The simple statement gave her pause, and she lifted her gaze to his.

"I pretend it's them."

Them— the guy who'd slit Quinn's neck or the mother who'd let it happen for her drug of choice? Both? "It seems we're both a little messed up."

A brief hint of a smile curled one side of Quinn's mouth, and she stared, wondering how she could ever have not thought him handsome. He was. Just in a hardcore, take-me-as-I-am, scars and all, kind of way. But wasn't that the case with everyone? Didn't they all want acceptance for the person they really were?

"Any time you need to take the edge off, call me. Day or night."

She shook her head, very sure he didn't know what he was saying. "Thanks but—"

"I mean it, Jolie. You want to cut, you call. Day or night."

She blinked at the promise behind his words, touched by the kindness. "Why?"

"Why what?"

"Why do you care?" she clarified, needing the truth, although she wasn't sure why. "The promise you made to Emma surely doesn't cover *this*."

Sitting as they were, so close, Quinn didn't have far to move to place his hand beneath her chin and lift so that she would look at him.

"I know your secrets."

She tried to look away but couldn't, not when he held her like this.

"You know mine," he continued softly. "So like it or not, we're in this together. That means no one gets left behind."

Jolie thought long and hard about his words while Quinn left to go get her some water. She used the chance to escape into the women's locker room, ignoring the curious stares of the women already there. She found a private cubicle to shower and dress in, going through the motions, her mind numb from exhaustion and yet ping-ponging through subjects, unable to focus for long.

She emerged ten minutes later, not at all surprised to find Quinn waiting for her. A big, silent soldier on guard.

Her soldier?

Or her scarred, unwanted protector?

The thought made her frown. She and Quinn had nothing in common— except for the violence they'd experienced in their pasts.

He handed her a water bottle without commenting on how she'd ignored his order to stay put.

"Thanks," she said, feeling a bit mellow despite the drama of the day.

"You going home?"

"I have to get back to work."

"You sure that's a good idea? Maybe you need to take a break. Come for a drive with me."

A drive with him sounded nice. And appealed way more than it should. "I'm fine now." She realized with a start that she actually meant it. Tired or not, the urge to cut was gone, and the shower had helped reenergize her. Besides, driving around town with Quinn... Not a good idea. Things were too complicated already to add small-town gossip to the mix. "But thanks."

They walked out to the parking lot together, and Quinn stayed by her side all the way to her car. She dropped inside her Maxima and waited, sensing he wanted to say something.

"I know it was bad," Quinn said quietly. "But you let him win every time you hurt yourself."

Quinn settled his palms against the base of the lowered window and leaned against it, and to keep from looking at him, she found herself staring at his hands. He had a workingman's hands, long fingers, a few callouses.

"Jolie."

She looked up, drawn by his tone of voice.

Quinn tilted his head to one side, his expression softening just a bit as he looked at her. In a ball cap and gym clothes, a day or two's worth of stubble on his cheeks and chin, Quinn looked rough-and-tumble. Big and brawny and rugged. Women stared when he passed them. Maybe at first because of the scar, but then... then because there was just something about him. Something fascinating and dangerous and innately protective.

"I tell myself that, too."

"Good. So next time, you'll call me," he repeated.

Some men ran from a challenge, but time and again, she had seen Quinn charge forward to face them. This was one of those times. And despite her embarrassment that he knew what he did about her, he still offered his help. His support. That meant a lot.

She started the car but paused after she put the vehicle into gear. "What about you?" she asked instead of making a promise to contact him. "What helps you forget the past? What they did to you?"

"Knowing God has a special kind of judgment for people like them."

She blinked at his response, surprised and yet pleased. "I didn't realize you are a religious man." She liked that characteristic. Because in all that happened, she was smart enough to know her bad choices had led up to what had happened that night. Not the rape itself, she was *not* to blame, but her mother was right. Had she been home in her bed where she was supposed to be, it wouldn't have happened.

Would she ever be able to forgive herself for such horrible decisions?

Maybe. Maybe not.

Only time would tell.

10

That afternoon Quinn reminded himself that he just had to pitch in until Emma returned. But then he remembered the look in Jolie's eyes, and everything in him wanted to wrap her up in his arms and carry her away. Protect her until she felt able to do it herself.

He knew he couldn't. Touching Jolie would've sent her over the edge. So he'd given her another outlet for her pain.

Jolie's near breakdown at the gym had torn him in two. She'd hit the mitts for all she was worth, over and over, eyes glazed with tears she'd refused to shed. Every punch packed with fury and too much pain.

He hadn't planned to do more than keep a watchful eye over Emma's friends while she was gone, but no way could he ignore what Jolie was going through. And the moment Duncan called with a name— God help the man who'd hurt her.

He'd meant what he'd said. He believed in God and in God's judgment, but he also believed in justice. Whoever he was, wherever he was, her rapist's days were numbered.

Quinn skipped his planned coffee stop at Cuppa Jo's since he'd seen Jolie at the gym, and headed back up the mountain after his workout. He grabbed a quick sandwich for lunch and repeatedly shook his head at himself as he focused on putting Tucker through training in an effort to keep his mind on track.

Tucker was smart. Quick. But the dog had his moments, responding well to some commands yet ignoring others. All the while looking at Quinn with an expression of *stupid human.*

Quinn had hoped to make more progress with Tucker before Ian returned from his honeymoon, but training proved to be time-consuming and slow. Like Ian had warned, training the dogs was a process that couldn't be rushed and one that had to be perfected before any canine could be considered completely trained to protect its human.

In English, Quinn commanded Tucker to stay, to come, roll over. Then he switched to Cherokee and ordered the dog to attack. Using a little-known language and hand signals for such important commands was key. It kept the dog and the person the animal guarded safe during moments of chaos.

Quinn fired off the commands once more, this time all in Cherokee. *Attack. Heel. Retreat.*

Tucker nailed every command, then came back to Quinn for a tail-wagging praise session. He petted and treated the dog and decided to end the training there for the day.

Quinn took Tucker into the house to relax, then went back out to the kennel to retrieve another of Ian's newly acquired dogs. This one was a cream and white Goldendoodle. Poodles themselves weren't typically aggressive dogs, but the mix proved to be extremely intelligent and protective of their owners— which was exactly what he and Ian wanted. "Come on, Bentley."

Bentley was a character. He looked like a giant teddy bear with a pink tongue constantly hanging out of his mouth. He was woolly and soft but trimmed short so that his fur didn't mat. Bentley was so new to Mad Dog, Quinn spent an hour or more patiently going over the most basic of commands, teaching the dog to sit. Lie down. Shake. Simple tricks to put on a show and fool most.

"Good job," Quinn called at the end of the session, when the dog managed to complete a couple commands in succession. "Playtime," he said firmly, only then picking up a stick and throwing it for Bentley to retrieve.

Bentley chased after it, and Quinn watched, his mind drifting once again to Jolie. Waiting around for Duncan to call was taking a toll.

Quinn called it a day after some playtime and took Bentley back to the kennel. Zack had already been there and cleaned the pens, and each of the dogs had plenty of water.

Inside the main house, Tuck waited for his dinner, bowl in mouth as he stared out one of the lower kitchen windows. Quinn laughed when he saw the dog's antics and fed Tucker his chow before grabbing a drink for himself and heading to Ian's office to use the computer. He wasn't as tech-savvy as Duncan or his VP, Owen Redd, but Quinn knew enough to use a search engine.

Like the other night, he saw nothing other than the handful of recent articles and news about Cuppa Jo's opening and one mentioning Jolie and Emma's *Besties*, written when the girls were teenagers. He reread the story, smiling at how the girls had dressed Emma up in mismatched clothes and taken her to the mall as payback because Emma had gotten a little too demanding of them.

Quinn took a long drink and stared at the picture of the *Besties*, all of whom looked young and innocent. They smiled for the camera, even Jolie, though she looked uncomfortable and stood back behind the others, as though she tried to hide. The article listed the girls' ages as fifteen, which meant the photo had been taken a year after Jolie's rape.

He searched a few more listings but came up empty-handed about the time Tucker finished chowing down and padded into the home office to find him, shoving his big head onto Quinn's knee for scratching. "What do you think?" he asked the dog.

Tucker let out a forlorn whine.

Quinn stopped petting Tucker and grabbed the keyboard again, entering *cutting* and *rape* into the search engine. This time, instead of a few articles, he found over *thirty million*.

After school, Kaylee showed up for work with bruises on her wrists, arm, and neck.

Jolie's fury grew as she stared at the marks, seeing them despite the girl's attempts to disguise them with makeup and bracelets and a trendy scarf.

Kaylee mixed up a white chocolate frappe while Jolie rang up the customer standing on the opposite side of the counter. "One seventy is your change. Oh, thank you," she added when the woman immediately added it to the tip jar. The coins bounced inside the container, reminding Jolie of the day Blake Parker had first appeared in her coffeehouse.

Despite her anger over Kaylee's condition, the urge to cut wasn't as gnawing as it had been. *Thanks to Quinn.*

The customer moved on to the serving area and waited patiently for Kaylee to finish before taking the drink and heading back out the door. Jolie watched the woman go, knowing as the evening progressed and the students from the university streamed in after classes let out her chances to talk to Kaylee would be fewer and farther between. "Kaylee, got a sec?"

The girl tried to hide her unease, but Jolie saw through the act. Jolie motioned for Kaylee to join her by the espresso machines.

"Um, sure. What's up?" Kaylee asked.

"You tell me. What happened to you?" Jolie asked, deciding a direct approach was best.

Kaylee swallowed hard, the bruise on her throat lifting and lowering back below the edge of the scarf.

"I don't know what you mean," Kaylee returned softly.

Jolie reached out and quickly snagged the girl's hand, shoving the bracelets back to reveal the bruises beneath. "Those," she said, pointing to the shadows on Kaylee's inner wrist, "bruises are made from fingers gripping you too tightly. They're on both of your wrists. What happened?"

Kaylee winced, her cheeks filling with color. "It's fine. I'm okay."

"Damien hurt you," Jolie said. "Didn't he?"

The girl bit her lip and shrugged. "It's not what you think."

"I think he *hurt* you," Jolie said. "The question is, why are you dismissing it?"

"Because he didn't mean to. I bruise really easy."

"Kaylee," Jolie said, incredulous that the girl would defend the guy.

"It's true! We were messing around," Kaylee whispered, her cheeks growing redder, "and wrestling and... things got kinda hot."

The similarity to her rape blindsided her, and Jolie felt herself sway on her feet. She leaned against the countertop and struggled for composure.

"I'm *fine*," the girl said. "You don't have to look so freaked about it. Nothing happened. We stopped."

For once, Jolie understood what it was like for Quinn to stand there and listen to excuses and know something was horribly wrong but not be able to help. Quinn probably felt even *more* helpless because her assault had taken place so long ago, but to have the evidence of Kaylee's injuries right there...

"I almost didn't come in today," Kaylee said softly. "Because I knew you'd see and make a big deal out of it. I didn't want to leave you hanging, so give me credit for coming in at least."

"I am. I do," Jolie said to the girl. "I'm glad you came in, but more important, I'm glad I saw the bruises. What are you going to do about them?"

Kaylee's eyebrows pinched together above her nose. "Do?"

"Yes, *do*. Did you tell your father? Break up with Damien?"

Kaylee gaped at Jolie.

"We were just messing around, and he *stopped*. It's fine. Just drop it already."

"No. Kaylee, you can't consider staying with someone who hurts you."

Kaylee looked away and crossed her arms over her chest, her body language making it clear she had heard enough and didn't appreciate the lecture. Jolie fought for calm and composure, knowing that railing at the girl wasn't going to gain anything other than resentment.

"It was an accident. He didn't mean to bruise me," the girl said.

"But he did bruise you. And what will happen next time? Will he stop then? Say it was another accident?" Jolie pressed. "You need to think long and hard about that. You have your whole life ahead of you. Is getting bruised and bullied really the way you want to spend it?"

The chime on the door interrupted them, and three of her regulars came in, followed by a longtime friend from high school. Jolie took their orders and rang them up, passing the customers on to a now-sullen Kaylee. "Austin Cantrell, is that you?" she asked when the man made it up to the register.

Austin looked a bit out of place amongst her clientele of college kids and business professionals, dressed as he was in his mechanic's coveralls and grease-stained hat bearing the name Cantrell's Garage. Austin and his brother, Homer, owned and ran a handful of businesses, but the garage was the brothers' favorite place to hang out.

"It's me," the man said, his backward tone that of the shy boy she'd known throughout high school because they'd shared the same homeroom. "Look at this place." Austin whistled softly. "Mighty fancy digs you have here, Miss Jolie." He plucked at his coveralls. "I'm feeling a mite underdressed."

"Stop it," she said, laughing. "This is nothing compared to you. How many businesses do you own now? Four? Five?"

Austin's face turned a ruddy shade, but he winked at her and grinned.

"Just opened up the Wash'n Spin. That makes six."

She smiled at his bashful yet proud grin. "That calls for a celebration. What can I get you? My treat."

"Well, now since you're offering... I wouldn't mind skipping the coffee in exchange for you answering a question for me."

"Oh?" she asked, curious.

"Do you happen to own that old cabin of your granddaddy's?"

She tilted her head to one side. "Maybe I do. Why?"

The man's excitement was tangible, and he practically rubbed his hands together there in front of her.

"Because my granddaddy's been telling me stories about the mighty fine deer hunting in that area. I was hoping I could talk you into letting me use it when the season comes in, so long as I follow the rules and all."

"I might be agreeable to that," she told him. "But I should warn you, the cabin's been neglected since I inherited it."

She hadn't thought about the cabin in ages. Along with the house she now lived in, her grandmother had left Jolie a tract of land bordering the state park and the log cabin her grandfather had used for hunting, camping, and writing.

A well-loved professor at the university as well as an author, her grandfather's favorite escape had been that cabin in the woods. It was where he'd written out his stories of mystical mountain moons and ghosts of Civil War soldiers that supposedly haunted the area. Just the thought of the cabin sitting there unused and unloved made her sad.

"I could take a look around. Fix things up if need be," Austin said. "It's the least I could do in exchange for you letting me use it."

"You'd do that?"

"Be happy to," he said. "Don't mind at all."

Austin's friendly smile split his face in half, and she remembered back to the days in high school when the girls made fun of Austin because of his stutter. She returned his grin, glad to have made his day brighter by uttering a simple yes.

The cabin would be safe in his hands. Austin had serviced her car from the day she'd started driving, and she'd been inside his business enough times to know he didn't abuse things in his care.

Unlike Kaylee's boyfriend.

"Do you have time to show me how to get there?" he asked. "I'm pretty busy at the garage right now, but I could make some time in the next month or so to make a trip and see what's what."

"That would be great," she said, meaning every word. With any luck, Austin might have the cabin in top shape before the weather got bad, and if he did...

She and the *Besties* hadn't spent a lot of time together of late. Maybe Ian would let Emma out of reach for a night, and they could hike to the cabin and have a girls' retreat/campout. That might be just the thing to help get them all back on track since life had taken them in so many different directions. "Let me get some paper, and I'll draw you a map," she told him.

After finding a pad of paper and pen, Jolie ran through the list of directions and landmarks to find the isolated cabin. She wrote them down, and then Austin read through aloud to make sure he understood them. That done, they chatted about friends from school and caught up on who was now married to whom and having babies, while Kaylee got Austin a coffee— minus the frou-frou extras.

Jolie introduced Kaylee to Austin and listened as Austin asked Kaylee about a couple teachers he and Jolie had had in high school and hadn't really liked. Kaylee's instant response of horror made them chuckle as Kaylee relayed the fact the teachers were still in class and just as mean as ever.

Chatting with Austin helped ease the lingering tension between Jolie and Kaylee, and Jolie was grateful that Kaylee seemed to lose some of her standoffishness.

Austin stayed a good twenty minutes to chat, but the next rush of college kids filing through the door drove him away. Jolie waved good-bye so she could take orders and payment, glancing outside the storefront window a minute later to see Austin standing outside watching her through the glass.

He ducked his head with a shy smile when she caught him looking and ruefully lifted the coffee cup in his hand as though saying thanks. She nodded and smiled— until movement caught her attention and she spotted Blake Parker as he passed by Austin on his way down the street.

Her pleasant mood faded instantly. She swallowed back her unease and the instinctive panic that threatened to choke her.

What was she going to do? She couldn't run from Blake every

time his shadow crossed her path. She couldn't *cut* every time she caught a glimpse of him. And this was twice she'd seen him in uniform meaning— Blake had to be a new deputy in town.

Thanks to Tasha once being engaged to a state trooper, Jolie knew Parker's being there most likely had to do with an open position or assignment by the state to fill a hole. Surely that was the case. Because Blake wouldn't have come to town had he known she lived there— would he?

One day very soon, you'll work up the courage to confront him. Then you can demand he request another transfer and get away from you.

Until then, she had to gather her reserves and build up the confidence to have that meeting.

Some of the many self-help books she'd read encouraged her to have mock conversations with the offenders in which she could say or do whatever she wanted. She'd always put off such a thing, but maybe it was time to work on that speech.

Jolie exhaled the breath she hadn't known she'd held once Blake was no longer visible and turned to find Kaylee watching her with an inquisitive stare. Desperate to get the girl's keen focus off of her, she said, "Kaylee, about earlier—"

"I'm fine." The girl grabbed a plastic tub and a rag before heading toward the seating area. "You've got it all wrong."

"Do I?" Jolie asked.

Kaylee made a huffy sound.

"Yeah, you do," Kaylee called from the table. "And you know, you're my boss and all, but Damien's right. You need to mind your own business."

Taken aback by the girl's words when she had only tried to help, Jolie stood there at the cash register in silence, watching as Kaylee moved deeper into the seating area to gather up the dirty dishes.

Was Kaylee right? Was she transferring her past onto Kaylee? Making too much of what might have happened?

"Jolie? You okay?" a male voice asked.

She snapped to attention, only then realizing Austin had stepped back inside Cuppa Jo's. "Hey. What— Yes, I'm fine," she said when her mind replayed his words. "Is something wrong? Need more coffee?"

"No, I'm good," he said, lifting the cup in his hand as though to prove it. "Actually, I was wondering... You want to go out sometime? I know you're busy getting this place up and running. I stay pretty busy, too. But we can't work all the time, right?"

She faltered but only for a moment. Austin was a nice guy. A *good* guy. Someone quiet and safe and unassuming. Was she really going to turn him down? Let the past keep her from fun? A future? Like Quinn had said, she gave the past power by cowering to it. Hadn't Rick and Blake Parker taken enough from her? "I'd love to," she forced herself to say, the words emerging a bit breathless thanks to her inner debate.

Dating had never come easy to her. She was awkward and stiff, always waiting for the guy to make a move. Preparing herself to fend the man off. But the date never proved worthy of the buildup of worry and anxiety and nerves, so she'd eventually stopped accepting the requests that came her way.

But maybe with Austin... She'd feel comfortable?

It was possible. She'd known him a long time. They were friends, too. And Gram had always said the best relationships began as friendships.

"Yeah? You'll go out with me?" Austin confirmed with a smile.

She nodded again. "I can probably get away from here a few hours Saturday evening. Will that work for you?"

11

*D*uncan called Quinn the following morning. The moment his cell phone rang and Duncan's number appeared, Quinn snatched up the phone and barked a hello. "What'd you find out?"

"Not a lot," Duncan said. "I'm still digging. Just wanted to fill you in on what I found so far."

"Which is...?" Quinn asked, more than a bit impatient that Duncan was taking so long to get to the point of the call.

"According to state records, she was homeschooled most of her life, made good grades, attended church every Sunday, and was part of the youth group. Mother stayed home; Dad worked at the plant in town. No history of domestic calls or other issues that had them on anyone's radar."

Which meant he had no more information now than he'd had before Duncan had called. Jolie had told him most of that herself. "What about neighbors? She said the guy was a neighbor a little older than her."

"I'm still looking, but her home address is surrounded by 'neighbors' so I'm weeding through them to locate the ones with kids

Jolie's age— which there are a lot of, as well. It takes time to narrow things down."

Quinn ran a hand over his head in frustration, Jolie's words, her expression as she'd told him about the rape in his head for all eternity.

"She didn't give you a name? A first name? That would help," Duncan said.

Yeah, it would but— "No. No names. She did talk about a pond that was between their properties. It was a party spot."

"That might help narrow it down some more," Duncan said. "Anything else?"

He racked his brain for things Jolie may have mentioned in passing that hadn't registered at the time as informative but could mean finding her attacker now. Still, he came up with nothing. "No. Duncan—"

"I know. You want answers now. So do I," Duncan said. "How's she holding up?"

Duncan's question left Quinn without words as he pictured her in the gym once more, pounding the mitts with a fiercely determined expression and glazed eyes. "She could be better."

"Quinn, given her age at the time, the statute of limitations is either over or almost over. If she's going to prosecute, she'll have to decide now and get things in motion. Given the timeframe, the odds are against punishment. The judge is more likely to throw the case out."

Quinn ran a hand over his face and rubbed hard. "She doesn't want to prosecute. I'm the one doing the digging. I want to know where he is now."

"Look, I don't like this any more than you do. Jolie is a sweetheart and one of Emma's closest friends, but if she's willing to let the guy—"

"I'm not willing," Quinn said bluntly. "He got away with it, but she's still messed up by what happened. Even if he doesn't serve time, he deserves to pay." And pay he would. There were ways to get a job done without anyone finding out. Ways to leave no evidence behind.

He might not be as skilled as Duncan when it came to computers and digging of that nature, but he was more than qualified when it came to hand-to-hand, guns, things of that nature. One of the reasons he'd made such a good living as a mercenary was that, once he accepted a job and a person to protect, he did so at all costs. He'd chosen well, worked for people who deserved to make it home to their families and homes, rather than those trying to screw their country over by charging millions for nothing just because the red tape would make it impossible to track. It was what made it okay to risk his life— at a very high price.

"Quinn..."

Quinn could hear the warning in Duncan's voice. The *don't do anything stupid* tone Duncan used sometimes. "I have training to do," he said, interrupting whatever inane lecture Duncan was about to attempt. "Call me when you find out more."

"Will do," Duncan said in a resigned tone.

Quinn ended the call and headed down the steps, into the kennel, and out the door, Tucker keeping pace beside him. Maybe driving into town every morning for coffee was taking Emma's request to keep an eye on her friends to the extreme, but in light of what he'd discovered about Jolie as a result, it was a habit he intended to continue, at least until he knew Jolie had a handle on her issues with cutting.

He yanked open the truck door. The dog leaped into the seat like a pro, turning and settling himself inside the cab with a goofy, tongue-hanging grin on his face because the dog liked to go for rides.

Quinn climbed into the cab and headed down the mountain. Thirty minutes later, he was in the gym working out when he spotted the guy who'd been in Jolie's coffeehouse that day she'd asked him to stick around. The guy chatted up the desk attendant signing people in and then began his workout on the equipment on the far side of the room. Quinn watched the guy for a while, amazed someone his height could squeeze onto a few of the seats.

He finished his reps and grabbed his towel, heading back across the room to do a few repeats on the machines near the man in an effort to strike up a conversation. "Hey, how's it going?" he said as he chose a machine two down from the other man and set the weight.

"Not bad. Gotta get the time in, ya know," the guy said.

"Yeah, yeah," a woman interjected as she walked up to them. "What he really means is that he's here to keep an eye on me."

"Got that right," the man agreed with a smile. "Can't turn you lose in a place like this. It's not healthy for my fellow man."

The woman shook her head and rolled her eyes, but her smile said the teasing pleased her.

"Ari is in the daycare and playing away. I'm off to aerobics. Have fun," she said, looking at Quinn before adding, "Don't know who you are, but if he tries to go over fifty pounds, remind him I'll kick his butt," the petite woman declared. "Doctor's orders."

"Bah," the guy grumbled. "Go to your class, woman."

The woman walked away, blowing a kiss to the man down from Quinn.

"Women. Think they can rule your life just because you put a ring on their finger," the man said in a good-natured tone.

"I heard that!" the woman called from the edge of the equipment area.

The guy laughed and shook his head.

"She'd be way too full of herself if she knew she was the best thing that happened to me," the other man said, settling back into the seat to do his reps.

"You been married long?" Quinn forced himself to ask. He wasn't a talker by nature, and making chitchat wasn't easy.

"Five years on Friday. You?"

Quinn shook his head. "Congrats, though."

"Thanks. Hey, didn't I see you in Cuppa Jo's the other day?" the man asked next.

Quinn didn't bother counting his reps. "Maybe. Jolie's a friend."

"Jolie," the guy repeated. "That wouldn't be short for Jolene, would it? Jolene Carter?"

Quinn paused and glanced at the guy, noting his intensity. "Something wrong?"

"What? No, no. She looked familiar is all. Just wondered if it was her."

Quinn released the weight grips and sat forward, his elbows digging into his knees. "Carter's her last name. You know her?"

The guy set his weights down with a mild *clank* and stood, grabbing his towel and water bottle.

"Yeah, I knew her. Long time ago. Guess that explains why she looked familiar, huh?" the man said before walking to the water fountain on the far side of the gym.

Quinn wanted to follow him but couldn't. Not without making it obvious he wanted more details of how and why the man knew Jolie.

He got up and headed for the front desk.

"Can I help you?" the attendant asked.

"Yeah, I can't remember if I signed in," he said, grabbing the board to scan the names. Three lines up, Blake and Kristine Parker had signed in, also checking off the box to say they were placing a child in daycare. "I guess I did sign in," he said, lowering the clipboard to the counter.

"You're too young to be forgetful," the female attendant told him with a smile. "Sure you didn't just need an excuse to talk to me?"

He took a quick glance as expected and mentally shrugged. Barflies and gym hotties were cut from the same cloth. "You know what they say, the mind's the first thing to go. See you around."

12

The next couple days flew by. Jolie kept a sharp eye out for Blake Parker, but thankfully he didn't return to Cuppa Jo's. She knew it was only a matter of time until Blake made another appearance and that she only postponed the inevitable, but she couldn't bring herself to go to the sheriff's department to confront the man.

She didn't want to have that conversation in public with curious town gossips trying to figure out what business she had with the deputy, and she most definitely didn't want to talk to Blake when no one else was around.

Basically— her hands were tied. At least that was the excuse she told herself.

Jolie stared outside the front window of Cuppa Jo's and watched the streetlights flick on. Friday night in a university town meant most of the college students had either headed home for the weekend, were hanging out at The Shake Shak, or hitting the local bars.

She wasn't a prude, but after what had happened to her with a single beer, she'd never understood the recklessness and stupidity that came with wanton drinking. She hadn't touched a drop of alcohol since that night, and she knew she never would again, her desire to drink permanently skewed by the attack and her part in letting things advance to the point that her teenage hormones had overridden her common sense.

Closing time finally arrived. Jolie waved good-bye to Elaine, who'd worked a rare evening shift since her kids were spending the weekend with their grandparents. Kaylee had gone to Damien's football game and the dance afterward at the high school.

Jolie made her way to her car, lifting her face to the sky to watch the lightning flash in the distance. The storm rolling in looked to be a doozy. She'd make it home just in time to pop some popcorn, turn out the lights, and watch the lightning streak across the sky.

Jolie kept an eye on the approaching storm and tapped her fingers against the steering wheel in time with the song playing on the radio. Tenth Avenue North's latest release hit home, and she found herself struggling to breathe.

A big, fat drop of rain hit her windshield, followed by several more, distracting her from the power of the lyrics. "Come on. Just a little longer." She didn't mind the rain, but she didn't necessarily want to get drenched trying to make it from the car to the house.

Thunder rolled in the distance, and lightning streaked across the sky. Jolie jumped and then laughed at her silliness. She wasn't afraid of storms, but that boom of thunder had rattled the very ground beneath her.

She caught every red light heading out of town and quickly resigned herself to getting drenched when the football game ended and cars spilled out of the high school lot, slowing her progress even more.

Finally she cleared the last light and turned onto her street when her car made a funny noise. Jolie frowned and punched down on the gas, but instead of picking up speed, the vehicle jerked and coughed. "Nooo! Are you kidding me?"

Jolie stared at the orange gas light on her dash and wondered how on earth she could've missed the fact the red arrow was several widths below the E.

The Maxima chugged along a final few feet before giving out. She coasted to a stop and shoved the car into Park, hitting her emergency flashers.

The gas station wasn't that far away, but it was closed. University town or not, some things didn't change, and Stone River was small enough that it meant getting gas before ten p.m. or else waiting for the station to open the next day. The truck stop on the far side of town at the highway entrance was open, but she obviously didn't have the gas to drive there to fill up.

A truck pulled up behind her and turned on its hazard lights. She sighed, but it was out of embarrassment more than anything else. Quinn. It had to be him, coming to her rescue. Great timing on his part, but since he already knew her secret for cutting, did she really want to be known as the woman of many issues?

A knock sounded on her window, but she opened her door instead, ignoring the blowing rain. "I'm out of gas," she told him.

"Put it in Neutral, and I'll push you off the road," he said, already drenched by the ever-increasing drops. "Head toward the church."

She waited until she saw his bulky shadow at the rear of her car before she took her foot off the brake. In short order, the car crept forward thanks to Quinn's strength, and she guided the vehicle into the empty church lot.

Thunder boomed above her head, and lightning lit up the sky. "I'm sorry about this," she said when Quinn opened her door.

"Lock up. I'll drive you home."

She gathered her things and managed to climb from the car, immediately drenched by the downpour. Quinn grasped her elbow in his hand, and together they made a dash for the truck. They ran side by side, and when lightning flashed with a sharp *crack*, she couldn't stop the small laugh that emerged from her throat.

"You're happy about this?" Quinn opened the passenger door and helped her into his truck.

"I love storms!" She raked her wet hair off her face. "Look at that sky. It's amazing."

Lightning streaked across the sky in multiple places, lighting the world around them. She turned her head and was struck by Quinn's expression, but when the light faded and came again, Quinn was gone, the door shutting her in darkness.

She huddled against the seat, the air conditioning inside the truck cold against her wet skin. The interior smelled like leather and rain and the man climbing into the vehicle beside her, a heady combination that left her senses whirling.

Jolie shook her head to clear it. She had accepted the date with Austin because he made her feel safe, but that was not how she felt around Quinn. At least, not when it came to physical contact. With Quinn, she was always out of sorts, and aware of him as a man. Not in a lustful way, necessarily, but as someone she could see herself with if... only things were different.

Jolie fastened her seat belt, glancing away from him when he lifted his shirttail to wipe the rain from his face.

When he finished, Quinn put the truck in motion, and Jolie laced her fingers in her lap and squeezed hard.

She couldn't sit there and stare at Quinn, so she looked out the window to watch every flash of lightning. They made her want to jump from the truck and stare up at the sky. Dance in the rain.

It was something Emma's mother had done one evening when they had gone to Emma's for a slumber party. Morgan had been afraid of the storm rolling through, so Emma's mother had encouraged the girls to leave the safety of the porch and dance in the rain. Now a storm didn't roll through without Jolie thinking of Lauren and that fabulous evening spent running around Emma's yard barefoot, soaked to the skin, and laughing.

In minutes, Quinn pulled up outside her house and stopped, but before she could thank him and make a run for her front door, he was out of the truck and rounding the front to her side.

Once again, she found herself dashing through the rain, only this time, the storm was right above them. The wind whipped through the trees around her house, the force slinging her hair across her face, blinding her. But Quinn's grip held firm as he led the way.

They made their way up the steps and under the porch roof, the pounding rain hitting the tin roof with a deafening roar.

Jolie had her keys in her hand, but it took two tries to get the door open because she kept getting distracted by the lightning. When she entered the house and turned, she wasn't sure what to do next. Invite him in? Say thanks, but he needed to go? What was the proper protocol for a friend of a friend who was now her... friend?

She opened her mouth to speak when Quinn took the decision from her and stepped inside. "Oh, um... yeah. Come in."

Quinn's gaze searched hers, intense as he looked at her. "You'd send me home in that?"

He waited in that ever-patient, expectant way of his, and she shrugged. "You don't strike me as the type to be afraid of storms, but I suppose since you drove me home, I'll let you stay until it blows over."

He plucked the wet T-shirt away from his body. "Thanks. I'll check your leg while I'm here."

"Oh... um... it's fine. There's no need."

"If you've healed, the stitches might be ready to come out. Lift your skirt."

She blinked at his audacity. "*Quinn...*"

Thunder boomed outside, and lightning flashed a mere second after, lighting the interior of her house. And Quinn's ornery grin. Was he being... playful?

"Better hurry before the power goes out."

Or what? He'd perform the task by feel?

The thought was enough to get her moving, but only because she didn't want him touching her any more than he had to.

To tell the truth, she liked this sense of friendship developing between them, and she didn't want anything to muck it up.

Like thinking her feelings for him could lead to more?

Even she knew Quinn's presence in Stone River was on a daily stay-or-go-when-he-wanted basis. Emma had told Jolie of the deal between Ian and Quinn, that Quinn had accepted the partnership Ian offered, but only if it came with an escape clause.

"Got a towel I can use?" he asked in his gravelly voice. "Otherwise I'm going to drip on you."

Jolie hugged her arms around herself, beginning to chill. "Yes. They're— Bathroom."

She was extremely aware of Quinn's presence behind her as she made her way down the hall to the half bath. She pulled a thick, white towel from the cabinet lining the wall next to the toilet and handed it to him, only then seeing the way Quinn looked at her, his gaze sweeping over her.

A glance down revealed her shirt plastered to her skin. Thank goodness she wore a camisole beneath so she was covered. "I'm, uh— I'm going to go upstairs," she told him, sliding by him and somehow managing to exit the small bath without making contact with him.

"I'll wait for you in the kitchen."

Once in the hall, she made herself walk to the stairs, but when he couldn't see her, she hurried up them.

Inside her bedroom, she locked the door and flipped on the light, hoping to calm the mad, uncomfortable fluttering of her pulse.

She pulled at her clothes, stripping down and shivering in the cool air of the house. Thunder rumbled outside and rattled the windows, speeding up her motions because if the lights went out... surely Quinn wouldn't come after her?

She yanked a T-shirt from her closet and then tossed it aside for another, inanely distracted by what to wear for her stitch removal. Another skirt? Sweats? Shorts were out of the question. She didn't own a pair, thanks to the scars on her thighs.

She settled on lightweight, baggy sweats for both their warmth and comfort. She was in the process of pulling them on when the power went out and her bedroom went dark. "Oh, crud."

"Jolie," Quinn called, his voice echoing throughout her house.

"I'm okay," she said in a rush. "I'm coming down."

She tied the sweats over her hips and slowly made her way to the door, a lightning strike aiding the process.

"Slowly," Quinn said from below.

"You mean I can't slide down the railing like I did as a kid?" Quinn didn't respond to her question, but she figured that was a response in and of itself.

"Where are your flashlights?" he asked once she had made it to the bottom of the stairs.

She led the way back into the kitchen and had to run her hands across the cabinet doors to count them to find the right one. "It's amazing, isn't it?" She found the large, lantern-style camping light. "How much we take for granted?"

With a press of the switch, light flooded the kitchen.

Outside the house, the storm raged on, and every so often, the wind whipped the overgrown crepe myrtle limbs against the siding and window.

"I *have* to trim that," she murmured, moving to the fridge and removing a pitcher of lemonade. She poured two glasses without asking Quinn if he wanted one, just to keep her distance from him. "It always beats against the house like it's going to tear it apart."

Behind her, Quinn pulled out a chair. Jolie turned, glasses in hand, suddenly frozen and unable to move.

"Ready when you are," he said in his gruff voice.

She couldn't imagine anyone going through what Quinn had, or living the circumstances leading up to the incident, but like her, his past had formed who he was now. And time had proven Quinn wasn't a bad guy. At least where some things were concerned. His past... Who was she to judge when she'd nearly killed Rick?

"Sit down. Let me see the cut." Quinn pulled out another chair to seat himself facing the empty one.

She inhaled deeply and focused on facts. As much as she wanted to deny him, the stitches did need to come out. She'd noticed that this morning after her shower.

Jolie handed him a glass and lowered herself onto the edge of the chair, setting her own glass on the table.

Head down, she pulled the baggy material of her sweats up her leg, folding it end over end all the way past her knee until the cut was revealed. It had healed nicely. Thanks to Quinn.

She braced herself for his touch and noticed his mouth curling down at the corners at her response. What a slap in the face it must be to him for one of Emma's friends to treat him that way. And given all he'd already done for her... "I'm sorry," she said softly. "As cliche as it sounds, it's not you. It's me."

He held her gaze and, after a few seconds, gave her a slight nod of understanding.

Quinn used the sanitizing wipes she kept on the table for quick cleanups on the knife as well as his hands. She bit her lip when he slid his palm beneath her knee and lifted her leg to rest atop his, sliding his hand higher on her thigh to hold the skin taut while he lightly snipped the stitches.

"Someone asked me about you today."

"Oh?"

Quinn lifted his head and held her gaze while he said, "Big guy. The same man who was in your coffee shop that day."

She struggled to maintain her composure. Quinn fished for information, a response. She wouldn't give him one. By the topic alone, she figured Blake was beginning to put the pieces together, confirm who she was. "It's a small town," she said, more than a little breathless due to her lungs seizing up. "I'm sure we will see him around."

He continued at his task of snipping the stitches and gently removing the threads one by one. Did he have to go so slowly? She wanted it done, wanted Quinn gone. And the longer it took for him to perform the task, the more aware she was of the gentleness of his fingers sliding over her skin.

"I talked to the guy."

"Stay away from him." The warning burst out of her before she could stop it, and as it lingered in the air between them, Quinn lifted his gaze back to hers.

"Why's that?"

Oh, why hadn't she kept her mouth shut? With four little words, she had opened up yet another Pandora's box of questions. "Um.... no reason. When he was in Cuppa Jo's, he gave me a bad vibe, that's all."

Quinn's green-eyed stare focused on her so intensely she fought the urge to jump up and run.

"That's it? A bad vibe?"

She managed a casual shrug even though her shoulders were so tense the act felt like a few bones snapped in the process. "I thought soldiers believed in such things?"

"I believe in following my gut. But are you sure that's all that bothers you about the guy?"

Quinn held her gaze a long, long moment as though willing her to continue, but when she didn't speak again, he finished his task.

"How's that?"

"Good. Didn't feel a thing." She looked up to find him close. So close she could see the deep green of his beautiful eyes and the little lines etched into his skin around them.

Everything stilled. The rain drilled into the tin roof above their heads, but the thunder rumbles were farther away now, the lightning strikes less intense and not as bright as before. They breathed in unison, and Jolie watched as Quinn's gaze lowered and fastened on her mouth. She stared, transfixed, as he leaned toward her.

The bright kitchen lights overhead flicked on, breaking the spell cast by the storm and lack of power.

Jolie drew back and glanced up at the ceiling, looking everywhere and anywhere but at Quinn. She quickly pulled her leg from atop his and shoved the rolled cuff of her sweats to her knee to cover the scars. "Let there be light, eh?" she said, forcing a laugh afterward.

She lifted her glass to her lips and drank, still too unnerved to look directly at Quinn, because unless she was mistaken, for a moment, it'd been like he'd wanted to kiss her?

Quinn picked up the pocketknife he'd set aside and cleaned it before folding it closed and standing.

"Good night, Jolie."

She nodded, watched as he moved silently down the hall, out the door into the rain.

Jolie followed him more slowly, waiting on the porch while Quinn climbed into his truck and drove away. That's when she came to a surprising conclusion.

Deep down. Way deep. A part of her was disappointed Quinn *hadn't* kissed her.

13

The following morning, Quinn's cell phone buzzed as he tightened the cap on a container of gasoline. He put the gas in the back of his truck to transport and dug his phone out of his pocket. "Quinn."

"It's Duncan."

Quinn climbed into his truck and started the engine. "What did you find out?"

"There were four farms around that area, and all of them had kids in Jolie's age range at the time she lived there. Plus, every farm had a pond for watering their animals."

Quinn swallowed back a frustrated mutter. "Were you able to narrow it down?"

"Some. Two of the farms had only girls, which left those owned by the Douglases and the Parkers."

Blake Parker. "Where are they now?" His blood began to boil. The guy at the gym hadn't seemed like the type to attack a woman, but Quinn was very well aware of what went on in the dark of night when the shadows gave power and turned normal men into monsters. "Where are the Parkers?"

"Rick Parker, thirty-four... He's in an assisted living home with brain damage," Duncan said. "Hospital report says he was swimming and hit his head on a rock. He's been hospitalized ever since. The younger brother, Blake Parker, twenty-four, is a sheriff's deputy. His last known assignment was Atlanta, but he's been transferred. The paperwork is backlogged so I couldn't find his new location."

"He's here," Quinn muttered. "I've seen him around, but not in uniform."

"You think it was him?" Duncan asked.

Good question.

He thought of the meeting in the gym, replayed the interaction between the guy and his wife. It wasn't often that people surprised him, but Blake didn't come across as being capable of rape. "I don't know."

"You keeping an eye on Jolie?" Duncan asked. "I can assign one of my men to guard her. I'd send Owen, but he's asked for some time off to be with his sister."

"No," Quinn said. "I've got this. I'll take care of Jolie. Just keep digging."

———

Quinn appeared on Jolie's doorstep and insisted on driving her back to the church parking lot where her car was parked. Once in his truck and on their way, she stared out the window and counted down the seconds until she could get out. Not exactly something a normal, red-blooded female did when spending time with a gorgeous man. But in the light of day, her regret over their missed kiss evaporated like the rain beneath the hot rays of the sun. Because with Quinn, a kiss wasn't just a kiss but an invitation to chaos she couldn't afford to have in her life.

"Jolie... about last night..."

She laughed silently at Quinn's choice of words. How many times had they been said the morning after? That didn't apply to her and Quinn at all, but she found it amusing just the same. "Nothing happened. There's nothing to talk about."

"I just wanted you to know I didn't mean to make you uncomfortable."

"You... It's fine. I mean, there's our friendship with Emma, right? I don't think either of us wants things to get weird in that respect."

"No," he agreed.

"Good. So we're on the same page." She forced a lightness and cheerfulness to her tone she certainly didn't feel. "Because we've got a lot of get-togethers with Emma and Ian in the future, and things would be... uncomfortable. I think you should keep your distance."

"That's going to be hard to do," he said softly, earning her full attention.

"What do you mean?"

"Blake Parker." He glanced across the cab of the truck. "I know he's here in town and that he's the reason you asked me to stay in Cuppa Jo's that day. You recognized him."

Jolie hugged her arms around her front, nails biting into her sides.

"Two neighboring families had boys around your age," Quinn continued. "You could make things simple and tell me who hurt you, or I'll keep digging until I find out for myself."

"You've been *investigating* me? You have no right!" What had he done? What if people found out he'd been checking into her past? What if it angered the Parkers? What then?

"You have to be protected."

"You don't think that's taking things a bit too far? What if I refuse? What if I don't want your help? What if seeing him was just a surprise because I haven't seen anyone from my hometown in fifteen *years*?"

He hit his signal in preparation of turning into the church lot.

"Is that what it was?" Almost as quickly, he shook his head, answering the question himself. "I didn't think so."

"You can't do this, Quinn. Stop interfering in my life."

"I will— when you explain everything to Emma."

Her sides were exploding from the pain she inflicted upon herself — until Quinn reached across the cab and grasped her wrist in his hand, yanking it away from her body.

"There are other ways, Jolie."

A laugh bubbled out of her chest but lacked any hint of amusement.

"I'll keep my distance if that's what you want, but you will be protected. Sweetheart, I won't let anyone hurt you."

He was hurting her. Didn't he see that? The past should have stayed the past, but he was bringing it up just as much as the sight and sudden appearance of Blake Parker had. "You have to stop. You can't keep involving yourself in my life without causing me more trouble," she said. "More people will find out, and I don't want anyone to know. I didn't want *you* to know! Gah, what a mess! Please, just drop it and leave things be."

When they arrived at her car, she realized Quinn had gone above and beyond once again when he lifted a container of gasoline from the rear of his truck and proceeded to fill her tank.

"How much do I owe you?" She grabbed her purse from where she'd set it on the front seat and dug inside for her wallet.

"There's only two things I want from you— the complete story, nothing held back, and confirmation of the man's name."

Her fingers clenched over the bills in her hand, and she yanked them out, then stuffed them into the pocket of his T-shirt. "This should cover it."

Too many people had been hurt because of that night. The last thing she wanted was for Quinn to take it upon himself to exact some sort of revenge against a *cop* because he felt honor-bound to Emma.

Quinn didn't even glance at the money. He met her gaze and stared hard, but she ignored the glare and got into her car. The moment he finished and tightened the gas cap, she started the vehicle, leaving the church lot as quickly as possible without letting herself look back.

An hour later, the chime on the coffeehouse door sounded, and Jolie glanced up, her body going hot and then cold in an instant. She blinked, praying the man approaching the counter was a figment of her imagination, because she didn't want to take his order. Not again. But unlike the last time, today there was no one else there to do it....

She considered running into the back room, simply ignoring him until he left. Instead, she grabbed a rag and wiped down a spotless counter, careful to keep her face turned away. "What can I get you?"

Blake requested a sandwich, a thermos of coffee, and a smoothie to go. She kept her back to him as she went to work, hurrying through the motions to get him out of her shop as quickly as possible. She kept her head down and totaled his order, refusing to place the change in his hand and laying it on the counter instead.

"Thanks."

She turned away as quickly as possible but heard him shove something into the tip jar. She wouldn't look. Refused. But her curiosity got the best of her, and she snatched the container up to peer inside. Having just handled the bills, it was easy to spot his tip. And instead of the change he'd left before, this time he'd left the remainder of the fifty he'd given her.

Once again, her body flushed hot and then cold as she glared at the offending pieces of paper. Ironically, it was the same amount she'd shoved at Quinn earlier. A God-smack if she ever saw one. Things like this... They didn't happen on accident.

The thought left her ill.

But why had he left so much? His total had been just under ten. To leave her both twenties she'd given him in return...

Did it mean Blake recognized her?

———

The morning and lunch rush had finally slowed by the time Kaylee showed up to work. Jolie took one look at the girl and swallowed hard. It was October in Georgia. Technically fall, but the days were nearly as humid as they were in summer. Yet Kaylee wore jeans and a tank top with a long-sleeve shirt over the tank. To hide more bruises? Jolie believed so, especially since the girl moved away every time Jolie got too close.

Jolie left the girl alone to work and settled herself in her office to focus on paperwork. Thankfully her supplies could be ordered online, but making sure she had enough without over-purchasing had become a balancing act she was still learning how to perform.

"Knock knock," Emma said from Jolie's office door.

Jolie looked up in surprise and then jumped up from her chair, racing across the room to hug her friend. "Hiii! Oh, I'm so glad to see you."

Emma laughed and returned the exuberant hug.

"Same here! I missed you guys. We were driving through town on our way home, and Quinn decided to stop for coffee. Are you busy? Do you have some time to come say hello while the boys talk?"

"Of course." She would never refer to Quinn or Ian as "boys" or believe Quinn's desire for coffee was anything short of making sure she and Emma connected again as soon as possible, but she still appreciated the gesture. "I didn't think you were coming home for a few days."

"We weren't, but we didn't want to get stuck in the middle of a hurricane. Have you seen the weather? Scary stuff."

"I haven't. But I'm so glad you're home." Jolie wrapped her arms around Emma and hugged her again. BFF hugs and chatter worked magic. This was proof. Jolie could feel the tension inside her lessening.

"Hey..." Emma said, pulling away to look at Jolie. "You okay?"

"Fine. Just tired and cranky." It was a struggle to maintain eye contact because now that Emma could see again, she had very rapidly picked up on reading expressions. Fake cheer didn't cut it anymore. Emma could see through that like nobody's business.

"Quinn said you've been working nonstop. And that you've had a few issues while we've been gone."

"I'm good. And I wouldn't call running out of gas an issue. More like— forgetfulness."

"But you aren't forgetful," Emma chided. "Jolie, you have to take care of yourself. You're running yourself ragged."

She ignored the fact that Quinn and Emma had apparently been discussing her and focused on setting Emma at ease. "I'm *fine*. I just hired a new girl. And as soon as I can, I'll hire another person, and then I'll be able to take more time off."

Emma linked their arms and tugged Jolie back into the main part of the building. Jolie's gaze immediately zeroed in on Quinn, who sat facing their return while talking to Ian at a table in the front.

"I could help. You wouldn't even have to pay me," Emma said. "Seriously. If you need help for a while, I'm here and happy to pitch in. Dad finally hired some waitresses to cover my shifts and Laney's at The Shak, and he knows now that I'm married, I'm going to be kenneling more than anything. I have the time, and you know you can count on me. Okay?"

It was an amazing offer. One she really couldn't afford to pass up, if only to get a day off to catch up on sleep. "You sure Ian would be okay with that?" Jolie asked.

"Okay with what?" Ian asked, turning in his seat.

Jolie could totally see why Emma loved Ian. Once, they'd shared the physical trauma of being blind and connected on a level few could as a result, but now they were even closer. It was sweet seeing them together because they fit each other so well. Complemented each other.

Both had dark hair and amazing eyes, though now Ian preferred to wear sunglasses when out in public. Ian was tall and muscular like Quinn, while Emma was average height, lean but curvy. But best of all, anyone could *feel* how much they loved each other. It was a strong, tangible vibe that surrounded them.

Jolie watched as Emma smoothed her hands over Ian's shoulders, not stopping until her palms rested on Ian's chest, his head nestled against Emma's stomach where she stood behind him. They were so in love sometimes it hurt Jolie to watch them. How could she ever have that?

"I told Jolie since Frank finally hired replacements for me and Laney, I can help her out here some so she could get some downtime. Just until she's ready to hire another person."

"You two just got back from your honeymoon." Jolie avoided Quinn's gaze. "Are you sure you don't want to take advantage of your father finally listening to you and finish your honeymoon since it was cut short?"

Emma's cheeks flushed a rosy red, and a chuckle burst out of Ian.

"I think we'll be fine," Emma said with a gush, earning more chuckles from her husband.

Ian turned in his chair and wrapped his arm around Emma's hips to tug her onto his lap. The gesture was simple yet sweet. Jolie watched, envious of her best friend's love for her husband. Of the tenderness they shared.

When Emma leaned down to give Ian a quick kiss, Jolie turned her head away to give them some privacy and found herself pinned by Quinn's steady gaze. In an instant, she thought of their near kiss, and she knew Quinn was thinking the same when his gaze lowered to the vicinity of her mouth. "Well, I should get back to work."

"No," Emma said, immediately turning to grasp Jolie's arm. "Please stay. Sit down. Tell me what all we've missed while we were away. Has Quinn kept an eye on you like I asked?"

The only available chair was beside Quinn. And she sooo didn't want to sit there. "Yes, he has," Jolie told them. "But I can't sit. I'm sorry. I really have a lot to do, but I promise we'll get together soon. Okay? I just wanted to come say hello."

"Jolie, do you have a sec?" Kaylee asked from the front.

Jolie welcomed the convenient interruption. "Be right there!" To Emma and Ian, she said, "See? I gotta go. But I'm so glad you're back."

She walked away, not acknowledging Quinn at all, and earned a frown from him in the process.

Okay, what happened while we were gone?" Emma demanded of Quinn once they'd made it back to the MacGregor house atop the mountain.

Instead of answering, Quinn unloaded the luggage and informed the newlyweds that he'd moved into the apartment above the kennel garage to give them some privacy but would still be around when they needed him.

Emma voiced the question again, but Ian distracted her, signaling with his hand for Quinn to make an escape while he could.

Quinn left the house and went out to work with Tucker, putting the dog through the commands and tricks the Lab knew so far and adding a new one to the mix. Tucker's performance rated better than average— until Emma emerged from the house and the dog spotted her. Within seconds, Tucker raced toward his beloved first owner, and all the dogs in the nearby kennel barked in greeting.

Emma petted Tucker as she walked toward Quinn.

"You're not going to get out of talking to me," she said bluntly.

One of the things he liked about Emma was her matter-of-factness. She didn't play the games some women played, and she was protective and loyal and friendly to a fault, especially where her loved ones were concerned. He'd never known anyone like her. Never had anyone care for him in such a way. It was... nice.

"Quinn? You and Jolie. What was that earlier today?"

He stared at her, wishing he hadn't promised Jolie to stay quiet. "What do you mean?"

Emma crossed her arms over her chest and hiked one of her eyebrows high.

"I didn't press things at the coffee shop *or* on the way home," she said, "but if you think you're going to avoid my questions, you're wrong. What's going on? What happened between you and Jolie, because I can tell something did."

He reached out to Tucker when the dog walked near and petted the large canine to keep from having to look at Emma. "Ask her."

"I'm asking you."

He frowned at the demand. Jolie's friends would want to know that she self-harmed and would want to help in any way possible, but he couldn't be the one to tell something that wasn't his to tell. "You need to ask her."

Emma was like a dog with a bone when it came to digging for answers. She'd proven it with Ian multiple times already.

Hopefully he'd left enough of a mystery in his response to guarantee Emma would dig deeper, not giving up until she learned about Jolie's secret so Jolie could get the help she needed.

"Okay, fine. I'll ask her. But now answer me this: Are you interested in Jolie?"

He straightened and signaled for Tucker to heel. "This isn't high school, Emma."

"Exactly. So don't be macho; admit or deny it. Are you?"

"No." He was attracted to Jolie. Intrigued by her. Curious as well as furious because she did the things that she did. She was beautiful, desirable— but not for him. He'd resigned himself to bachelorhood a long time ago. Women served a purpose in his life, but he never stayed in one place long enough to develop a relationship, not that they were his thing. What did he know about love? Commitment?

In his opinion, Jolie needed a man capable of being that steady constant in her life. A counterbalance to her out-of-control emotions that caused her to cut. That wasn't him.

"Oh," Emma said, disappointment layering her tone. "Well, I just thought you should know I'm okay with it if you are. I mean, I know you and Jolie are very different, but I thought I saw something there."

He'd have to be more careful of his reactions to Jolie whenever she was near. "You're mistaken."

"Am I? Or are you pretending there's not for some weird man-reason you think I won't understand?"

Man-reason? He wasn't going to touch that one. "Emma, you're a newlywed. Newlyweds want everyone to be as in love as they are."

"That's so not it," she said in protest. "Much... Okay, so maybe it is a *little*," she said with a rueful smile, "but it's not the only thing. You and Jolie—"

"There is no me and Jolie," he told her, fastening the leash in his hand to Tucker's collar to make sure the dog knew it was time to get to work.

"If that's the case, then why all the tension between you?" Emma called after him.

"She's your best friend," he said over his shoulder. "Ask her."

14

$\mathcal{E}$mma arranged for a meeting of the *Besties* later that evening. Jolie was surprised by the texted invitation to appear at her coffeehouse so soon after Emma's return, but then the group never stayed away from each other for long. It was an unwritten rule.

"So, tell us," Morgan said once the group was settled around a table in the front, where Jolie could keep an eye on things. "How was the honeymoon? Did Ian let you leave your hotel room to explore the islands at all?"

"Morgan!"

Emma's face bloomed with color, and Jolie was pleased to note her friend looked insanely happy.

"It was wonderful, and yes, we left the room. Ian's friend arranged for a private tour, and we went all over the island," Emma told them. "It was amazing. I even got to go snorkeling. You wouldn't believe all the colors of the fish. They were amazing."

"Did Ian go into the water?" Tasha asked, the question no doubt stemming from Ian's Navy SEAL days. Ian's blindness had forced him to face his claustrophobia. Blindness was Ian's personalized hell as it trapped him in his head with his worst nightmares.

Emma shook her head and frowned. "No. He stayed on the boat

and fished, though. And he's promised to swim with me at home," she added, her excitement at Ian's progress written on her face.

Across the way, Jolie watched as Kaylee bent to pick up a few napkins that had fallen on the floor. A grimace flashed over her pretty face as she straightened. Jolie frowned, the tension inside her growing by leaps and bounds.

"Hello? Earth to Jolie?" Tasha said, getting Jolie's attention. "You okay?"

Through a force of will, she pulled her nails from her skin and soothed the nail-rimmed area with light strokes of her fingertips. "Fine."

But when Jolie glanced around the table, she noticed Emma looking down, staring at the half-moons now embedded in Jolie's skin. She quickly repositioned her fingers and hid them from view, but from that point on, Emma's enthusiasm dimmed, and Jolie knew her time of reckoning was closing in fast. Emma's expression and the long stares she sent Jolie's way made it clear Emma had questions.

Over the next hour, Tasha filled them in on the latest anecdotes of being a vet in a fairly small town. Morgan broke the news of her plan to forego job hunting to place herself and the kids at her ex-husband's mercy regarding alimony and child support, and explained her plan to practice for the big baking competition to be held over the holidays.

Since Jolie didn't have anything to add other than how many hours she'd worked, she listened and laughed and commented where appropriate, leaving the conversation several times to help Kaylee close up.

Once the door was locked and the lights dimmed, she suggested the *Besties* move to the other side of the fireplace and the more comfortable couch and chairs.

"This is really nice," Tasha called out from behind the wall. "Cozy and comfortable. I totally get why people hang out here. It's beautiful and functional."

"Thanks," Jolie said, pleased by the compliment. She'd tried hard to make the interior of the coffee shop homey. The front consisted of basic tables and chairs where fast lunches and quick email checks could take place, but the back was designed with lingering in mind.

Before rejoining her friends, Jolie made herself another cup of decaf tea, just to give herself some quiet time and space.

"What's going on, Jo-Jo?" Emma asked quietly.

Jolie stilled. "Huh? What do you mean?"

"Seriously? Spill. I mean it. What was up with... that?" Emma tilted her head toward the now-vacated table where they'd sat moments ago.

Jolie fought a futile battle against the heat rushing into her cheeks. "Nothing."

"I *saw* you. Cut the pretense and tell me what's wrong, what's going on," Emma ordered.

Emma grabbed Jolie's arm and turned it over, revealing the half-moon crescents still imprinted in her skin. They weren't as deep as before but weren't completely gone, either.

"Jo... Talk to me," Emma demanded. "Since when do you do that?"

Jolie reminded herself to be thankful for Emma's caring and friendship rather than angry that she was being questioned about something so personal— again. "It's nothing. I just reacted."

"To what?"

Jolie jumped at the chance to take the focus off herself and decided to seek advice from her friends. "Kaylee."

"Your new girl?" Emma clarified, her eyebrows pinched over her nose.

"Hey, are you guys coming over or what?" Tasha called from behind the fireplace.

"Yes! Be right there," Jolie said. To Emma, Jolie added, "Come on. I'll explain."

Minutes later, they were situated in two chairs and the couch, and Jolie told them what little she knew of the girl and her boyfriend.

"You think he's abusing her," Emma said softly.

"Yes. At least it looks that way to me," she told her friends. "What else explains the bruises? But when I asked her about them—"

"She denied it all," Tasha said softly.

"Yeah." Jolie nodded, shrugged. "The last thing I want to do is push her away. Not when this may be her safe place."

"What about home?" Morgan asked, her hands wrapped around a frappe. "Her parents?"

"Her mother is dead. It's just Kaylee and her dad. From what I've gathered, he's a professor at the university, and he works a lot."

"So he may not even know what's going on with his own daughter," Tasha murmured. "If you've tried talking to her and she's shutting you down, I say go to him. She's underage. More reason to talk to the dad. If he's not aware of it, he'll thank you, and if he is..."

"Then what? Pretend it's okay then? Normal for her to have bruises?" Jolie shook her head, feeling her blood pressure rise just from talking about it.

"Jo," Emma said, reaching across the distance to Jolie's arm, squeezing it gently. "This is horrible, and yes, we'll do our best to help you come up with a solution, but you can't control what she does or what her father allows. And you can't get so upset that you... react like that."

"Like what?" Tasha demanded. "Am I missing something?"

"Me, too," Morgan said, staring at Jolie before looking back at Emma. "Did something happen?"

Jolie could feel Emma's stare boring into her. Could sense the unspoken questions whirling about in the air between them. This was her chance to open up to the *Besties* about everything— if she wanted. If she could.

But how could she explain self-harming without going into the pain of *why*? "It's nothing. Emma just saw me do something."

"What?" Morgan asked, blunt as ever.

Jolie inhaled and let the breath out slowly. "Emma saw me... dig my nails into my skin because I got angry. It's okay. I'm fine. See?" She flashed the back of her hand so they could see for themselves no permanent damage had been done. When she finally worked up the nerve to glance at her friends, she found the three of them exchanging worried looks.

"That's pretty intense, Jo. Have you ever done anything else?" Tasha asked. "Worse?"

A nervous laugh escaped her. "This isn't about me. It's about Kaylee," Jolie said.

"That's avoidance," Emma said, her voice strained. "You have, haven't you? You've... *hurt* yourself?"

"Oh, Jolie. *Seriously*?" Morgan asked, her mouth parting in visible shock.

More than aware of their combined censure, Jolie got up from the table and paced across the floor toward the fireplace. She stared down into the dark, empty well and thought of the childhood fairy tale of the girl who slept in the cinder box to keep warm. She'd read the story numerous times, but she'd always wondered— What if it wasn't just to keep warm? What if the fairy-tale princess slept there because that dark, small place welcomed her more than the world with all its cruelty? That there, in her black-sooted box, things were what they were and perhaps didn't seem quite so bad?

"Jolie, I'm sorry," Morgan said. "I shouldn't have sounded so... whatever. I'm just surprised. You know we love you, and we will do anything we can to help you with whatever is going on. We're just..."

"Hurt," Emma murmured. "We're your friends. Your *best* friends. How long has this been going on? Why haven't you told us?"

"I'm telling you now," Jolie whispered, knowing it wasn't enough.

"Yeah, but you've never once indicated that something was wrong," Emma said.

"Because I didn't want anyone to *know*," Jolie told them.

"But look at you." Morgan lifted and waved her hand in Jolie's direction. "Sweetie, you've got it all. You're tall and thin even though you practically live here, and... you're beautiful. Not to mention kind and sweet." Morgan shook her head, her long earrings flashing beneath the lights over their heads. "I would never in a million years have thought you would hurt yourself as a way to... Why *do* you do it?"

Jolie shrugged, uncomfortable with the praise, with the question. This was a mistake. She'd kept her secret so long for a reason. She didn't want to share it. Didn't want to have to explain. "Stop. Please. Just forget I said anything."

Emma walked to where Jolie stood. "We can't do that. We won't. Jolie, you can tell us anything. Absolutely anything. We'll understand."

Could they? Really? Because it was obvious they didn't understand. That they thought differently of her now.

"Jo-Jo?" Emma said, her tone pleading. "*Talk* to us. We're here for you, and we're not leaving until you tell us the truth. What's going on? How badly have you... hurt yourself?"

Jolie took another deep breath, her heart pounding against her ribs. *Just say it.* "Sometimes I... cut."

Morgan's gasp was loud, almost but not quite covering Emma's strangled inhalation. And Tasha... If she made a response, Jolie didn't hear it.

"Jolie, why?" Morgan demanded, sounding an awful lot like Quinn in that moment because her voice was so low and harsh. "Doesn't it hurt?"

A laugh huffed out of her chest before she could stop it. "That's the point."

The couch scooted on the polished concrete floor, and Jolie turned, along with Emma and Morgan, and watched as Tasha grabbed her purse and rounded the fireplace in a near-run, rushing to get out of the coffeehouse.

"Tash?" Emma called. "Tasha, don't leave!"

Tasha ignored the request and flipped the lock on the front door, seemingly unable to get out of there fast enough.

"She just needs time," Emma said, trying to cover the silence left behind.

"So do we," Morgan said, "but we didn't—"

Morgan broke off when Emma shot her a quelling glare.

"Jolie, you know we have questions. Like why you do it," Emma asked. "When did you start?"

"I don't know why," she said honestly, unable to look at either of them. She stared at the hearth, at the safe, dark cinder box.

"Sometimes it's anger, sometimes it's frustration. It builds up, and I just do it."

"How long? Since when?" Emma asked.

"I started doing it at fourteen, but I stopped ten years ago. I stopped for a long time," she said, feeling more than a little defensive.

"But you're doing it again," Emma said. "Aren't you?"

Jolie didn't answer, but she felt her silence was answer enough.

"Where do you... you know, hurt yourself?" Morgan asked next.

Jolie leaned her forehead against the smooth, varnished wood of the mantle. "My legs."

"I've always wondered why you wear skirts," Morgan murmured. "That's it, isn't it?"

Jolie nodded, still not looking at them. "Partly. And because they're comfortable. But in the beginning, jeans would irritate the cuts and... shorts revealed them so..."

Emma wrapped her arms around Jolie without speaking, and pretty soon, Morgan joined in on the group hug. And as much as Jolie appreciated their physical show of support, Tasha's departure was a slap in the face. "It'll be weird now," she told them. "With Tash."

"No," Emma countered. "We won't let it. She'll be fine. She's sensitive, Jo-Jo, and she hates to cry in front of us. You know that. I imagine she couldn't stand the thought of you hurting so much you'd do that."

Maybe that was it, but when Tasha'd left, she hadn't looked at all like she was about to cry. She'd looked angry. Disappointed. Like Quinn, Tasha had seen the dark side of humanity. Cared for animals neglected and abused. Animals had no choice, but the glaring fact remained that she cut by choice. Not the best of responses or how she wanted to cope with things, but she chose to think of herself as a work in progress. A sinner was a sinner, after all. And like it or not, self-harm was hers.

Morgan's phone went off on the table.

"That's my alarm. I promised Mom I'd be home by eleven." Morgan looked at them, her expression torn between friendship and maternal duty.

"Go," Jolie said firmly, somehow managing to produce a smile. "Keep your promise so your mom won't regret telling you she'd babysit while you do that contest."

Morgan's bracelets rattled together as she ran her fingers through her hair.

"I just hate to go now. Jolie..."

"I'm fine," she told her friend, forcing herself to make eye contact. "We'll be heading home soon."

"Em?" Morgan asked.

"I'll be here for a bit," Emma said.

Seemingly reassured by Emma's statement, Morgan grabbed her purse and phone and jog-walked back to where Jolie and Emma stood, hugging them both again.

"I love you, Jo-Jo," Morgan said. "But please don't do it anymore."

Jolie carried enough guilt without making a promise she didn't know whether she could keep no matter how hard she tried. "I love you, too."

With a final squeeze, Morgan left them and hurried out the door. Jolie followed to lock it once again, aware of Emma's silence as she gathered up mugs and plates and forks and carried them to the counter and the sink beyond. "Em, don't. I'll get those."

"I've got them," Emma said, setting them down with a clatter before yanking open the dishwasher door to load the trays.

"You're angry, too." Jolie smoothed her hands over her hips. "I should've kept my mouth shut."

Emma dropped one of the plastic plates with a clatter.

"No. You shouldn't have. And yeah, I'm angry, but only because you *didn't* tell us before now. *You didn't tell me.*" Emma stared at Jolie, tears in her eyes. "How should I feel when you've seen me at my absolute worst? You were there when I lost my mom *and* my vision. You watched me have to learn everything all over again. When I was mad at the world!"

Emma snatched the plate up once more and shoved it into the dishwasher.

"But you were there for me, and you wouldn't leave me alone no matter how badly I wanted you to, but you— *You* couldn't trust me enough to tell me you needed help? You couldn't confide in me? Do you know how it makes me feel to know you chose to hurt yourself instead of talking to me?"

Emma's anger and upset were tangible. Legitimate. Every word Emma said was true, but losing her sight and her mother's death had been accidents. Horrible, tragic accidents. Whereas the rape was brutal and deliberate, and something she couldn't express to others, especially not then, so soon afterward. How could she describe being pinned down in the mud? Feeling Rick's body rip through her insides, her virginity? "It's not like that."

"Then tell me what it's like, because I don't understand," Emma said, her voice raw. "Why do you do it? What happened to you to make you start?"

She gripped the back of a chair with her hands to hold herself up. "I couldn't deal with being raped," she heard herself whisper.

Emma wanted the truth? There it was.

"You... *Raped*?"

Emma barely managed to get the words out. Tears flooded Emma's eyes and trickled down her face, but Jolie didn't let herself falter. She couldn't cry. Not anymore. Not over Rick and Blake. Not over her parents' response to what had happened to her.

She couldn't. She refused to shed another tear.

"But you said you started cutting when you were— No," Emma said softly, shaking her head. "Oh, *Jolie*. That's why you moved here to live with your grandmother?"

Jolie nodded, aching inside because of the way Emma's voice broke when the details sank in.

Emma raced across the floor toward Jolie, but Jolie didn't move. Not even when Emma hugged and petted and cried copious tears.

Dry-eyed and weaving, all Jolie could do was stay on her feet. Because, come hell or high water, she wasn't going to let Rick and his brother destroy her now.

After a time, Emma drew back and lifted her hands to frame Jolie's face.

"Any more secrets?" Emma asked, her voice hoarse. "Because now's the time to spill."

Jolie shook her head, numb to her core. "Not a one," she whispered. "Think I'm a freak?"

Emma immediately pulled Jolie back into a fierce hug.

"Oh, sweetie. I think you're the strongest of us all."

15

Quinn was waiting for Jolie when she emerged from the coffeehouse ten minutes or so after Emma's departure. It was well after midnight, and the last thing she wanted was to talk to another person, much less Quinn.

Emma had wanted details of the rape, but Jolie hadn't been able to go into them. Thankfully Emma had understood.

Maybe one day she could talk about that time in her life, but for today, she'd shared enough.

The sight of Quinn leaning against his truck, thickly muscled arms crossed over his massive chest, sent a frisson through her despite her fatigue and exhaustion. Being emotionally drawn to someone mattered more than physical chemistry that could fade, but she'd be lying if she said she didn't find Quinn's looks appealing.

Quinn was a good-looking man. He was too hard to be considered handsome, his features too angled and sharp to be considered classic. But there was something about him, a ruggedness that drew her gaze whenever he was near. "Where's Emma?"

He tilted his head to one side and studied her closely.

"Emma asked me to drop her off so she could check on Tasha."

Jolie nodded, wondering what Tasha had to say about the

disclosure that had taken place tonight. "You don't have to follow me home. I'll be fine." She unlocked her car with a press of the key fob and put her purse and laptop inside the backseat, slamming the door before opening the driver's.

Quinn moved toward her, closing the distance separating them.

"Stop hovering, okay? Yes, I told them. I even told Emma why," she said pointedly. "I knew if I didn't, you probably would," she added, practically sneering the words.

He snagged her arm before she could drop into her seat.

"I gave you my word, and I've kept it. *Jolie*," he said when she tugged her arm away.

"I know! I know," she repeated, knowing deep down that Quinn *was* a man of his word and she was lashing out at him because her emotions were so raw. "It's just the way they looked at me. And then when Emma wouldn't drop it and kept asking why, I told her, and I swear it was almost like it had happened to her."

"She loves you. And I doubt there is a woman in the world who couldn't sympathize with what happened to you."

Jolie closed her eyes and covered her face with her palms. "Nothing will ever be the same."

"No, it won't," Quinn murmured close to her ear. "But now it's out in the open, and you can really begin to heal."

Bubbles of laughter lodged in her throat at the statement. How was that possible when Blake Parker now lived here? Was a Stone River deputy!

Quinn growled something under his breath, tensing.

She lowered her hands and turned to see a car slowing by the lot where they were, the metallic flash of an emblem on the side of a souped-up Dodge Charger making her heart race. The cop's window was down, the streetlights bright. And as though he'd been conjured up by her thoughts, she saw Blake Parker looking at them.

A combination of panic and horror filled her when she saw the car turn into the lot, lights flicking on. "I'm sorry," she said in a rush before plastering herself to Quinn and yanking his head down. She meshed their mouths together too hard and flinched from the pain of one of her teeth scraping her lip. But she didn't care. She wound her arms tighter, ignoring the way Quinn didn't kiss her back.

"Everything all right here?" Blake called from his open window.

Jolie released her hold on Quinn's neck but let her hands slide down his chest. She stared up at him, unable to face the man behind her. "F-fine," she said softly.

"Just saying good night," Quinn said in his damaged voice.

Jolie lowered her forehead to Quinn's chest, praying he wouldn't let go of her. Quinn had placed his free hand on her waist during the kiss, and now he rubbed his palm up and down her back in a soothing motion. Surprisingly, it helped ease the fear and anxiety flowing through her veins.

Blake was silent, no doubt assessing the situation. Jolie willed the man to go away, pressing her face into Quinn's chest like some lovesick teenager in the hopes Blake would think he'd interrupted a make-out session. *Go. Just go. Please, go.*

"Well, I'll leave you to it then," Blake said. "But don't linger too long, or I'll be getting calls from the neighbors."

"Understood," Quinn said.

Jolie waited, leaning against Quinn's body for support until the cruiser's headlights swung around and the vehicle left the parking lot.

The moment the cruiser picked up speed, she sagged in relief.

"You want to explain that?"

"No." She pulled away, but Quinn quickly ended her retreat by sliding his palm beneath her hair. "What are you doing?"

He lowered his head with purpose.

"Showing you how it's done."

Unlike her rash, smash-and-hold kiss, Quinn lightly rubbed his lips against hers. He didn't rush, and he didn't press hard enough to bruise. Light and easy, his mouth moved over hers.

She told herself to pull away, but she didn't. Couldn't. Because in all her life, she'd never been kissed like this. Quinn was gentle yet masterful, claiming more and more of her mouth and her senses with every second until she forgot to be afraid. In Quinn's kiss, she found heat and pleasure and the growing flicker of desire. The tiny, flickering wonderings of *what if?*

Quinn lifted his head and stepped away, leaving her dazed. She shook her head in an attempt to clear it, thankful he'd come to his senses. "You should go. Emma will be waiting for you."

"Emma's fine," he said. "Jolie—"

"I have to go home. I open tomorrow morning." She turned toward her car, but Quinn moved faster, planting a hand on the roof above her door so that she couldn't get in.

"What was that about? Who is he?"

"No one."

"Don't lie to me. You kissed me to avoid facing him. To make an impression. Who is he to you?" Quinn demanded.

She blinked up at him, the guilt of her lie weighing heavily on her heart. How could she possibly explain?

"Answer me, sweetheart."

She shook her head, her entire body quaking with a surge of adrenaline and fear.

"Jolie— Is *he* the guy who *raped* you?" he asked next. "Is that why you kissed me?"

Once again, she shook her head in denial, but she knew Quinn didn't believe her. And really, why would he when the reality was like splitting hairs. Rape. Accessory to rape. Was there a difference? The act was done. Blake had been present during it. A participant for a time— and a very real reminder in the flesh.

"Look at me, love."

Lashes lowered, she grasped his wrists in her hands and forced him to release her. "I have to go."

"Sweetheart, it's not your fault."

"Let *go*. You have no right to stop me," she whispered.

"I can't let you drive home like this. I'll take you."

"No. You have to get Emma. You—" Emma. Oh, what would he say to her? Jolie hated the thought of being discussed in low tones and whispers. Gossiped about like... like her mother had feared, one of the reasons she'd insisted on keeping the rape a secret.

As though he read her thoughts, Quinn shifted the hand against the roof of her car and gazed down at her, waiting for explanations she couldn't give.

"Another secret your friends don't know?" His eyes narrowed. "How have you fooled them all this time?"

"I haven't fooled them." She'd simply tried to pick up the pieces.

"You haven't told them the truth."

"They know more now than they did. And not everything should be shared," she added huskily. How could she tell them the complete story? Why would she? Her friendship with the *Besties* meant the world to her, and it would devastate her to think they might view her differently if they knew *every*thing.

Pity. Disgust. Horror. Blame?

Her friends were wonderful but... even she knew she held some responsibility for going against her parents' rules by sneaking out to meet Rick for underage drinking and partying. "Maybe I don't want to be defined by my past. Maybe I just want to look toward the future. I would think you, of all people, would understand."

She braved a glance at Quinn's face and faltered. Because instead of repulsion and the long list of adjectives she expected, she saw... anger— and admiration? No, that couldn't be right.

"Maybe I do. But you're still going to tell me who he is to you."

Every brutal, gory detail? "No."

"Then I'll find out from him."

Find out from— "*No!*" She swallowed hard and reached out, grabbing Quinn by his shirt. If Quinn went to Blake and demanded answers, what then? She'd be forced to acknowledge Blake, and she wasn't ready to face him. Not yet.

"Jolie, make a decision. You tell me— or I go to him," Quinn said, his head lowered so that his nose nearly brushed hers as he stared into her eyes. "But make no mistake, I will know the truth."

"Please," she begged. "Please, please, *please,* stay away from him. Quinn."

"You can't leave me hanging like this, wondering how he's involved."

She'd worked so hard to bury it deep, deep inside, but having told Quinn everything else, the desire to unburden herself of every single aspect of that night shot to the surface, desperate to be free. "I can't. I *can't* talk about it," she whispered. "Quinn, try to understand how much it hurts. I can't go there."

Quinn closed his eyes and pressed his forehead to hers, his hand on her nape. Her hands rested on either side of his waist. They probably looked like a couple snuggling at the end of a long night, but the reality was far different. He held her up, while she held him there to keep him from charging after Blake.

"If it's that bad, then why is he walking free?" he demanded. "What was his sentence? How could he become a cop?"

She flinched at his tone, shame filling her as it always did when she thought of that night and all that had transpired. "Please, drop it. Just leave it *alone*."

"How do you expect me to do that when you're terrified of him? You kissed me to let him think we're together, so that he'd think you weren't alone and unprotected."

She tried to argue, deny what Quinn said, but she couldn't. Maybe she hadn't consciously planned for that result, but that was exactly what had occurred. Quinn intimidated people. And maybe kissing him had been rash and she had no business dragging him into this mess only to deny him information, but she still prayed Blake would stay far, far away now that he'd seen them together.

"I will protect you, Jolie. I won't let anyone hurt you."

She blinked, her resolve faltering. Confiding in someone would be a relief. Talking about that night and what took place... But if she told Quinn the truth, what guarantee did she have that Quinn wouldn't go after Blake anyway? That her secret wouldn't be revealed because of Quinn's anger? It was too high a risk to take. "You need to go get Emma," she whispered. "You need to just... *go*."

Quinn glared at her and sighed, and she knew he realized she was right. Ian would be worried.

"I'll take Emma home and drive to your house. Wait up for me."

"Is that really why you want to come to my house?" She hugged her arms around her front and squeezed tight. "I used you earlier, just like you said. So he'd think... But if you think something is going to happen between us, it's not."

He glowered down at her, his mouth drawn into a tight line.

"I don't expect you to take me to bed. I just want answers."

"And I want time to think," she countered, forcing herself to stare into his gaze. "To decide whether or not I can give you those answers without my life imploding yet again."

16

"Quinn? Did something else happen?" Emma asked on the drive up the mountain. "I know you left after you dropped me off at Tasha's. Where did you go?"

Quinn firmed his grip on the steering wheel, wondering how he'd gotten so entangled in Emma's and Jolie's lives when all he'd done was agree to be Ian's eyes while training the dogs. "Tell me exactly what you know of Jolie's past."

"I think a better question is, what do you know?" she asked, sliding an inquiring look at him across the expanse of the truck.

"Everything," he said simply, fighting the desire to race up the mountain to deposit Emma as quickly as possible, forcing himself to take the dark, dangerously curvy drive at a much slower speed. Jolie wasn't the only one who needed time to think. To process things.

To calm down so he didn't wind up in jail for murder.

Jolie's fear of the deputy had been tangible, and it brought back every bad memory he possessed from his so-called childhood. Watching his mother put up with losers just so she could shoot up. Tending her wounds after they beat her, used her. Dumped her on the floor like trash.

Things happened, but that didn't make it easier to understand—or to stomach the violence.

"Everything?" Emma murmured, her tone holding more than a bit of surprise.

He considered his promise to Jolie void since she had revealed the news of her rape and cutting to Emma. "She confided in me."

"Why? No offense, but that surprises me. Jolie's not a sharer."

"It wasn't her best moment. I think she regrets it," he admitted grudgingly.

"I see."

"I know about the rape, Emma. And the cutting." He didn't look at Emma. Couldn't. Not when he knew she could probably see too much on his face now that she actually could see again.

Emma was quiet for a quarter mile before she inhaled and exhaled loudly.

"I can't believe she didn't tell me." Tears thickened her voice. "All these years, she's kept her secrets, and I didn't have a clue."

"She wasn't ready," he murmured, focusing on the road and trying to wrap his mind about the statement.

"Yeah, but what changed?"

"Does it matter?" he muttered. "At least she's talking."

"True," Emma agreed. "I honestly don't know much about her life before she moved to live with her grandmother. Jolie hasn't ever talked about her childhood very much. I thought it was because she and her parents don't seem to get along, but now I know that's when it happened. The rape. She said that's when she started cutting."

He nodded, glad to hear Emma confirm what he already knew. "Do you know if she chose to move here, or did her parents send her away afterward?" The answer meant the difference between Jolie wanting to escape what had happened to her and feeling as though her parents blamed her for it. Whatever had happened to her— and he would get her to tell him everything— had been brutal. He'd seen the darkness in her eyes. The pain and suffering she had endured and sought to escape now.

"I'm not sure," Emma said. "I know Jolie was homeschooled by her mother during grade school and that they were very strict. But I have no idea if she decided to move or if they... You don't think they *made* her, do you?"

"Family dynamics aren't my specialty," he said, angry on Jolie's behalf. He needed more information. Fast.

"I just can't imagine it. I mean, she moved between eighth and ninth grade. My mom and her grandmother were friends, and they introduced us so Jolie would know someone at school when it started. I introduced Jolie to Morgan and Tasha. Then Mom and I had the accident. Things are a little vague for a while, but I remember Tasha and Morgan saying how weird and sad Jolie seemed. It made me feel sorry for her, and when I returned to school, Jolie and I were made lab partners. How could I not have guessed what she'd been through? What she was doing to herself?"

He leaned his elbow against the door and rubbed his fist over his mouth to smother the bitter words springing to his lips. Emma hadn't been able to guess because Jolie had been so good at hiding her pain, swallowing it down and holding it in to survive.

"Does this change how you feel about her?" Emma asked.

He made the turn into the long driveway leading to the house. "There's nothing between us, Emma."

"But if you didn't know all the stuff she has going on," Emma pressed, "would it make a difference?"

"She's not to blame."

"Not about the rape, no, but—"

"She's not to blame," he repeated, ending whatever Emma was going to say next. "We all cope differently. Eating, drinking, sexual depravities. Cutting is Jolie's method. If nothing else, we have to respect the fact she doesn't open fire on innocent bystanders in movie theaters. She doesn't harm anyone else." Including the monster who'd hurt her.

"You make it sound like it's okay," Emma said.

"No. I'm simply saying she could do more damage if she chose to. We all could."

While Emma pondered his words, he realized all of this

reaffirmed his instincts to steer clear of Jolie. Getting involved with her meant having every aspect of their connection, of a friendship or relationship with her, paraded before the *Besties* and talked about as a group. Jolie's friends loved her, cared for her, and would always be in Jolie's "business" because of that.

The fact that Jolie had kept her secret this long meant only that she was desperate to keep their view of her pure, and not be judged or pitied because of what had happened. He understood her need for privacy. To compartmentalize that part of her life and bury it deep. The problem with that was never knowing when something would pop up and rattle the foundation. Which was exactly what had happened earlier tonight when she'd kissed him, just to avoid facing the deputy.

But his regret? Kissing her again. He'd hated the hard, painful grind to be what she thought of when she remembered kissing him. That's why he'd gone against his hands-off rule.

"I think you know more than you're telling me," Emma said.

He wasn't going to confirm or deny. And he definitely couldn't hint at the deputy's involvement—whatever that was—when the *Besties* were likely to form a lynch mob and go after Parker themselves.

Quinn stopped outside the front door for Emma to get out of the truck, but she didn't budge.

"Fine. Don't tell me. The suspense is killing me but— whatever." She slanted a look across the truck's interior that pinned him to the door. "Just promise me— Whatever's going on, you'll look out for Jolie? Be there for her? She wouldn't have talked to you if she didn't trust you."

He couldn't agree since he'd threatened blackmail to gain answers, but he stared into Emma's worried expression and nodded. "You have my word."

"And if you ever need to talk about it... You know, get advice? You'll—"

"*Emma.*"

"Fine, fine. I get it. I don't like it," she murmured, "but I get it."

Emma climbed out of the truck and shot several more glances over her shoulder toward him as he waited for her to reach the house. Once she'd let herself in, he drove back down the mountain, his thoughts for Jolie's well-being battling his need to track down Blake Parker and beat the man to a pulp.

He'd met his share of good, honest policemen who'd signed up because they wanted to serve and protect. But he'd also met more than a few who hid behind their badges to serve and protect their own agenda. That had to be the case here. Otherwise, Jolie wouldn't be afraid.

But why was his gut telling him the guy was harmless? That didn't fit the scenario.

Quinn turned into Jolie's driveway and parked behind her Maxima. The house was dark, but he knew she was awake. A flutter of the curtain by her front door confirmed it.

He took his time getting out of the truck. Used every second to try to calm the edginess inside him. She would tell him the truth, or he would go straight to the sheriff's department and get the answers he wanted. Her choice. "Open up," he said when he stood on her threshold.

A long moment passed before he heard the deadbolt turn. Jolie pulled the door just wide enough for him to see her face.

"Go home, Quinn. I'm not—"

He planted his hand on the flat surface and gently pushed until she backed up a few steps.

"Can't we just forget about it?" she pleaded.

"Forget you kissed me— or forget why you kissed me?" He watched the various expressions flicker across her face. She tried to hide her thoughts but failed. Her fear and unease revealed themselves in her eyes. What was the saying about a person's eyes being the gateway to their soul? That was definitely the case for Jolie.

"Quinn—"

"No," he said firmly, following her retreat into her home and shutting the door behind him. "You're going to tell me what happened, or I'll track that deputy down and find out for myself."

She shook her head repeatedly in denial.

"Please, just drop it."

"He raped you, Jolie. How do I forget that?"

She closed her eyes and released a frustrated sound.

"He *didn't*. It wasn't... It wasn't him."

Relief poured through him at her words, but it still didn't explain her response to the man.

A low huff left her chest, and she turned to pace into the kitchen. Quinn followed her, fighting the urge to draw her into his arms but needing to get facts first.

She turned and leaned her hips against the countertop behind her, arms crossed over her front protectively. Jolie refused to look at him, and he knew he would never forget the image of her standing there in the dark of her kitchen, bowed beneath the weight of her past.

"Start at the beginning. Who raped you?"

She made a mournful noise in her throat that slipped beneath his skin and tugged at the heart he'd long ago hardened to such sounds in an effort to keep his focus. Quinn moved toward her, not stopping until he stood toe-to-toe. "Talk to me."

Jolie turned away and slowly walked into the living room. Once again, he followed, silent. Watchful.

A low huff escaped her.

"You're hovering."

"I'm waiting. And being patient about it, too." He continued to wait for her, willing her to tell him the entire story. "I've never told anyone about my mother. About my life before I joined the service. But I told you. That means something to me."

He couldn't get any more honest than that. Relating the events around that time of his life had taken some doing. Having a drug addict and crack whore for a mother wasn't something to be proud of. Foster homes, teachers, principals, social workers... Once they read his file and knew his history, he'd often been pulled aside to be read the riot act over what was expected of him and how one slip would send him packing. How they were doing him a *favor* by letting

him stay in their presence. Jolie had simply accepted him, past
and all.

She turned to look at him, her thick hair falling over one
shoulder.

"A part of me wants to face him and order him to leave town, but I
have this fear," she said, lifting her hand to her chest and rubbing it
over her heart, "that instead of going he'll— that *everyone* will find
out."

He hated that she lived with that fear. That constant unease of not
knowing when the bomb was going to explode.

She fingered the necklace at her throat, the silver chain glinting a
bit in the low light of the room.

"You don't know what I did. What I'm capable of."

"Tell me."

"That night... I went to the pond. Rick was there with his little
brother. Rick offered me a drink with this look on his face, like he
didn't think I would. And because I wanted to look grown up, I drank
the whole thing. It was summer and hot, so we stripped down to our
underwear and went swimming. Blake, too. It was fun. No big deal.
But then Rick and I started splashing and playing and... kissing.
Then we were on the edge of the water making out. I thought that
would be it because his little brother was right there, but then Rick...
He wanted more. I got s-scared. I told him to stop because I didn't
want to, but he just... laughed. He said I wouldn't have come there if I
didn't w-want to."

Quinn's nails bit into his palms, and fury bombarded him on all
fronts. He didn't move, though. He didn't want to do anything to
interrupt Jolie and possibly stop the words she finally gave voice to.

"I fought him," she whispered, her voice low, strained. "I fought
him, and I almost got away because we were in the mud, but Rick
caught me and— He just kept laughing. Even when he— When he
ordered his brother to hold my arms."

Curses sprang to mind, and Quinn bit them back, needing to hear
the details.

"Blake was a-a big kid. H-he was only t-ten, but he outweighed me by a hundred pounds. And he adored Rick s-so... I don't remember everything. Just the pain a-and being afraid and how big the moon looked. I kept fighting and got my hands loose. That's when I g-grabbed a rock and hit him as hard as I could. Rick fell on top of me, and I screamed and screamed until Blake helped push Rick o-off. That's when I saw the blood."

Quinn remained silent. He just didn't have the words. He wanted to leave, track the men down, and kill them with his bare hands. They deserved it for hurting her the way they had. But then she lifted her lashes and looked at him, and he folded her against his chest because he couldn't do anything else but hold her.

Jolie gripped his shirt in her fists, her breath hot where it penetrated the material next to his skin. She trembled and shook, and he knew he couldn't leave her. Not now. "You aren't to blame for what happened."

"But I *am*."

He smoothed his hands up her arms and palmed her face, rubbed his thumb back and forth beneath her lower lip to soothe the quivering. "You are *not* to blame."

A laugh bubbled out of her throat.

"I almost killed him."

"Jolie, he raped you. You had every right to defend yourself."

"I just wanted him to stop. I wanted him *off* me."

She removed his hands from her face and pushed them away.

"Rick had brain damage. He was in a coma. And if I p-pressed charges against him, his parents were going to charge me with assault a-and attempted murder. They said they would tell everyone."

"Tell them what? It was self-defense."

"Who would believe me? I was at the pond drinking with him. And the way I was dressed... How I had flirted with him... It was my word against a man who couldn't defend himself from the accusation. So my parents and his talked, and they came to an agreement. No charges against me so long as I didn't sully their name by mentioning rape."

In other words, her parents had made a devil's bargain. And at what cost? By hiding the rape and not talking about what had happened to her, sending her away, they'd damaged Jolie, almost as much as Rick and Blake Parker had. "How did they explain his injury?" he asked, already knowing the answer.

"They said he'd gone swimming and slipped, hit his head on the rock."

"And the brother? He wasn't punished, either?"

She shook her head. "He told them he thought Rick and I were wrestling. Playing, like we'd been playing in the water. Maybe he told the truth. He was *ten*. Maybe he didn't understand what was really happening."

"Maybe not then, but he knows what happened now." Quinn stared at her, more questions filtering through his mind because of Blake Parker's presence. Bad enough the man was part of the family who had so badly hurt her, but to now be a cop and in a position of authority. How had that happened?

No wonder Jolie hadn't wanted to be recognized. She'd moved away to escape the torment of living in the same town as her rapist's family only to have the guy's brother show up here. No man should ever be able to hurt a woman and get away with it.

As though reading his thoughts, Jolie lifted her head and met his gaze.

"You can't say anything to Blake," she said firmly. "You can't *do* anything, Quinn."

He lightly gripped her long hair in his hands, rubbing the soft silkiness between his fingers. "Do you know why he's here?"

She closed her eyes briefly, squeezed them tight.

"No. I haven't been brave enough to confront him yet."

"Don't. Stay away from him." He didn't want her anywhere near the man.

She leaned against him, and he welcomed her weight and the trust she placed in him with the act.

"I will if you will," she said softly. "Quinn, please. I couldn't stand it if you got into trouble because of me."

"I can take care of myself."

She spread her hands over his chest, the heat of her touch blistering his skin beneath the cotton material. He watched her gaze as it shifted, moved to the area of the scar on his neck.

"I mean it. Please stay away from him. Maybe Blake doesn't recognize me. It's been fifteen years, so it's possible."

"Not likely." The moment he uttered the words, he wished he could take them back. She didn't need to be frightened any more than she already was by the man's presence in town. When she met his gaze again, he added, "I won't do anything stupid."

As he'd hoped, Jolie's expression softened, some of the tension easing, replaced by wry amusement.

"Thank you. I didn't think it would help to talk, but I think it has. You and Emma…"

He liked being lumped into the friend group with Emma, refusing to acknowledge that he wouldn't mind being thought of as more. "Maybe next time, you'll listen to me." Quinn cuddled her against him in a show of support, a part of him amazed that she let him and pleased that she seemed to welcome his touch. But the moment he inhaled the scent of her, his mind warned him to keep his distance.

He silently recited the many, many reasons they couldn't be more than friends, even as he pulled her closer, hugged her tight.

Emma and the ever-intrusive *Besties*.

Jolie's issues with cutting in the aftermath of the rape.

His own past and a lifestyle that didn't lend itself to relationships.

But in the dark of her living room, all of those reasons faded away, and he only knew that he wanted to kiss her again, comfort her from now on. "I'm sorry they hurt you."

"I don't want to think about it anymore."

Quinn cuddled her closer, reined in his base desires to focus on offering her the support she needed from him. "Are you going to tell Emma the details?" he asked. "About the rape or Blake being in town? I can do it if you like, if it would make it easier for you to talk to her once she knows."

Jolie was quiet a long moment, her head buried against his shoulder.

"No. I-If I decide to tell her, I'll do it. Don't say anything."

She'd answered his questions, shared her story. Opened herself up to him in ways she hadn't with her friends or anyone else. He couldn't ignore that or break her trust in him. "I will protect you," he promised. "You're not alone."

She lifted her head, used her hands to balance herself against him so that she could brush her mouth against his. He felt the tension inside her change from unease to... something he was afraid to name on the chance he would get it wrong.

When she broke the kiss to draw in a shaky breath, he kissed her cheek, not pressing too hard or too fast but allowing her to get used to his touch. Because somewhere along the way, between promising Emma he'd watch over Jolie and now, he'd crossed a line he couldn't uncross.

"Quinn?" she whispered, her breath blowing hot against his ear.

He immediately drew back and stared down at her averted face. "No pressure. Not from me. Never from me, sweetheart."

"I'm sorry."

He stroked his fingers over her soft cheek. "Don't be. It was just a friendly kiss."

"Thank you. You don't want more, trust me," she added, backing up a few steps. "I've tried before t-to... to date and k-kiss, but I panic. And then there's Emma and— things could get awkward."

That they could. Didn't mean he liked her pointing it out, though. "It's fine."

She shook her head repeatedly.

"It's not. I wanted to say thank you, but I shouldn't have kissed you, especially not when I-I have a date with someone else tomorrow night. I mean, this evening," she said, wincing as she looked toward the clock on the wall by the door.

He let her words bounce around in his brain and tried to wrap his mind around them. She had a date. Later that day. What happened to her panicking when it came to those types of things?

He didn't like it. "Cancel."

"What? No," Jolie countered, not hesitating in the slightest before voicing her response. "You said yourself that"—she waved her hand in the air between them—"was just a friendly kiss."

Jolie shot him a wry smile over her shoulder as she walked to the door and opened it. Definitely his cue to leave.

"He's actually a really good guy. I've known him a long time. He's... safe."

Safe.

The description left him feeling frustrated, knowing she was willing to settle for less than she deserved.

Quinn moved toward her and crossed the threshold, wondering how he'd gone from being a protector to a confidant to the guy listening to her talk about dating another guy, all in one night.

17
____

The following morning, Jolie felt every second of her up-too-late and then ultimately sleepless night.

Quinn's words rang in her mind long after he'd left her house, and she wondered where he'd gone afterwards. Back up the mountain to the apartment above the kennel? Or had he driven around town looking for Blake?

Tommy came in to work the breakfast and lunch hours and went on his way, leaving Jolie to cover things until Kaylee arrived. The busyness helped keep her mind off Quinn and the fact she'd kissed him. Again. But nothing kept the memory of those kisses, and all she'd shared with him, at bay for long. *Why* had she kissed him? Why had he kissed her twice? Weren't things complicated enough?

Alone, Jolie scrambled to take care of the long line behind the register. In the midst of chaos, Emma walked in along with Morgan. Both took one look at Jolie and slipped behind the bar without asking.

While Morgan took food orders, Emma marked cups for Jolie to fill, ringing up patrons with ease thanks to her many years tending The Shake Shak. By the time the mass had thinned and no customers waited, all three of them sagged against the counter.

"Wow," Morgan said. "Talk about a crush. I had no idea you did this in a day."

"A day? That was just an hour," Emma added with a glance at her watch. "Where's your help?"

"Good question." Jolie scanned the storefront for any sign of Kaylee. "Kaylee's never late, and I would've thought she would call if she wasn't coming in."

"Hope it's nothing serious," Emma said, a worried frown puckering her eyebrows. "You don't think it has anything to do with the boyfriend, do you?"

"Oh, I hope not." But it was a possibility. Whatever the reason, the girl needed to provide an explanation. "I'll call her cell and see what's up."

Jolie found Kaylee's number and called, but it went straight to voice mail. Jolie tried calling Kaylee's house next. "She's not answering. Think I should call the university and track her father down?"

"She may have just forgotten she was supposed to work, or mixed up the times," Emma said. "Happened all the time at The Shak."

"I suppose," Jolie agreed.

"Seriously," Morgan said. "Maybe her dad got sick or something, and it slipped her mind because she's taking care of him. Or maybe she got sick."

"Or maybe she just forgot," Emma said again, giving Jolie a pointed look. "It happens. I'm sure she's fine."

Maybe she *was* overreacting to Kaylee's absence. Just because something bad had happened to her didn't mean Kaylee would also be a victim. The teen had repeatedly said that Damien had stopped when asked. Jolie had to give the boy credit for that instead of labeling him with Rick Parker's sins. "I'm sure she is too. Something just came up. I don't doubt Kaylee will call when she can. Thank you both for pitching in. Hopefully it'll be a slow night for Elaine, or I'll have to cancel."

"Cancel what?" Emma asked, picking up on the specification. "Is something going on?"

Since their last conversation had involved dark, gloomy things and more than a little upset, Jolie managed a smile. "Yeah, actually. I have a date." Morgan and Emma stared at Jolie, visibly shocked. "Come on, really? Is it that hard to believe?"

"Uh, yeah," Morgan said, the words holding quite a bit of attitude. "Especially when you've always said there's nothing between you and Quinn."

Jolie glanced at Emma, her smile fading at the sight of Emma's pleased expression. "Stop. Both of you. I'm not going out with Quinn."

Emma's smile fell.

"What? Then with whom?" Morgan demanded.

"Austin. And stop looking at me like that. You're always telling me *to date*. Why do you look like I've lost my mind now when I finally am?"

"It's not that, Jo," Emma said. "It's just the timing."

"Yeah," Morgan added. "Should you be dating when you're upset and..."

When Morgan's words trailed off, Jolie finished the statement. "Cutting? Guys, I slipped. Okay? I made a mistake, but that has nothing to do with me accepting a date with Austin."

"Austin Cantrell?" Morgan clarified.

Jolie nodded, watching her friends' reactions to that bit of news. Austin really was a nice guy. The kind of guy she could see herself actually having a future with— eventually.

But the memory of Quinn kissing her blasted through her mind, scattering all thoughts of Austin. Quinn, with his fierce expressions and scar. With his tattoos and heat and strength.

"Jolie? Hello? Earth to Jolie?"

Morgan snapped her fingers in front of Jolie's face.

She blinked back to awareness, blushing at the amused expressions her friends wore. "Yes, Austin."

"Oh, she totally zoned out and missed the question," Emma said with a laugh.

Question? "What question?" Jolie squirmed beneath the intensity of their combined stares.

"How did all of this come about? And when?" Emma asked, obviously setting her desire for Jolie to date Quinn aside—at least for the time being.

"Austin came in the other day, and we talked and…"

"And?" Morgan pressed.

"And then he left," she said, unable to keep from smiling when her friends looked horrified. "But then he came back inside and asked me out. I'm not sure what we're doing, but I told him I could probably get away a few hours this evening. At least, that was before Kaylee failed to show up for her shift. I guess I should call the repair shop and cancel."

"No way," Emma said. "I'll help Elaine. You're going."

"Definitely," Morgan said with a nod. "I'll stay and help, too."

Jolie tilted her head to one side and studied her friends. "You have Ian to deal with," she said to Emma. "And you have your kids," she added to Morgan. "Neither of you have time to stay."

"We'll make time," Emma said.

"Yeah." Morgan winked and fluffed her hair, her bracelets jingling. "You help all of us out, all the time. You've earned more than a few favors. We'll handle things here while you kiss the stutter out of ol' Austin."

Jolie could feel the color seeping up her neck into her face long seconds before Emma and Morgan giggled at her embarrassment. Kissing Austin might be fine and fabulous, but once again, the thought of kissing any man had Quinn's image flashing in front of her eyes.

Last night's kisses had been sweet, but they'd contained a headiness and allure that promised much more. Quinn had held himself in check, a fact for which she was eternally grateful. But a part of her couldn't help but wonder what it would be like to experience Quinn's passion unfettered by her fear and her past and all the baggage she carried.

But since marriage wasn't an option because he wasn't the marrying kind...

"Oh! I almost forgot to tell you my news," Morgan said. "That's why Emma and I came by. Well, we wanted to check on you, too. Make sure you were okay after our talk."

"I'm fine," she said, meaning it. "In a way, it helps that you know. I feel more accountable to not cut because I know it will upset you—"

"Got that right," Morgan said.

"And know I need to pray and find other, more productive outlets," Emma said, pretending Morgan hadn't commented. "What's your news?"

"I made it to the next round!" Morgan jumped up and down in excitement, her blond hair bouncing around her shoulders. "I can officially enter the contest."

Jolie shook her head, confused. "What? I thought you had already entered."

"Well, I sent all the information in, but there's a review process and a selection board just to narrow things down. But anyway, I made the first cut— Oh, wow. Bad pun under the circumstances," she added, making a face. "But you know what I mean."

"I do. And that's great, Morgan. I'm happy for you." Jolie opened her arms and gave her friend a hug. "So what happens now?"

Morgan drew back with a grin.

"Another elimination round. If I make it through that, I get to submit more photos of my work, and my business plan."

"Business plan?" Emma asked.

Morgan nodded, either completely oblivious to Emma's concerned glance or else choosing to ignore it.

"Yeah. For a bakery or something. I have to figure out exactly what I want and what's feasible. But the prize money should cover the cost."

Jolie schooled her expression into one of total support. Maybe Morgan was getting in over her head, but she obviously thought she was ready for such a move, despite her recent divorce and juggling parents and kids. Jolie wasn't about to be the naysayer. "I'm sure you'll do great."

Morgan checked her watch and grimaced.

"I have to get home, but I'll be back once I get the kids ready for bed. You going to be okay for now, Jolie?"

"I'll stay," Emma said. "I'll call Ian to let him know what's going on. He and Quinn can have some male bonding time or something before they come to get me at closing."

"Or I could drive you home," Jolie offered. "After all, I'll be back to lock up. It's no problem," she said, desperate to avoid another run-in with Quinn. Plus, driving Emma up the mountain and dropping her at her door was the least she could do for her help tonight.

Morgan gave both Emma and Jolie a hug before she gathered her purse and the shopping bag she'd carried in earlier and headed toward the door with a wave over her shoulder.

"I'm worried about her," Emma said.

"You and me both."

"You don't think she can do it?" Emma asked.

Jolie returned to the counter and began cleaning up in the lull between waves of coffee addicts. "It's not that I don't think she can, I just wonder...at what cost."

"Explain," Emma said, grabbing a few dishes and carrying them behind the counter to be washed.

"Emma... look at me. I love this place. It's my life and I'm fine with that. I knew going into it that I'd work long hours and rarely catch a break for a long, long time until things get going really well. I'm willing to make the sacrifice. But Morgan... She has kids. Young kids and elderly parents. How does she think she's going to work a business from the ground up?"

Various expressions flickered across Emma's face.

"I see what you mean. I guess whatever happens is meant to happen. If she wins, which we both know is kinda a long shot, then we'll just have to help her figure things out and pitch in where we can. Isn't that what *Besties* are for?"

It was. And how like Emma to remember that and point out that fact.

"Jolie, are you too stressed from working so much? Is that why you... slipped?" Emma asked pointedly.

"I do it when I get overwhelmed, yes." Jolie avoided the subject of the rape and Blake entirely. Emma would do something, say something to the man. She wouldn't be able to help herself because that's just who she was. Passionate, protective, and loyal. "It's not one specific thing, but a combination of frustrations and feelings and things I can't really explain. I'm not proud of it; I don't *want* to do it. Sometimes I don't even think about it. I just do it and regret it later."

Emma nodded as though she understood, even though Jolie knew Emma didn't comprehend at all. Still, Emma was willing to accept the explanation at face value, and Jolie loved her friend for that.

"You know I'm here for you whenever you need me," Emma murmured. "Whether it's to work or to talk or— to go with you to see someone? Maybe you have and I don't know about it, but—"

"I haven't."

"Okay, so... maybe we could find a professional who might be able to help in a way I can't? I'm speaking from experience here. I had counseling when I lost my sight. I hated it at the time, but it did help."

Jolie stared into Emma's worried eyes and saw love. Caring. And even though she was embarrassed by her go-to instinct to self-harm, she was glad, in a way, that Quinn had forced her hand in telling Emma. "No promises, but I'll think about it."

Emma's relief was obvious as she stretched out her arm and placed her hand over Jolie's.

"I love you."

"I love you, too."

"Good. Because if you wind up with Austin, it means the guys are going to have to become friends. I refuse to let anything or anyone keep us apart."

"Let's not get ahead of ourselves," Jolie said, shaking her head at Emma's goal setting.

"Oh, boy. Looks like the movie theater just let out. Here we go again," Emma said, moving to stand behind the cash register. "When's Elaine coming in?"

"Half an hour," Jolie said.

"Looks like it's going to be a busy thirty minutes."

You have a nice voice," Jolie said to Austin, staring at him in amazement as they stood on the outskirts of the university's main lawn.

Austin had stopped by the coffee shop to pick her up, but instead of driving, they'd wound up walking to the university for a concert featuring a few local country bands.

She didn't like the crowds or the obvious partying going on, but once the bands started playing, she began to enjoy herself. Standing beside him, she'd heard Austin singing along to the more popular songs. "I never knew you could sing."

She watched as Austin's face turned a ruddy shade of red, and a shy smile turned his average features into more.

"I can't, not really. When I was a kid, it was part of my speech therapy," he said. "I probably ruined that whole set for you."

"Not at all." She nudged his arm with hers with the finesse of a fifth grader with her first crush. Dating, flirting... How did women do this? She never knew what was too over-the-top or— "Oh," she said, seeing a barely twenty-something woman lift her shirt to flash the band and everyone nearby.

Jolie wasn't sure what to do other than stand there and ignore the younger woman.

"You, uh, wanna go get something to drink?" Austin said near her ear.

She nodded, probably a little too vigorously. "Yeah, sure."

They quickly left the crush of people near the stage and moved to the sidelines then down toward the far end of the open lawn.

"We can stay back here if you want," Austin said. "It's a little less crowded."

She nodded again, more than a little relieved. "The concert's great."

"But not really your thing," he said, giving her a searching look.

Jolie decided to be honest. After all, if she started a new chapter in her life by coming clean about cutting, she had to tell the truth in other areas, too. "Crowds make me a bit nervous. I'm sorry."

Austin's low laugh sounded warm and rich and inviting, like his singing voice.

"They make me nervous, too."

"Really?" she asked, surprised by his response and wondering if he said that to set her at ease.

"Yeah. I hate'em. Give me a quiet garage and a car any day. I thought you'd want to be up front, though, so..."

She laughed at the way they were both so nervous and trying to be polite, to do what they thought the other person would enjoy. "Staying back here sounds great to me."

"Next!" a voice yelled from within the concession booth.

"What would you like?" Austin asked, opening his wallet.

"Water, please."

Austin's eyes lit with his smile as he pulled some bills from the folds.

"A water, a Coke, and a giant pretzel," he said to one of the people operating the booth.

Jolie bit her lip and shifted her weight from foot to foot, absurdly pleased by his order. The stand offered an assortment of beer along with sodas, and she'd be lying if she said she wasn't a bit worried that Austin might get as smashed as some of the others there, just because he could.

They found an empty bench along one of the walkways. Austin split the pretzel in half and handed her one of the large pieces. "Thanks."

"I'm not sure bread and water really counts as a date," he said, watching her. "I'm thinking I still owe you a nice dinner sometime.

Someplace quiet, with thick steaks and water in a fancy glass instead of plastic. You interested?"

Jolie stared at Austin's smile and shoved aside the thoughts of Quinn crowding her brain aside. Quinn was complicated whereas Austin was surprisingly... not. "Yeah. Yeah, I am."

18

---

*I*an threw the dart at the board where it landed with a resounding strike. Bulls-eye.

Learning to play darts blind had been a challenge Ian had issued to Emma several months ago when his brother had hired Emma to help Ian cope with the loss of his eyesight. Ian had thought the task impossible, a diversion voiced to get Emma's mind off the loss of her beloved pet. But Emma had devised a way and forced Ian to cooperate with her, earning all of their respect in the process. "Do you ever get tired of winning?" Quinn muttered, staring at his friend's score.

"You ever get tired of losing?" Ian's chuckle rubbed salt into the wound. "You're distracted. Have anything to do with a certain tall brunette?"

Quinn dropped into the leather recliner inside Ian's den and flipped the lever for the footrest, a loud signal that he was throwing in the towel for now. Tucker immediately bounded over to have his ears scratched. "How do you know she's a brunette?"

Ian slowly made his way to the dartboard, smirking even more as he felt his darts' positions and tallied the score.

"Emma's described her friends to me," Ian said, pacing back to the throwing line taped to the floor. "She also filled me in on Jolie's past."

Quinn wasn't surprised. Ian and Emma were extraordinarily close due to all they'd weathered together. No doubt, Emma had confided in her husband as a way of coping with her own feelings and anger over the rape and the inability to help Jolie.

"She okay?"

Quinn rubbed his free hand over the scruff on his chin. "She works too hard trying to forget it happened, and she cuts herself when she gets upset. That sound okay to you?"

He'd done some research on Deputy Blake Parker. The man had a spotless record, had already won a few commendations for actions in the line of duty, and on the sheriff's department's website, it listed Parker as the replacement for a deputy who'd retired several months ago, leading Quinn to believe Parker's presence in town wasn't an orchestrated move on his part.

Ian's throw drilled into the board.

"So your distraction has nothing to do with her being on a date with another guy tonight?"

Quinn glared at Ian, wondering how a blind man saw so much.

Tucker looked back and forth between the two humans, his tongue sagging out of the side of his mouth. The dog grunted out a sigh and lowered himself to the floor, unamused by them.

"Ahhh," Ian said, grinning.

"If you want a fight, I'd be happy to take you on," Quinn warned. "Throw your darts, and mind your own business."

"Did you mind yours when I lost my vision? No. Better think again if you think I'm passing this up."

Another dart struck the board, the sound echoing in the room.

Quinn pinched the bridge of his nose and screwed his eyes shut. "There are a billion and one reasons Jolie and I wouldn't work. We're dysfunction at its worst."

"Excuses." Ian lifted his hand for another shot. "If you want something to work, you make it. She's been hurt. She needs someone—"

"Who knows what it's like to be normal," Quinn interjected. "Ian, she lives in a Victorian with a white picket fence out front. I've never owned anything in my life. I don't know what it's like to make someplace a home. This is the longest I've ever lived in one spot, and I've told you more than once our partnership is a trial run. Emma would kill me if I led Jolie on only to take off in a month."

"So don't leave. You've got to settle somewhere. Might as well be here," Ian said, his words followed by the thud of the dart.

Quinn opened his eyes and glared at Ian again, not that his friend could see it. "It's not that simple."

"Can be if you want it to be."

"You're as bad as Emma. All the honeymooning has messed with your brains. Both of you want everyone to be a happy couple. Aren't you and Emma and Tasha and Owen enough?" Quinn flipped the lever on the chair to close the footrest and lunged to his feet. "I need to check on the dogs."

Ian's chuckles followed him out the door and into the hall.

"You can run, but you can't hide," Ian called after Quinn. "The fact we're talking about her is proof. Sure you don't want to run into town and pick Emma up? She said she was staying at Cuppa Jo's until Jolie made it back from her date."

Quinn picked up his pace and left the house, but the cool night air did nothing to clear his senses. He made his way to the rear of the kennel and the stairs to his apartment but paused when Goliath's massive head appeared above the gate.

The Great Dane stood on her rear legs and draped her paws over the wooden barrier, her entire body moving with each wag of her tail. "What do you think?" he asked, moving to pet Goli's head and scratch under her ears in the dog's sweet spot.

Shaking his head at himself, Quinn released Goli and grabbed his keys from his jeans. "Don't laugh," he said to the dog, pointing a finger at an inquisitive Goli for good measure as he left the kennel behind.

An hour and a half later, Quinn sat in his truck outside Cuppa Jo's and watched as Jolie and her date strolled down the sidewalk toward her business.

Seeing her with the other man set Quinn's teeth on edge. The two of them laughed and smiled and talked with ease. Until they reached the edge of her storefront and the guy reached out to keep Jolie from walking on. They were in the shadows, along the brick edge where one shop ended and Cuppa Jo's began. The perfect spot to— "Ah, man."

What was he doing? Was he really going to sit there and spy on her like some stalker? Watch to see if the guy kissed her good-night?

Quinn forced himself to look away and stared at the people walking alongside his truck. Stone River was busy tonight, crowded like something big was happening on the Zailer campus.

He tapped his fingers against the steering wheel and stared at more people until, drawn despite his best intentions, he looked back to where Jolie and her date had stood and found the spot empty.

He quickly straightened in the cab of the truck and scanned the sidewalk in front of her shop, then gazed inside the well-lit coffeehouse, spotting Jolie talking to Emma, Morgan, and another woman. He turned in the seat, finally eyeing Jolie's date getting into a flashy muscle car older than either of them. Even worse. It was kind of hard to hate a guy with great taste in women *and* cars.

The interior of Cuppa Jo's dimmed. After a bit, the woman Quinn didn't recognize left the building and drove away. He waited impatiently, debating whether or not to interrupt Jolie's conversation. He could always use the excuse that he'd come to drive Emma home to save Jolie the trip up the mountain— and maybe catch a few comments about how Jolie's date had gone.

The low rumble of a new-model Camaro rolling slowly past the coffee shop ended the mental debate because the driver also seemed interested in who was inside the business. Quinn watched in his mirrors as Kaylee's boyfriend pulled to the side down the street and turned off his lights but didn't leave the vehicle.

Quinn's instincts gnawed at his gut. Something wasn't right. According to Ian, Emma had stayed to help out at Cuppa Jo's because

Kaylee Forbes hadn't showed up for her shift. So why was the boyfriend there if she wasn't?

A flash of light drew his attention back to Cuppa Jo's as the women emerged, the streetlights reflecting briefly as the glass door opened and closed. Emma and Morgan waited while Jolie locked up, and then they walked toward the parking lot at the side of the building— the angle providing the Camaro's driver with a good view of what was going on. Seconds later, Morgan's minivan left the lot and headed in the direction of Rose Hill. Jolie's Maxima appeared soon after.

Quinn started his truck, noting the Camaro's lights flicked on as well. He waited, watching as the car pulled out behind Jolie, but when she turned to take the mountain road, the Camaro continued on. He left Emma in Jolie's capable hands and followed Kaylee's boyfriend— all the way to Jolie's house, where the kid parked in the shadows and waited again.

J olie dropped Emma off at her house and declined the offer to come in for a bit. Between working and the date, not to mention her restless night, she was worn out.

On the way down the mountain, she turned off the radio and took her time driving, not wanting to get into such a hurry that she missed a curve.

The dark mountain road might intimidate some, but she'd spent her whole life in the country, where the only light came from the night sky.

Some of her anxiety and worry lessened along the way as she prayed for guidance, and she reminded herself she could only do so much. People made choices. Some good. Some bad. She'd made more than a few bad choices herself, but spending the evening with Austin had been a good choice. Since she'd known him so long, she'd been comfortable with him. And after the initial awkwardness, and that flasher at the concert, they had both relaxed and had fun, talking nonstop as they got reacquainted with one another.

Austin still liked to read sci-fi and work on cars, and his music tastes ran more toward classic rock than the pop music of their childhood. He preferred hunting to fishing, played a bit of guitar, and cheered for any team who played against the Jayhawks due to a rivalry with a cousin from Kansas.

Jolie turned into her driveway and gathered her things only to pause when she spotted Quinn's truck parked a little ways down her street. He was there, even though she'd driven Emma home?

She left her car, locking it with a press of the key ring on the way to her porch. Close by, an engine roared to life, and the flash of headlights drew her attention. Tires squealed, and she paused as Damien Bennett's sports car drove past with a low thump of the radio. He slowed at the end of her driveway, then hit the gas and took off down the street.

What on earth? Had Damien followed her *home*? Waited there for her? Why?

Was that why Quinn was there?

Quinn's truck began moving, taking the same path as Damien. She waited on her porch until Quinn passed before hurrying into the house and locking herself inside. At first, she'd thought it strange that Quinn was there, but now... now his presence gave her comfort. She might have been oblivious to Damien, but Quinn had been paying attention, and she knew he would make sure she was safe, protected. Just like he'd promised.

Across the room, her answering machine blinked twice in rapid succession. She dropped her things to the floor and rushed to press the button.

"Jolie, it's— It's Kaylee. I'm okay," the girl said.

Jolie heard someone speak in the background. Damien?

"I won't be coming to work. I'm sorry. I should call the coffee shop and say this to you in person, but this is just easier. I'm sorry," she said again. "Damien doesn't like me working there and— Please don't be too mad at me. Um... I have to go. I'm really sorry. Bye."

Jolie stood there and stared at the machine. Damien had demanded the girl quit her job? And Kaylee had done it!

Her choice.

The machine beeped for the second message, this one recorded two hours after the first.

"Jolie, it's me again," Kaylee said, sniffling. "I wanted to call back and say thank you. For caring. It— It means a lot."

The girl's words were choked and barely audible due to her crying.

"I'm sorry. I'm really, really sorry I didn't listen to you about Damien. You were right," Kaylee whispered, breaking into sobs. "You were right about everything. I broke up with him. Just wanted you to know."

The phone clicked loudly as Kaylee hung up, and after a second, the answering machine reset itself.

Jolie grabbed the desk chair and sat down before her shaking legs could give out. Kaylee had sounded so upset. Was it too late to call her now? Just to check on her?

Jolie glanced at her cell and grimaced. She and Emma hadn't left the coffee shop until late, and the drive to take Emma home had taken over an hour round trip. It was nearing one. Too late to call Kaylee's home without waking the house and causing problems. Still, she picked up the phone, her hand hesitating over the numbers.

She set the phone aside to grab her cell, deciding to text instead so Kaylee would see the message if she was awake, but it wouldn't bother her otherwise. *Call me if you want to talk.*

Jolie sent the text and waited anxiously to see if Kaylee would respond, but the girl didn't. As upset as she'd sounded, Kaylee had probably cried herself to sleep.

Jolie walked to the window and pushed the curtain aside, searching the darkness for any sign of Damien or Quinn. When she didn't see either of them, she double-checked that the door was locked and went through her nightly routine before heading back downstairs to see if Quinn or Damien had returned.

Apparently it was going to be another sleepless night.

J olie wound up falling asleep on the couch. She missed the church service but thankfully her internal clock woke her in time to get ready for work. She rushed through her shower, determined to stop by Kaylee's house on her way.

She pulled into the empty driveway and frowned. Kaylee's father was either a Sunday morning church-goer or an early riser. Or maybe he'd seen his daughter's upset and taken her somewhere last night? A getaway of some sort?

A knock on the door received no response. Jolie knocked again, giving up when she heard nothing from within the house. She got back into her car, worried about Kaylee even though she barely knew the girl. Who wouldn't be worried, though?

She backed into the street and spotted Damien's Camaro parked in front of his house. Jolie hit the brakes, debating whether or not to pay the teen a visit. Especially since he'd taken it upon himself to *visit her* last night.

Was Kaylee over there? Had she changed her mind about the breakup?

It was possible. Anything was possible where teenagers were concerned. Which was exactly why she shouldn't be involved. She wasn't Kaylee's parent and couldn't control the girl's decisions. Worrying about Kaylee was only adding stress to Jolie's life. Stress she really didn't need.

Please, Lord, show me what to do.

She released a frustrated sound and grabbed the gearshift, glaring at Damien's car as she shoved her Maxima into Drive.

She'd call Kaylee from work. Better yet, she'd run by the small university on her way to Cuppa Jo's, and if Kaylee's father was there, Jolie would inform him of the bruises Kaylee sported so the man knew the issues his daughter faced with the breakup were indeed serious.

Then she'd mind her own business.

Unless Kaylee made contact again and wanted help. Asked for it.

Jolie drove to the university and found the correct building with relative ease. The campus and building were both virtually empty due to the day, but she managed to find a tired-looking janitor who pointed her in the direction of Professor Forbes' office. The man also relayed that Kaylee's father was indeed there.

Jolie checked her watch and frowned at the time. She had to hurry, but Kaylee's safety was more important than pouring coffee.

She knocked several times on the professor's office door and heard shuffling and noise on the other side. "Professor Forbes? I'm here about Kaylee. Could I please have a few minutes of your time?" she called through the door.

The dark-stained wooden panel finally swung open, and an older man appeared, looking disheveled and ill-kempt.

"What is this about Kaylee?" he asked. "Is something wrong?"

The balding man tucked his shirt into his creased pants and blinked at her with sleepy eyes. Had he slept there? Left Kaylee home alone? "I'm... My name is Jolie Carter. Kaylee works— worked," she corrected, "for me at Cuppa Jo's."

"Oh, yes. Nice to meet you."

Jolie fought her frustration and the southern manners that required niceties before blunt conversation. "Nice to meet you, too. Professor, Kaylee called me last night very upset."

"Yes, she and the Bennett boy are having a spat."

So Kaylee's father did have a clue what was going on? "Yes, Kaylee left a message saying she had broken up with Damien."

"Ms....?"

"Carter," she supplied once again.

"Ms. Carter, Kaylee's an emotional girl. I appreciate your concern, but she's fine. I talked to her after the breakup, and she said she was going to spend the night with a friend from school."

Relief poured through Jolie. Of course. Any girl fresh from a breakup sought comfort from her *Besties*. Kaylee was no different. And no doubt that was why Damien had driven by her house. He'd been looking for Kaylee because the girl was supposed to have worked. "I see. I'm very glad to hear that." Seeing the man's confusion, she added, "I was worried because Kaylee was so upset, and when I stopped by your house this morning to check on her, no one answered."

The professor straightened a bit and smoothed his hand over his sleep-mussed hair.

"I spend the night here sometimes when my research requires it. With Kaylee at a friend's, I saw no need to traipse home only to come back again this morning."

The man stepped back into his office and opened the door a bit wider for her to step inside. Jolie hovered just over the threshold, noting the stacks and stacks of books lining the floor and bookcases along the wall, flanking a couch with a pillow and blanket the man had apparently used the night before. "Um... I'm not sure how to say this so I'm just going to blurt it out," Jolie said softly. "But I was wondering if you've noticed the bruises Kaylee's had recently?"

Once more, the professor ran a hand over the longer hair on the sides of his head, smoothing it back behind his ears. "Can't say that I have. What kind of bruises?"

Oh, this was going to get awkward. "Some on her wrists and on her neck. I asked her about them, and she told me they were from Damien."

The man's face turned ruddy. "I see."

Jolie clasped her hands together in front of her and took a step forward. "Professor Forbes, I'm only here because I like Kaylee, and I'm concerned for her safety. I witnessed Damien and Kaylee in an argument outside my store, and he was very...aggressive with her, grabbing at her and ordering her around. To be honest, I was not unhappy to hear she'd broken up with him.

"I guess what I'm saying is that maybe you could talk to her about it or... something. I don't know. I just know that if Kaylee were my daughter, I would want to know what she's going through so that I could help her. That's all." The moment the words emerged from her mouth, Jolie faltered, transported back in time to that hospital room where Rick's father had berated her for injuring his son while her parents had stood by without saying a word.

Her parents had been shocked by her behavior, shocked by the events that had transpired, of that she was sure. But to this day, she still couldn't believe they'd let Rick's father say such horrible, awful, damaging things to her and not defended her or—simply made the man stop.

Professor Forbes nodded but didn't make eye contact with Jolie. He stared down at his desk, at a picture frame and photo she couldn't see.

"I hear what you're saying," he said softly. "I'm afraid Kaylee takes after me in that she doesn't like to show her emotions. When she gets upset, she likes to be alone to gather her thoughts and lick her wounds."

"It's a characteristic I know well," she told the man, lowering her guard a bit because she could see how much he loved his daughter. "Kaylee is a bright, beautiful girl. She's already proven that by ending things. I'm sure she'll be fine."

"Yes. Yes, me, too. She didn't want me to worry, which is why she called last night to let me know she was going to stay with her friend. I'll talk to her when she comes home."

Knowing she couldn't expect anything more, Jolie smiled and glanced at her watch. "I have to go. It was nice to meet you. And, please, tell Kaylee to call me if she needs to talk or— if she wants her job back."

"You fired her?" the man asked, sounding surprised.

"No. No, not at all. Damien demanded that Kaylee quit so... she did."

The man scowled at the statement, and Jolie felt bad about dropping that bombshell and taking off. "I have to go open my coffee shop," she said, moving to the doorway. "Please have Kaylee call me, even if it's just to tell me she's okay."

Kaylee's father didn't respond, so Jolie turned and left the building. She hurried back to her car, relieved the meeting was over.

She drove to Cuppa Jo's, passing Austin's garage along the way. Austin was standing outside dressed in his Sunday best, and he lifted his hand when he spotted her.

Jolie smiled and waved, her mood lifting immediately when she thought of the fun she'd had with him on their date.

She pictured them attending church together, but her smile faded when Quinn's image intruded on the happy picture.

Quinn attended worship services on occasion, mostly when Emma and Ian needed a ride down the mountain and Duncan wasn't available. But Quinn claimed he was a Believer and she accepted his word at face value, knowing not all Christians regularly attended church, while some non-Christians did.

Thankfully the rest of the day was busy enough to make time fly. Emma ran the register and bussed tables while Jolie and Tommy handled the coffee making and food prep.

Jolie kept busy, her mind occupied and off of Kaylee. Professor Forbes seemed like a nice man, one who would handle things given what Jolie had told him.

Closing time finally arrived, and Emma hurried to dim the lights and change the sign before someone could sneak in. There was something about that last five minutes before the doors were locked that had people hankering to stop in despite the posted closing time. "Ready?"

Emma nodded and smiled. "Oh yeah. And just so you know, Quinn's outside. You won't have to drive me home."

"I don't mind, Emma."

"I know," Emma murmured, sliding a sly smile in Jolie's direction. "But when you drop me off without coming inside..."

What? Was Emma suggesting this was Quinn's way of getting to see— *her*? Could it be? "He's just making sure Kaylee's boyfriend isn't outside. That's all."

"If you say so," Emma said, looking a bit disappointed by Jolie's lack of enthusiasm.

"I know so." Quinn was the other person Jolie had been thinking about all day. Despite his presence outside her house last night and the way he'd taken off after Kaylee's boyfriend, Jolie had expected Quinn to call or visit to fill her in on what was going on. But he hadn't.

Because things were awkward now that they'd kissed?

She could certainly understand if Quinn felt that way, seeing as how keeping an eye on her had taken on a life of its own he probably hadn't expected.

Emma frowned and held the door while Jolie set the security system for the night.

"Well, you can't blame me for trying," Em murmured.

"Actually, I can," Jolie said, forcing a laugh as she stepped onto the sidewalk. "I'm good, Em. Quinn and I are... friends. I don't think we should mess that up," she added, locking the door with a twist of her keys. She turned to face Emma and found Quinn standing right there, his expression making it clear he'd heard her response. "Um... Hi."

Quinn dipped his head in a nod and took a step toward his truck.

"We'll follow you home to make sure Kaylee's boyfriend isn't around," he told Jolie.

Emma's head pivoted from Jolie to Quinn and back to Jolie before Em sighed and moved to wrap Jolie in a hug.

"I love you. Let me know whenever you need me," Emma said.

"I love you, too," Jolie whispered, squeezing Emma tightly.

The moment Em stepped away from Jolie, Quinn headed to the passenger side of the truck to open Emma's door. While he did that, Jolie walked to her own car and climbed inside, pulling out of the lot without another word to either of them.

At her house, Jolie hurried to open the front door as quickly as possible, just so Quinn could leave.

The look on Quinn's face when she'd said what she had about them being friends... Was it just her or—had Quinn not looked pleased at being relegated to the friend zone?

19

Jolie opened bright and early Monday morning. Tommy was there to pitch in, and Emma arrived soon after, even though Jolie hadn't said to come. Between the three of them, they kept the line of Monday morning caffeine addicts to a short wait, providing coffee fixes and breakfast sandwiches until lunch kicked in. Finally a lull came between the afternoon classes at the university and the high school's dismissal bell.

Jolie kept an eye out for Kaylee, hoping the girl would come by to talk, maybe ask for her job back. But she didn't show.

Thankfully Tommy was able to cover Kaylee's shift. He left the counter to clean tables and retrieve dishes, while Emma manned the counter so that Jolie could email her order for the week. She lowered herself into the office chair with a grateful sigh, legs aching from being on them all day.

Jolie took a careful look at the form and made some tweaks. She hit send and got up to return to the front just as a knock sounded on the door.

"Ms. Carter?" a male voice said.

Jolie lifted her head with a smile of greeting, thinking one of her customers had taken a wrong turn on the way to the restrooms. Instead, the very ground beneath her feet tilted and swayed, and she clutched the desk to keep herself upright, staring in horror at Blake Parker. He stood dressed in his deputy's uniform, one hand holding a small, black notebook and the other resting on the utility belt around his waist.

"I'm sorry if this is a bad time—"

"Yes," she managed, biting the word out between her clenched teeth. The shock of having this meeting forced on her was too great. She couldn't move. Couldn't blink. She stood frozen, hunched over the desk.

Blake glanced down the hall toward the front of the coffee shop before he stepped into the room.

Seeing him come toward her left Jolie scrambling back. She knocked into the office chair, sending it rolling across the floor, and tumbled back another step until her shoulders hit the wall behind her. "S-stay away from me."

The chair banged against the metal filing cabinets and noisily bounced off, sliding toward her once more. She ignored the chair and opened the desk drawer, grabbing the scissors in her shaking hand.

"Put those down," Blake said softly.

"Stay away from me," she told him. "Get *away* from me."

"Ms.— Jolene, please. Put that down before you hurt yourself. I just want to talk to you."

She shook her head rapidly. "I'll scream if you take another step."

"Don't," he said, his voice low. "Come on now. You don't want that any more than I do. I'm here about the girl, Kaylee Forbes."

She blinked at him in confusion, the past tangled up in the present. "What?"

"Please, put that down. I'm not here to hurt you. I wouldn't be here at all, but I didn't know how to explain to my superior why I couldn't come see you without it bringing up questions I don't think either of us want asked."

"You mean you," she breathed, her throat tight, words hoarse. "How is *that* even possible?" she asked, referring to his uniform with a wave of her hand.

Blake lifted his broad shoulders in a shrug. "It's a story I wouldn't mind telling you sometime, but right now I need to ask you what you know about the missing girl."

Missing girl? "Kaylee's *missing*?"

Blake nodded, his expression solemn and wary.

"Her daddy reported her missing when she didn't return from school today. He found out she hasn't been with the friend she said she was staying with. He also said you paid him a visit yesterday morning and told him about Kaylee and her boyfriend having issues."

A laugh bubbled out of her chest before she could stop it. The irony was just too much. "You're here about Kaylee," she repeated in disbelief. "About someone *hurting* Kaylee. Is this a joke?"

"Jolene—"

"Ms. Carter," she said firmly.

Blake nodded and took another glance out the door before turning back to her.

"If someone sees you like that, they're going to ask a lot of questions. Is that what you want?" He stepped to the side and leaned against the blank space by the light switch. "I'll stay right here. Put that down, and let's talk about Kaylee Forbes."

All of the panic and worry and terror pulsed through her veins, every heartbeat pounding hard against her ribs. The person who'd pinned her arms and allowed his brother to *rape* her— wanted to talk.

"I know this is uncomfortable for you. It is for me, too."

"*Don't.* Don't you dare say it's uncomfortable for *you*," she whispered.

Blake nodded again. Was that all he could do?

"This wasn't the way I wanted to do things," he said. "When I realized it was you—"

"Stop talking and leave," she ordered. Begged. Pleaded.

Blake actually looked regretful when he opened the pad he held and stared at it.

"I can't. Not until I find this girl. Then I'll never bother you again if that's what you want."

"If that's what I want," she said, incredulous. "You shouldn't *be* here."

"Do you know where Kaylee Forbes is?" Blake asked, ignoring her words.

"No."

"Has she contacted you in the last forty-eight hours?" he asked next.

She bit her lower lip to still the trembling she felt and glared at him. If Kaylee was really missing... Oh, what had happened to her? Where had she gone? "Kaylee left two messages on my answering machine. One saying she quit and the other saying that I was right about her boyfriend and that she'd broken up with him."

Blake made notes on his little pad of paper.

"What were you right about?" he asked.

Jolie lowered her tired arms but still clutched the scissors in her hands. "One day I asked Kaylee about the bruises on her wrists from where her boyfriend had hurt her," she said hollowly. "I asked if he bullied or abused her. She said no because, even though things had gotten rough between them, when she'd said no— he'd stopped."

Parker's pen stilled over the paper, and his gaze flicked up to lock on hers.

"Jolene—"

"I don't know where she is. I haven't seen her; I'm not hiding her," she related dully, grazing her thumb across the blade of the shears. Back and forth. She could actually feel the tiny, individual lines of her fingerprint. "But if she's missing, the person you need to talk to is Damien Bennett."

"He's being sought for questioning now."

She scraped her thumb over the edge again. "Good."

"I'll leave my card here." He pulled a business card from the interior of the leather pad he held.

Blake took a step forward, but when she flinched back, he paused, then stretched out his hand to toss the card onto her desk.

"If you think of anything... And, Jolene, I would like a chance to talk to you about—"

"You stay away from me. You have nothing to say that I want to hear." Jolie watched as Blake turned and left her office, but she didn't move until she heard the chime sound on the front entry. Had he gone? Was he still there?

The metal biting into her hand brought her to awareness. She dropped her weapon onto the desk and stared down at the red line imprinted across her palm where she'd squeezed the scissors.

She had to get out of there. Had to leave.

Had to go somewhere and pray and deal with the urge to cut and cut and *cut*...

———————————

Quinn pulled into the parking lot beside Cuppa Jo's and jumped out of the cab before the dust of his arrival had settled.

He and Ian had been at Tasha's vet clinic for Tucker's physical and shots when Emma had texted Ian to ask how things were going, mentioning that a deputy had gone into Jolie's office to talk. Quinn knew it had to be Parker.

Sure enough, Blake Parker looked up from the laptop he had sitting atop the hood of the cruiser and eyed Quinn with the right amount of wariness as he approached.

Parker was big, a monster of a guy. Every bit of six feet six and three hundred pounds. It was easy to imagine him as a kid. A bully who had—

"Hey. Something wrong?" Parker said.

"Depends on if you're here to hurt her more than you already have."

The good deputy was quick to catch on to the fact Quinn knew the truth—and had the decency to pale to the point of looking sick.

"That's right. I know what you did to her," Quinn added, holding the man's gaze, moving closer. "And I'm telling you now to stay away from her, or I'll ignore that badge and take great pleasure in killing you myself."

"You're threatening a cop?"

"I'm threatening a rapist," Quinn countered, never breaking eye contact.

Blake lowered his gaze and shook his head. "I didn't—"

"You may not have committed the deed, but you and I both know you didn't get what you deserved."

Quinn waited for Parker to defend himself and make excuses, but after a moment, the man merely nodded. In agreement?

"Next time you see me out of uniform," Parker said, "have at it. I won't stop you."

Quinn narrowed his gaze, unable to figure out the guy's angle and taken aback by the statement.

"I'm serious," the deputy continued. "Meet up at the gym. No charges will be filed." The man smirked at Quinn's confusion. "And I've already promised Jolene that I'll keep my distance unless she wants to talk."

"Why would she want to do that?" Quinn demanded.

Blake closed the laptop with a soft snap before he pulled a business card from a case and handed it to Quinn.

"Because there are multiple sides to every story—including that one. I know what I did. And I know what I didn't do. Now, if Jolene thinks of anything in response to the missing girl, I need to know. Call me if she can't."

Quinn watched as Parker climbed into the cruiser and pulled out of the lot. And even though it went against everything inside him, Quinn let the man go unheeded.

Attacking a deputy in broad daylight on a busy street in front of a dash-cam would only lead to prison. There were ways to go about making sure Parker received the punishment he deserved. And even though it might mean returning to the life of violence he'd thought he'd left behind, so be it.

Not seeing Jolie's car, Quinn climbed back into his truck and headed for her house, figuring the gym would be second on her list.

Jolie was upset. Rightfully so. But since the *Besties* didn't know about Blake, she would probably want privacy to think and—

He punched the gas, his gut twisting into a hard knot when he thought of her cutting herself. Minutes later, he parked behind her Maxima and ran up her porch steps, surprised to find the door unlocked. "Jolie," he called, letting himself into the house. "It's me, Quinn. Where are you?"

Quinn quickly checked the downstairs but found it empty. Pausing in the kitchen, he heard a sound upstairs.

He took the steps two at a time and listened but didn't hear anything more. He searched the two front bedrooms, their open doors and small space making it easy. He turned toward the doors on his right.

The hair on his neck stood on end, and he braced himself for what he might find as he pushed the bathroom door open. He spotted the Bible first. The pages highlighted and marked—stained with blood.

His stomach fisted, and he barely managed to hold back his shout of pain. But then he realized the bloodstain was dark. Old?

There was an impression in the page, like something had been kept in between. His mind worked in slow motion, but it didn't take him long to comprehend the shape as the razor blade in Jolie's shaking fingers.

His gaze shifted from the blade to her eyes, dark and tortured. "Put it down."

Her mouth trembled and tears streaked her cheeks, but at his words, her fingers tightened over the blade.

"Jolie?" Deciding he had to take action, he reached out and simply grabbed the blade, uncaring if he cut himself in the process.

"No, stop," she said weakly.

"Get up," he ordered, tossing the blade into the trash before dragging her to her feet.

Jolie didn't fight him. That was probably the thing that scared him most was that she didn't fight. Like she didn't care. Not anymore. "Did you cut yourself? *Jolie?* Answer me."

She lifted her head and wouldn't look at him.

"I couldn't do it," she whispered. "I *wanted to* but— I p-prayed a-and thought of you a-and Emma and... I couldn't."

Relief left him weak in the knees. "That's good. Ah, baby, that's good," he told her, snuggling her in close. "You're strong. Stronger than you've ever been. You don't have to do that anymore."

She shook her head, wet her lips, lifting her hands to his waist. Quinn sucked in a harsh breath when she slid her hands up his chest. "Jolie, what are you doing? Sweetheart, stop."

She dragged him low for an open-mouthed kiss that rocked him to his soul until he forced himself to pull away.

"Please. Make me forget."

Her words were a desperate plea. Another strike ripping down his defenses where she was concerned. "You don't mean that."

He recognized her pain. He'd been there. Knew the burning need to implode and escape the tormented memories that wouldn't let go.

Jolie kissed him again, ran her hands over his chest and back, scorching him wherever they touched. But he couldn't make love to her. Wouldn't. Not in the state she was in. Not without his ring on her finger and vows allowing him to claim her as nothing less than his wife.

Something he *couldn't* do because she deserved better.

But he could give her the safety and security she craved. "Trust me," he said, swinging her up into his arms.

$\mathcal{J}$olie shut her eyes, uncaring of where Quinn took her. She was tired of caring, tired of fighting. Tired of remembering it all over and over again and the shame that came with the memories.

She'd held the blade to her thigh a long while. She'd made a few practice scrapes, dragging the blade along her skin without drawing blood. But then she'd remembered telling the *Besties* and pictured Quinn's expression when he'd seen her scars and realized what they were. But she'd *wanted* to. So badly.

Yet something else to be ashamed of.

She was vaguely aware of Quinn carrying her down the stairs, the treads beneath his feet squeaking with their combined weight. She ought to be self-conscious. She wasn't a tiny, petite woman. But it was yet another thing that didn't matter at the moment.

Quinn settled them into a chair with her draped across his lap, holding her like one would rock a child. And that's exactly what he did. With his lips pressed against her forehead, he rocked her, back and forth. Back and forth. After a long while, he whispered, *"Do not be afraid."*

He surprised her with his knowledge. Verse after verse, promise after promise. Quinn murmured them all while rocking her back and forth.

How easily she'd been manipulated by fear.

Peace stole over her, calmed the raging chaos inside of her, and brought her back from the edge of temptation to self-harm.

The words and verses began to blend together in a beautiful song with no tune, just highs and lows of Quinn's damaged, raspy voice.

She wasn't sure how long Quinn held her and quoted the verses. She was amazed at his memory, his knowledge, blessed by the gift of his friendship and comfort. His strength.

She'd seen the look in Quinn's eyes when he'd found her, as if he'd understood her wild thoughts and temptations, the darkest parts of her soul, because he'd lived it himself. The connection was real. Something tangible in a world where nothing made sense.

And what would your parents have to say now? Dating one man, cradled in the arms of another.

She stiffened just as the cell phone in Quinn's pants pocket began to vibrate. He murmured an apology and fished it out.

"It's Ian. I left him and Tucker at Tasha's clinic."

Jolie glanced at the clock on the far wall and frowned, more than ready to use the excuse to put some distance between them now that she remembered Austin's presence in her life.

Besides, it was closing time. Ian and Emma would both need a ride home. "Go," she whispered, straightening to sit up on his lap and then awkwardly get to her feet. "Drive them home."

If Quinn didn't take Ian and Emma home, Emma might call Jolie for a ride and— she couldn't handle that. Emma would know immediately that something was very, very wrong. It would require explaining why she'd left work in such a hurry, why she hadn't returned.

What the deputy had said to upset her so.

A part of her was mortified and embarrassed at what Quinn had witnessed, but at the same time, she couldn't regret what had just happened. Not after the way Quinn had responded and cared for her.

"I can stay if you need me to."

If she needed him to, not because he wanted to. "I don't," she said quickly. Maybe too quickly given the way Quinn's expression tightened. "I'm fine now. It was a momentary lapse," she said with a cheer she didn't feel. "I didn't think it was possible but— what you did helped me feel safe with you."

"You didn't feel safe with me until now?"

"Uh..." This time there was no mistaking his upset. "It's just... I mean... Quinn—"

"You felt safe enough going out with that Austin guy but you didn't feel safe being alone with me?" He straightened to his full height and turned toward the front door.

"Stop," she said, not that he listened. "You're twisting my words."

"Am I?" He stopped at the door, his hand on the knob. "Because it seems as though you're ignoring what's happened between us and still looking at me like everyone else."

"Quinn—"

"Forget it."

But without a word, Quinn turned and walked out the door, leaving the house and her behind with a not-so-gentle slam.

Oh, what had she done? She'd turned something wonderful into a nightmare she couldn't undo with a simple sorry. All because she was so messed up inside. Maybe Emma was right. Maybe it was time to seek real, professional counseling because her past impacted every one of her relationships. "I trust you. I *do*."

But how would she ever convince him now?

Quinn made the mistake of first picking Emma up from Cuppa Jo's. The moment she got into the truck, the questions began.

"Have you talked to Jolie?" Emma demanded. "What's going on? Why did she leave like that? Is Kaylee really missing?"

Quinn punched the gas and made the turns to Tasha's vet clinic, desperate to get there as quickly as possible. "Yeah, Kaylee's missing. Jolie's upset but okay."

"So you've seen her."

"Yes."

Emma's stare bored a hole in his profile. "That's it?" she said from the passenger seat. "That's all you're going to say?"

Quinn slid a glance in Emma's direction and saw her frowning at him.

"Quinn— Did something happen between you and Jolie?"

"Stop trying to matchmake," he growled out.

"It *did*, didn't it?" she cried, ignoring his response. "Tell me everything."

He tightened his grip on the wheel and ignored the nearly orange stoplight as he sped beneath it, comforting himself with the fact the intersection was empty except for his truck. "Go get your husband," he said, pulling into Tasha's parking lot in record time.

"Quinn, you can't do this to me. It's cruel. If something happened between you two, I have to know."

He pinched the bridge of his nose. "Why?"

"Um... well, because. It's Jolie— and you. And you two are both very big pieces of my life so— It's important to me, too."

He absorbed that for a moment and then shrugged. "Nothing happened." At least, nothing he wanted to talk about. How could he when Jolie had only kissed him because she'd needed an outlet for the pain? Holding her, reciting the verses he'd memorized to get himself through the dark times, had been the only thing he could think of to keep from kissing her again.

The whole scenario infuriated him, made him want to track the cop down, dash-cam or no.

"Why don't I believe you?"

Emma's expression was a mix of concern and worry and disbelief. But telling her what had happened would only make things worse. "Go get Ian so I can get you guys home."

Emma was slow to get out of the truck. Slower still to close the door.

"You promised you would protect her," Emma reminded. "I'm holding you to that."

He nodded once. He was holding himself to that promise as well — which was exactly why he'd left.

21

———————

*J*olie hurried back to Cuppa Jo's to double-check that things were as they should be. She had complete faith that Tommy and Emma had taken care of closing, but as the owner, she wanted to be sure.

Her favorite radio station cranked out a few tunes, followed by a weather update. The hurricane making landfall along the coast would bring rain and substantial winds inland to their area tomorrow afternoon.

She groaned at the news, hoping the winds wouldn't bring a loss of power. She couldn't afford to lose her food and dairy products if the refrigerator and freezer were down.

She let herself inside the coffeehouse and ran through her nightly routine. The cash drawer had been counted out, the prep completed for the morning.

Jolie entered her office and saw Emma had left her a note concerning a few minor details, but they were easy to address while she was there. Finished with those, she wondered if she should call someone about a generator, just in case.

Ian had a full-house generator atop the mountain since downed trees and power outages weren't unusual. Maybe she could call

Quinn and get information on the brand of generator. Use that topic as an excuse to break the ice and talk to him. Apologize for—what? Needing a friend?

Is that all he is? All you want him to be?

She pressed her fingers to her temple and rubbed. Quinn wasn't the type of man who would ever be interested in her. He was adventurous and daring while she was—

Safe.

There was that word again. But the desire to feel safe wasn't a bad thing. Was it?

Wanting his company once more, she debated the wisdom of driving up the mountain and refusing to leave until she and Quinn straightened things out between them. But doing so would definitely gain Emma's attention.

And until she figured out how to handle Quinn and Austin and her thoughts about both men, she didn't want to see any of the *Besties*. What could she say, after all?

Lord, help me.

She'd screwed up. And she didn't have a clue how to fix it or apologize because Quinn's expression had revealed the depth of his anger and *hurt*. Not an emotion a man like him allowed others to see very often, if at all.

She picked up the phone, but instead of calling Emma's house, she wound up dialing Kaylee's home number. Her father answered on the first ring.

"Kaylee?"

"No, Professor Forbes, it's Jolie Carter. I'm sorry to call so late, but I was wondering if you'd had any news?"

"No. No, I haven't. The police have questioned her friends, but no one has seen her," the man said, his voice breaking on the words.

Jolie winced at the sound, her heart in shreds over the man's despair. Her problems were nothing compared to a missing child. "Has, um, Damien said anything? A-a policeman stopped by here today, and he said that Damien was going to be questioned."

Professor Forbes sniffed and cleared his throat, gathering himself in a brief silence. "I thought so highly of him. I encouraged Kaylee to see Damien. She was so sad after her mother's death, and Kaylee had had a crush on the Bennett boy for years."

"It's not your fault," Jolie told him.

"Damien admitted to hitting her," the man continued, his voice growing harsh with his emotions. "He admitted to *punching* my little girl."

Jolie pressed her fingers over her mouth to hold in a cry of rage. Professor Forbes didn't need her distress added to what he already experienced as a father who'd not known his daughter was being abused.

"He was… quite intoxicated still when they questioned him. He said he left her here at the house after their fight, and that he didn't get her note about breaking up with him until the next day when he woke up."

Which explained why Quinn had seen Damien lurking outside Cuppa Jo's and her home. He'd been looking for Kaylee. "Where is Damien now?"

"Home. His father posted bond even though I begged the man not to. I told him it was only right that Damien stay in jail until Kaylee is found."

She agreed, but unfortunately when it came to families with money and power, right didn't always win. "I see."

"I don't want to tie up the phone line in case she calls. If you hear anything, Ms. Carter, please let me know."

"Yes, of course," Jolie whispered. "I'll say a lot of prayers for her safe return. Please keep me posted, as well."

After murmuring good-bye, Professor Forbes hung up, and Jolie was left staring at her phone, heartbroken over the news. *Oh, Kaylee, where are you?*

Kaylee obviously needed some time to cope with all the emotions she was feeling. It wasn't easy wrapping your mind around the fact that someone you cared for could hurt you in such a way. Jolie knew that from experience. But wherever Kaylee had gone, there was still the danger of her injuries being more serious than Kaylee might have believed. What if she'd passed out? Had internal bleeding from the blows she'd sustained?

You'll drive yourself nuts with the what-ifs.

Knowing it was true, Jolie stood to leave when she noticed the business card Blake had left behind. She didn't want to touch it but found herself picking it up, images from the night of the rape seeping past her ever-present mental walls.

She'd been devastated by Rick's actions. His brutality. But almost as bad was Blake's participation in it. In *holding her down*.

Oh, later she'd heard his words of defense, but she hadn't believed them. If she hadn't gotten loose and managed to grab the rock, she wouldn't have gotten away. Not until Rick had finished with her.

And then what? He wouldn't have wanted anyone to know what he'd done. Would the violence have continued? Would he have used the rock on her to shut her up? Made it look like she had slipped and hit her head?

She ripped the card into multiple pieces before throwing them into the trash, wishing it would be as easy to rid herself of Blake's presence in her life.

Jolie locked up and turned to go home when she spotted Tasha walking down the street, a golden retriever on the end of the leash Tasha held.

Their eyes met, and Jolie braced herself. "Hey."

"Hey, yourself." Tasha slowed to stand in front of Jolie. "I heard about Kaylee. Any news?"

Jolie blinked at the question and debated whether or not this was Tasha's way of making peace. They hadn't talked since the day she'd confessed to cutting, but she'd take any attempt to smooth things over. "No, none."

"I'm sorry," Tasha murmured, shifting a bit awkwardly from foot to foot. "I'm sure she's okay."

"I hope so." Jolie stood there, feeling lost and sad and guilty because she had altered their friendship with her news.

"Gah— Jo-Jo, why?" Tasha asked, tears catching on her lashes. "Is there anything I can do? Say? How can I help you? Make you stop? I can't stand the thought of you doing that to yourself."

The expression of torment, the helplessness on Tasha's face, tore through the barriers Jolie had erected over the years.

Cutting was always about her, for her. For power and control. Relief. But she was beginning to see herself through her friends' eyes. Beginning to understand how hurting herself... hurt them. She loved the *Besties*, would do anything for them, and now she put herself in their shoes, forced to stand by and do nothing while she cut.

It was cruel. Something she certainly wouldn't want them doing to themselves. "I'm trying, Tash. I really am. I slipped up. But I'm trying to do better. Can you accept that— accept me?"

"I love you."

"I love you, too."

"But I *hate it* that you hurt yourself."

"I do, too." She wished she had never discovered cutting or that such a thing existed.

Tasha made a sound and closed the distance between them, hugged Jolie for a long time, sniffling.

"I'm sorry I ran out on you like that," Tasha said, her voice choked. "It hurt too much to picture you doing that."

"I know. It's fine," Jolie told her. "I know it's hard to understand."

"It's not fine. I'm a doctor. I should have had a better grasp of what you were saying, going through. I should've been more supportive."

Jolie squeezed Tasha tightly and then released her. "You're here now. That's all that matters." Forgiveness was easy to give Tasha. So why wasn't it easy to give to her parents?

They had tried to talk to her several times in the years since, but she'd shut them down quickly, making it clear she was upset with them. But Quinn's accusation took root, and she faltered. Maybe her parents hadn't handled things well, but was she really angry with them for trying their best to protect her? Now that she saw Kaylee through her father's eyes... The man was reeling—just like her parents had been.

Jolie walked with Tasha for a bit, the subject changing to lighter topics. When neither of them could hide yawns, Tasha walked Jolie to her car and gave her a final hug.

"Love you, kid. Just please—"

"I know," Jolie said. The *Besties*, Quinn. They cared for her, otherwise they wouldn't be upset with her over the issue of self-harming. She wasn't only letting herself down by giving into the temptation to cut but them as well, and she didn't like the way it made her feel. "I'm... going to get counseling," she decided. "Things are different now, and I want to be better. I owe it to myself, and to a lot of other people."

Tasha frowned up the inch or so separating them in height.

"Are you okay? Is something else going on?"

"Just worried about Kaylee," Jolie said, not about to discuss what had happened with Quinn when she wasn't capable of processing it yet herself.

Jolie said good-bye and watched as Tasha and the dog in her care slowly crossed the street in the direction of Tasha's clinic.

Jolie climbed into her car and quickly locked the doors, unnerved by the thought of Damien lurking somewhere in the shadows.

Pushing away the emotions gathered within her, she started the engine, frowning at the radio announcer's discussion on the local state park.

The last severe storm had caused major damage to the forest due to tree loss and flooding, and officials were warning hikers and campers to clear the park immediately in preparation of the approaching storm system.

Jolie hit her brakes at the edge of the parking lot, the rocks beneath her tires causing her to skid slightly.

The state park. Her grandfather's cabin. She and Austin had discussed the cabin *in front* of Kaylee. Could the girl have gone there? Would she have gone there?

It was a long shot at best. But what if Kaylee *was* there? If she'd gone there to hide out a few days and get her head together, planning to return before school on Monday so no one would be the wiser— but couldn't make the return trip because of her injuries? Not only that, but Jolie seriously doubted the girl had sense enough at the time to carry a radio.

Jolie took her foot off the brake and guided the car into the street, toward the mountain road. But as she came to the intersection before Cantrell's Garage, she slowed. Quinn hadn't been able to get out of the house fast enough. Proof to her that he very much regretted what they'd shared. How needy she must have seemed. How awful and pathetic. No doubt he regretted his friendship with her, because of all the dysfunction between them. Whereas Austin...

Logically, Austin was the better choice to help her in this situation. A hunter, someone used to the woods. To the area. Someone whose head was clear of emotion and able to focus.

Asking Austin for help would also give her time with him to clear her head of her thoughts regarding Quinn. Time she desperately needed.

Jolie whipped into the driveway beside the garage and ran for Austin's door. She banged on the wood, every second that passed making her more and more certain that Kaylee was indeed at the cabin— and they had to get to her before the storm hit. "Austin! Austin, it's Jolie. Open up!"

The porch light clicked on before the door opened with a yank.

"Jolie? What's wrong?"

"I have to go to the cabin. Right now."

Austin tilted his head to one side and stared at her like she'd lost her mind.

"Do you know what time it is?"

"It doesn't matter. I have to go."

"Why? What's going on?"

"It's Kaylee. She's gone missing, and I think she might be there."

Austin scowled and ran a hand over his face. "Jolie, it's too dangerous. Have you seen the weather reports? Even if we left right now, we'd be lucky to make it there and back before the storm rolls in."

She nodded, wishing time were on their side and praying that God would see them through the darkness and the night ahead. "I know. I'm sorry, and I wouldn't ask, but I just know she's there, and if she is, she's hurt. Her boyfriend admitted to beating her. I have to go. You talked about hunting on our date and how you used a four-wheeler. I understand if you can't get away or don't want to go at all, but can I please borrow it?"

Austin leaned his shoulder against the door and frowned at her.

"Have you ever been on a four-wheeler?" he asked, his gaze dropping to her long skirt.

"No, but—"

"Come in."

"Austin, you said yourself there's no time."

He backed up a step and held the door for her. "Get in here. I'll get the four-wheeler loaded up while you change. Then we'll pack some gear and be on our way."

Relief filled her. He was going to take her. "Thank you."

"Don't thank me. It's crazy going into those mountains at night. But I wouldn't be able to live with myself if I let you go alone."

Quinn managed to endure Emma and Ian's inquisition on the way up the mountain, but the moment they arrived, he made an excuse and left the house as quickly as possible. He made his way up the steps to the apartment feeling older than his thirty-four years.

He dropped down onto his bed and stared up at the ceiling. His mind immediately began to replay the day's events and how it had felt when Jolie had kissed him. The sound she'd made. The way she'd clutched him closer in a momentary lapse of self-control.

She hadn't considered him "safe" until he'd held her and recited verse after verse to her, but feeling safe to be in the same room with him and *safe* to be intimate were two wholly different things.

He knew she felt the connection, the attraction, but her past kept her in bondage, filled with shame and regret. Safe to Jolie meant not making another mistake with a man who would use her and toss her away. And like it or not, he used to be that man. His history, his job—he could blame both, but the truth was Jolie was right about him—until now.

Holding her after she had fallen apart... Aware that she was as broken inside as he had been for so many years.

He wanted to be the man she chose. Had to be. But how could he prove to her that she was just as much his saving grace as he was hers?

He was ready. Ready for more. Ready to admit he loved her. Ready—for the next step in the life. Unless someone lived through abuse, they truly didn't *get* the darkness of it.

He did. He understood her pain, the longing to be free of it so that it would slink away in the darkness from which it came.

It was time to step up or risk losing her.

Jolie's words had infuriated him, but had she not said them, he wouldn't be here now. Ready to make that next move. He wanted to be the man she chose. Had to be.

He got to his feet and paused in the middle of the floor. He didn't know what to do, and the decision left him pacing.

It was too late to go to the house for some time with Ian's punching bag, not to mention how doing so would open him up to more questions from his friends. Things he couldn't talk to them about because of all the history that was tangled with it.

Quinn sat on the edge of the bed momentarily before jumping back up to pace some more.

Images bombarded him until he groaned and headed toward the door.

Now would be a really good time to run into Blake Parker.

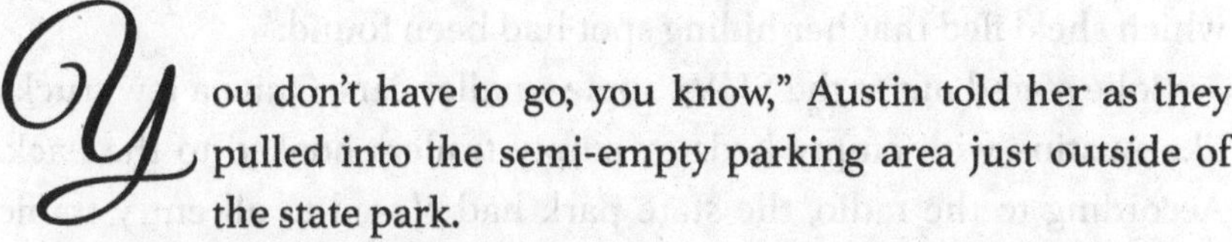

ou don't have to go, you know," Austin told her as they pulled into the semi-empty parking area just outside of the state park.

It had taken just over a half hour to load the ATV and gather supplies. A brief stop at a twenty-four-hour truck stop near the state park exit had taken care of what Austin didn't have on hand. Extra batteries, trail bars, water. Jolie had been so focused on getting to the cabin that she'd completely neglected to consider taking supplies, even though Kaylee doing the same had been one of her worries.

Her only concern had been getting there, but as the backpacks were filled and the weather reports relayed the severity of damage along the coast, she was grateful for Austin's experienced and more level-headed presence. She was grateful he was taking this so seriously and thinking things through since her brain only seemed capable of worrying about Kaylee— and Quinn.

She stared down at the jeans and T-shirt Austin had loaned her, both feeling rough and alien against her skin.

Better protection against the woods than a skirt.

"Jolie, I can go to the cabin and find out if she's there."

"No. *You* wouldn't be going if it weren't for me."

For the first time, she saw Austin battling his temper.

"It's the middle of the night," he said, pointing out the obvious. "And I'm going to be honest, I think this is a wild goose chase. If she's hurt like you said, how did she make the trip? It's an all-day hike for a healthy person."

Good point. But every time Jolie thought about Kaylee's presence during the discussion about the cabin, it made sense that Kaylee would go there, especially after Professor Forbes' comment about Kaylee always seeking places to be alone to think.

It was what she would've done. After the rape, when she'd dragged herself out of the mud, she'd hidden in the woods by the pond for a long time. She'd watched Rick and Blake's parents arrive with help. Heard her parents calling her name, even though she hadn't responded. It wasn't until Blake had pointed the direction in which she'd fled that her hiding spot had been found.

Jolie stared out at the SUVs, some smaller cars. Quite a few trucks like Austin's with empty beds or empty trailers hooked to the back. According to the radio, the state park had closed to all entry traffic and was only letting people leave. And since the cabin was perched on the edge of her grandfather's property bordering the park, that meant parking even farther away from the cabin. "You're not going without me," Jolie said. "Kaylee will be more receptive if I'm there. She doesn't know you."

Austin stared at her from behind the wheel, his expression lined with concern.

"It's not going to be an easy trip. Especially not on the way back if we get caught in the storm. You should stay, take my truck back to town."

"I'll be fine. And if it gets bad, then we'll ration the supplies and stay in the cabin until it blows over. Austin, I'm asking a lot of you. I understand if you've changed your mind."

Austin reached over the console and grasped her hand in his, squeezing it gently. "Don't forget those backpacks."

Jolie gathered the backpacks and supplies while Austin unloaded the ATV. In short order, they had helmets on and were on their way up the mountain in the dark.

The first trail closest to the park was well traveled and rutted. Jolie held on to Austin's sides as he maneuvered the four-wheeler up the path, every bump jarring her teeth and her tailbone.

Despite the early-morning hour, it was hot beneath the jacket. She knew not to take it off, though. The brush scraped over them on both sides at times, and without the protective helmet and clothing, her skin would be ripped to shreds.

It took an hour to make it to the turn-off point of the trail. Austin paused where the cleared state park's trail veered before guiding the ATV around the No Trespassing signs marking the edge of the park and her grandfather's private property.

The strain on Jolie's back to hold herself upright began to take a toll. She wasn't used to doing things like this, and she was already getting stiff.

"Hurting?" Austin asked when he caught a glimpse of her face. "Lean on me. Like this."

He took hold of her hands and pulled her arms farther around his waist.

"Rest your weight on me."

"Won't that make you hurt?"

He looked at her over his shoulder, his eyes smiling at her from within his helmet.

"Not my first ride," he said, gently knocking his helmet against hers. "Just move with me and go with the flow of the machine."

She nodded her understanding and held tightly as Austin guided them down the mountain. The wheels skidded part of the way, but Austin kept the ATV under control.

They crossed a shallow creek and started up the other side, and she wondered how he found his way in the dark, with only the light from the four-wheeler shining in front of them and the moon overhead. She knew all the landmarks, but in the dark, they were nearly impossible to see, much less recognize. And while Austin paused a few times to get his bearings, she knew from her many childhood trips on this same journey that he was headed the right way. Especially when the forest thickened to the point the ATV was no longer usable and they had to leave it behind.

She turned to watch the sun rise, wondering if there was anything as glorious as those first rays peeking over the treetops.

"Hope you're ready to stretch those legs," Austin said as he cut the motor.

She leaned back on the seat, every bone in her body protesting the punishment she was putting it through. Her eyes were gritty with fatigue, and she was more than aware of the fact she wasn't eighteen anymore. Having worked most of the day, then stumbling her way through a traumatic evening first with Blake and then with Quinn, her body was ready to quit. She just couldn't let it because they didn't have time to waste. "I need caffeine. Then I'll be good to go."

Climbing off the ATV was as strange and awkward to Jolie as climbing on had been. There was something insanely intimate about riding behind Austin, especially given the kiss she'd shared with Quinn only a few hours ago.

The thought of Quinn sent her mind reeling down paths she couldn't comprehend at the moment.

Quinn was angry with her for what she'd said, and she hated that her words had upset him. But now wasn't the time to be distracted by something she couldn't fix.

Quinn leaving was for the best. It wasn't like Quinn was the type who dreamed of a wife and kids. In fact, it was all too easy to see him as a loner for life. Whereas she... wanted more. A husband. Kids. But when had her thinking changed? When had she healed enough to consider something other than spinsterhood as her life?

She was too tired to try to figure that out.

She and Austin took turns making discreet trips into the trees. While Austin took his turn, she grabbed her phone, hoping to see a response from Emma regarding the text she'd sent in the truck on the way to the parking area. She'd asked Emma to go to Cuppa Jo's to help Tommy open and explained briefly that she had an idea of where Kaylee might be hiding.

"No signal out here in no-man's-land," Austin said as he rejoined her.

She nodded, frowning at her phone. "So I see. But how does the GPS work if there's no signal? Haven't you been using it?"

"Yeah. But it comes from satellites, not cell towers."

They grabbed the backpacks and started hiking, with Austin using his handheld GPS to guide them through the forest and up the steep ridge. If she was right, once they made it to the top, the cabin was in the trees on the far side. But the top was a long, long hike away. "You know," she said from behind him, panting, "I considered myself to be in good shape until this."

"Now you know why there's no one tougher than mountain folk," Austin said with a grin. "Can you imagine our ancestors doing all of this on horseback or with wagons?"

She couldn't. Not at all. "I know the answer but— Are we there yet?"

Austin's chuckles filled her ears and brought a smile to her lips. Austin was fun, easy to be with. Even now, under such trying circumstances.

"Also," she said, talking to help keep herself awake and aware of her surroundings because she was reaching the point of being dizzy from lack of sleep. "Are you going to be furious with me if she's not there?"

"Nah," he called over his shoulder. "But you may owe me a few kisses to ease the disappointment."

She stopped climbing to look at Austin's back as he continued up the ridge, realizing for the first time she may have made a huge mistake.

Her stomach knotted in unease because kissing him didn't feel right, even though he was the kind of man so many women would love to have as a husband and father to her children.

She knew it as clearly as the sun rising higher in the cloud-spotted sky. Maybe she had recently pondered a future with a man like Austin, but faced with Austin's teasing, the fact dawned that... he wasn't the man she wanted to kiss.

Austin must have noticed she wasn't walking, because he turned to look at her.

"Hey? You okay?"

"Yeah, fine," she said, forcing a weak smile. If she told Austin kissing wasn't an option, what would he do? Get angry? Leave her there? Do something else?

Austin tilted his head to the side and stared at her a long moment. "This wouldn't have anything to do with that guy who was at your house yesterday, would it?"

She swallowed hard, searching for the right response. "Um... huh?"

"I went out on a tow call and noticed his truck there." Austin turned to walk again.

"I'm sorry," she whispered, unsure of the proper response.

Austin paused again and waited for her to catch up with him.

"Why are you sorry?" he asked softly. "Unless there's something to be sorry for?"

She closed her eyes, well able to feel the heat rushing into her face.

"I see," he said simply.

She hurried after him. "Austin, wait. Please."

"Why? So I can be the nice guy and tell you to go for it with some other man?"

"I'm *sorry*," she said. "Quinn and I are—were— just friends but—"

"But now you're more than friends? I get it." He took a few more steps but, just as quickly, glanced back at her. "No, I don't get it. If you and this guy are together, why isn't he here instead of me?"

Good question. A wonderful question. A telling question because Quinn *wasn't* there. "Look, full disclosure is... we've kissed but we're not together."

Austin planted his hands on his hips and looked away from her, shaking his head.

"Then he's a fool."

Jolie followed Austin up the steep ridge in silence for a while, but she could only stand it for so long. "I'm sorry," she said, knowing she was more or less talking to herself. The wind picked up, rustling the leaves over their heads. "Maybe I should have asked Quinn but— I couldn't. He's angry with me."

Austin didn't say anything for several steps.

"Why?" he called over his shoulder.

"It's complicated."

"Gonna be a long walk."

She trudged a few more steps, every one of them stealing more and more of her anger until all that was left was her need to come clean. "He's upset because I said he'd made me feel safe and I didn't think it was possible." She shoved her hair out of her face.

Austin paused again and stared at her, and once more, her face filled with hot color.

"Safe," he repeated.

"Yeah, like you." In an instant she knew she'd said the wrong thing yet again. What it was about the word that the men found so offensive. Quinn was upset that he wasn't "safe," yet Austin seemed upset that he was?

"Safe," Austin muttered before shaking his head and trudging on up the incline.

She groaned in frustration and huffed behind him, trying to keep up. "Why are you offended by it? Why was he? I don't understand."

"Obviously," Austin said without slowing his pace.

She breathed so hard from talking and climbing that she paused to give her heart and lungs a rest. "Okay, fine. You want the truth? Something bad happened to me in the past. Something really, really bad," she blurted. "And I haven't ever been able to move on. But I want to."

"With me?"

"Yes. I mean, maybe."

"No."

No? "But—"

"I might not be the b-best-looking g-guy," he said, his stammer appearing due to his frustration, "but I'm a g-good man."

"I *know* that. I agree."

"That means I want to be more than your 'safe' g-guy," he continued.

What on earth? "Austin..."

"No. Jolie, look, I... like you. A lot. But I deserve a wife who feels passionately for me. By saying I'm safe, you're saying you don't feel that way about me."

"Being thought of as safe isn't bad," she argued. "I'm sorry. I don't mean to hurt you. I never expected this to happen, because he's *Quinn*, and if you knew him, you'd understand what all that means, but I... When he walked out yesterday, I got scared and angry and freaked out. It hurt so bad that he wouldn't even *try* to understand where I'm coming from, but when you said I owed you kisses, it made me realize I needed to tell you." She dragged in a deep breath because she'd said all of that in a gush. "I... like Quinn. A lot," she admitted, dazed by the truth of it. "But he's irritating and more than a little scary in a lot of ways because... he understands me so well."

"And you told the guy he's *not* safe," Austin repeated.

"What is it with that word? I was scared! I can't believe I'm even having this conversation with you, but when Quinn and I... I couldn't go to him when I figured out Kaylee might be at the cabin. I needed time to figure things out."

"Sounds to me like you have."

She blinked and looked up at Austin, hating the expression he wore because it tugged at her heartstrings. He was *such* a nice guy. But not *the* guy. Why couldn't Austin have been the one?

"Look, Jolie, I would've walked away, too. I mean, I wouldn't want to, and I'm sure he didn't, either, but nobody wants to be that guy."

"He'd never hurt me. I know that."

"Then he must be safe in the way that matters or else you wouldn't have tested him."

The truth of his statement sank in and left Jolie reeling. Austin was right. "You're saying I said it on purpose? To test him?"

"I don't know. Did you? How did you think he'd react?"

"I don't know. I wasn't thinking clearly," she admitted, trying to sort through her emotions. "Maybe— Maybe I did say it deliberately. I was overwhelmed, and I guess I knew he'd react and..." *Things would end.* And end they had— with Quinn walking out the door.

"Look, Jolie, if he's any kind of man, it would kill him to be with you thinking he couldn't give you something you need. Even if it's a feeling of security. And seeing that security is what he does, that had to be a blow to the old ego."

Could it be true?

She had to acknowledge that her doubts and fears had crowded her, overtaken her. She could've been more tactful, if nothing else. "How do I fix this?"

Austin released a weary laugh and ran his hand over his mouth. "Can't help you there. I might be a gentleman, but I refuse to be the guy who helps the girl get another guy."

23

"Where did she go?" Quinn demanded that same morning in Ian and Emma's kitchen.

"Watch it," Ian murmured.

The order was stated calmly, but since Quinn had practically growled the words at Ian's wife, Quinn knew it wasn't to be ignored. Ian might be blind, but as a former Navy SEAL, he was still deadly.

Quinn raked his fingers through his short hair and fought the urge to pull. Jolie should've come to him for help. But then why would she when he'd acted like such a jerk and left her without so much as a good-bye?

"I don't know," Emma said, frowning down at her cell phone. "The message just asks if I will help Tommy open Cuppa Jo's because Jolie had an idea of where Kaylee might be and was going to look for her at the cabin."

He lifted his head at that. "What cabin?"

"I guess her grandfather's? It's the only cabin I've ever heard Jolie mention," Emma said.

"Where is it?" Quinn asked next.

"I have no idea," Emma said. "Only that it's near the state park."

Quinn fought his frustration and scrubbed his hands over his gritty eyes. Sleep had eluded him last night. He'd barely managed to restrain himself from going to Jolie's house because he knew how hard she worked and how tired she always seemed. He'd needed time to come to terms with what she'd said, too. But now she was gone—somewhere inside a state park with the remnants of a hurricane headed their way. "Think. What has she said about it?"

Emma grimaced and leaned her cheek against Ian's hand when he placed it on her shoulder.

"I don't know. I mean, she's mentioned it in the past because her grandfather liked to write there. And she said she'd like us to go sometime for a girls' weekend but not until— Austin," Emma said, the name emerging in a gush.

"Come again?" Quinn urged, hating that the name kept popping up.

"Austin Cantrell. Jolie told me recently that she gave Austin permission to use the cabin during hunting season, and in return, he told her he would fix it up before the season started so she could go visit. Jolie said she drew him a map. If Kaylee was there at the time... That has to be why Jolie thinks Kaylee might be there."

Quinn grabbed his phone and did a search for Cantrell's Garage, finding the number and the emergency number with ease. Given the hour, he didn't think the garage was open yet, but the emergency number rang until Austin Cantrell's voice mail kicked in, telling the caller to leave a message. "No answer."

Quinn stalked to the kitchen doors.

"Are you going after Jolie?" Emma called.

"Yeah. But first I'm going to talk to Cantrell and get my hands on that map."

Half an hour later, Quinn stared at Austin Cantrell's driveway and groaned at the sight of Jolie's Maxima. Either Jolie had spent the night with Cantrell, because why else would she be there at seven in the freaking morning, or she'd gone to the other man for help in getting to the cabin.

Quinn hit the steering wheel with his palm, jealousy eating at him. How would he find her now?

They made it to the cabin by seven thirty, and by then, the wind had really picked up speed. The land had grown up over the years since her grandfather's death, and it was barely recognizable from the memories she had of it as a child. Still, the rush of the waterfall over the rocks into the lake below drew them to the area, and it was easy to locate the structure once they were there.

"Hang back. Let me take a look inside," Austin told her in a low voice.

"Why?"

"Because, believe it or not, mountain men do still exist, and you could have a squatter— or some other creature inside. Let me take a look first."

She appreciated Austin's attempt to protect her, but she was the one who'd brought them here in the first place. And after his albeit reluctant acceptance of her discussion about Quinn, the least she could do was be right there to help if something happened.

Austin shrugged his shoulders to remove the heavy backpack he carried and removed a pistol from within his jacket pocket. She was surprised she hadn't felt the weapon during the ride but not that he carried one. Austin was right. One never knew what trouble one might find in the woods, be it human or animal.

"Anyone home?" Austin called out. "Don't mean no harm. Just saying hello."

Jolie refused to stay where Austin told her to and crept along behind him, looking for any signs of life inside the cabin. No one responded to his call, but something scurried off the porch, scaring Jolie enough to make her jump and latch on to Austin's back with her nails. "Sorry."

He chuckled at her response.

"That raccoon will never be the same." Austin eyed the spot where her nails gripped him. "Glad I didn't take the jacket off yet."

Austin looked at her and smiled like the good-natured guy he was, but in her peripheral vision, Jolie caught a flutter of movement by the window. "Wait— *Kaylee*?"

Austin immediately forced Jolie behind him until they heard a weak, feminine call from within. Austin made it up the two steps onto the narrow porch first, but Jolie shoved him aside the moment they made it into the dark, musty cabin. *"Kaylee."*

Jolie barely recognized the girl. Kaylee's face was swollen, both eyes blackened. Her cheeks shades of yellow and purple. The girl's lip was split and caked with blood, and she moved with the slow deliberateness of someone in a great deal of pain.

"Hey," Kaylee said simply.

"Oh, sweetie." Jolie moved closer to where the girl sat in her grandfather's old leather recliner. It looked as though Kaylee had slept there instead of the bed.

"It wasn't so bad when I started," Kaylee told them softly. "I wanted some time to think, where Damien couldn't find me. I thought I would be better and back home by Monday, but then on the way here, I fell."

Jolie watched as Kaylee pulled up her pant leg and showed them her ankle, swollen two to three times its normal size.

"I took my shoe off, and then I couldn't get it back on," the girl told them.

"It's okay," Jolie whispered, barely able to look at Kaylee because of the fury she felt on the girl's behalf. If Damien hadn't hurt the girl, she wouldn't have left town, wouldn't have fallen and gotten hurt even more. "We're here. We'll help you get back."

Kaylee's eyes filled with tears that trickled over the bruises on her cheeks.

"I don't want to go back. I don't want anyone to see me like this. Especially not my dad."

Jolie knelt on the dusty cabin floor, her hands braced on Kaylee's knees. The girl was covered in scratches and bruises, mosquito bites. "Your dad is worried out of his mind," she whispered. "He won't care about anything but the fact you're safe."

"But I don't want him to see me," the girl said, breaking down in sobs. "Can't we stay here? Just until it's not so bad?"

Austin had been walking around the small cabin while Jolie talked to Kaylee, and he reentered the main room with a frown.

"'Fraid not." His gaze met Jolie's. "She needs proper care. If we stay, we'll be here for days once the storm blows through because the trails will be destroyed. We have to head back. Now."

Jolie looked around the cabin, saddened because she wasn't going to be able to linger. She hadn't stepped foot in the structure since her grandmother's death ten years ago, but nothing had changed. The walls were still plastered and smooth, the wooden floor rough beneath the dust and dirt. Everything needed a good scrubbing, but fixed up, it would be comfortable and full of good memories.

This was the place where her grandparents had brought her to heal. To get away from everything and everyone to listen to nature and breathe the fresh air and just be. This was her safe haven. So why had she stayed away so long?

All this time, she'd thought she was coping, but in reality, she'd been hiding.

"I'll carry Kaylee down. You bring the supplies," Austin said, moving toward the teen. "Hate to say it, honey, but this ain't gonna be fun."

Jolie grabbed the backpacks, her sore back straining under the weight as she shouldered them. Austin stooped down in front of Kaylee and picked the girl up to carry on his back, mindful of her very swollen foot.

Jolie held the door and then gave the cabin one last look as she followed them outside. The wind blew her hair into her face and mouth, and after a few steps, she dragged the mass back and used the hair tie she habitually wore on her wrist. Leaves blew through the air, and the treetops swayed with the gusts.

It didn't take them long to walk to the top of the ridge, but the moment she saw what they faced, her stomach dropped. How on earth was Austin going to get Kaylee to the bottom without falling?

Kaylee must have been thinking the same thing because she told Austin to stop.

"We'll take it a step at a time," he told the girl.

"I'd rather go down on my butt than for us to go tumbling down like Jack and Jill," the girl told him.

"That will take too long. Look up," Austin said.

Kaylee and Jolie both lifted their faces toward the sky, and Jolie grimaced at the dark purple clouds in the distance. The wind was really starting to howl, slapping limbs and leaves together and creating quite a bit of noise. "We have to hurry, Kaylee. Let him try. I'll walk in front of Austin. He can hold on to me to steady you both."

"Then we'll all three fall!" the girl cried, tears beginning to leak out of her eyes. "I'm sorry. I'm so sorry. I shouldn't have come here."

Jolie and Austin exchanged a look before Austin hefted the girl higher on his back.

"We're not getting anywhere standing here. Let's go and see what happens. Jolie, might as well leave those. You'll travel faster without the weight."

Leaving the backpacks behind wasn't easy, but Jolie knew Austin was right. The weight of both packs was too much for her, and with no sleep, she was fighting for every step.

After several feet, it became clear that Austin wasn't going to be able to carry Kaylee down the ridge. He lowered the girl to her uninjured foot and wrapped her arm around his shoulders, walking beside her and helping her maneuver the rocky, uneven ground, holding on to Kaylee with one arm while grasping tree trunks for leverage and balance. Jolie lagged behind, downing a power bar and water to counter the exhaustion leaving her light-headed.

It took four times as long to make it to the bottom of the ridge as it had for Austin and Jolie to hike to the top. Finally they made it back to the ATV, and Jolie was never so happy to see a piece of machinery in her life.

According to the sticker on the ATV, two passengers were prohibited. She wondered what the manufacturers would think of it hauling three. But in this case, it couldn't be helped. With every minute that passed, the sky darkened, the storm making its way inland.

Kaylee sat behind Austin on the cushioned seat, while Jolie sat on the rack on the rear. And here she'd thought the ride to the cabin was bad....

They crossed the creek with teeth-clenching bounces and lurches, but when they made it to the other side and started up the mountain, the ATV began to spin its wheels in the same spot as it had before. Austin tried several times to make a go at the incline, but nothing worked. "Let me off," Jolie said. "You can take Kaylee to the top. I'll walk."

Austin didn't look pleased by the suggestion, but he nodded. Jolie watched as Austin and Kaylee fought the loose rocks and trees and brush until they were too far ahead of Jolie for her to see them. She walked as fast as she could, following the trail the ATV left behind.

She had to stop several times to rest, and before she caught up with them, the first sprinkles started to fall, a weak imitation of what headed their way.

Jolie was still trying to make it up the mountain when she heard the ATV coming toward her. She paused again, needing another rest.

Austin was alone on the four-wheeler.

"I left Kaylee at the top. Come on, we're going to get caught inside the park unless we hurry."

Jolie thought of the terrain they had left to traverse and shook her head. "Go."

"What?" Austin said, looking as though he thought he'd misheard her.

"There is another big mountain ahead, not to mention all the distance between here and the road. Take Kaylee and get her some help."

"Jolie, I'm not leaving you here. Get on," Austin ordered.

"No! You know it will be faster if you do it my way. You can't haul all three of us, and waiting for me to walk will take too much time," she said. "I'll pick up the backpacks and go back to the cabin to wait out the storm."

"It's too dangerous."

"Standing here wasting time is too dangerous," she countered. "Kaylee needs help, and I can't drive that thing, so you taking her is the best solution." Jolie moved close to the ATV and wrapped her arms around Austin, hugging him tight. "I'll be okay. I can make it back to the cabin in time. I'll be fine. Promise. Just make sure you don't forget I'm there when it's all over."

Austin returned the embrace, and Jolie ignored the wind and the raindrops trickling down from the canopy of trees above their heads. When she drew back, she hesitated, then leaned forward and gave Austin a kiss on the cheek. "You really are an awesome guy, you know that?"

His dark expression didn't change.

"You're pretty awesome yourself." Austin tugged on a lock of hair that had escaped her tie. "Don't stop," he said. "Go straight to the cabin. Leave the bags behind if they're too heavy. Just get out of the storm, and stay in the cabin."

"Will do."

"Here. Take this." He dug into his pocket and took out the gun. "You know how to use this?"

"I'm a country girl. Of course I do."

"Good. You need to use it, use it. Don't hesitate. Safety's on," he said, showing her the lever, "and the clip is full."

"Thanks. Austin?" Jolie waited for him to make eye contact. "For what it's worth, I'm sorry. You're going to make a lucky girl very happy one day."

Austin gave her a sad smile and hugged her again.

"For what it's worth," he said, "I knew it wasn't me when we kissed after our date and it was like kissing my cousin."

She laughed at the face he made and stayed there long enough to watch Austin turn the machine around and head back up the mountain. Her pulse raced at the eeriness of the sky and the sounds the wind made in the trees, and adrenaline kicked in, erasing her exhaustion and getting her to the creek in record time.

Walking across the moss-covered rocks wasn't easy. She slipped several times and wound up with soaked shoes and jeans, and once, she fell in all the way up to her waist before scrambling to her knees and out of the water, thankful the gun stayed dry.

Her jeans were heavy and water-weighted as she began the hike back up the ridge, and she said a lot of prayers for safety in the hopes that an animal hadn't already discovered the backpacks.

Finally she made it to the top. She wanted to collapse into a heap and let her trembling legs rest, but the wind and rain were getting stronger, and she knew if she stopped, she wouldn't be able to get started again.

Weeds and fallen limbs dragged at her legs, and she tripped over the soaked hems of Austin's too-long-for-her jeans more than once.

Thunder began to rumble, and lightning flashed across the sky, and she used the fear of getting struck as incentive to move faster, grabbing the packs and not stopping until she made it to the porch and shoved open the cabin door.

She dropped the backpacks to the floor and sagged against the door, every bone, muscle, and tendon in her body trembling in fatigue. But she had made it. She was safe.

For now.

24

Quinn was unloading his gear in the parking lot closest to the state park when Austin and Kaylee arrived on the back of an ATV. Quinn barely managed to wait until Austin was off the four-wheeler before grabbing hold of the guy and slamming him against a truck. "Where is she?"

Austin narrowed his gaze on Quinn from behind the helmet he wore.

"You must be him."

"Where is she?"

"Jolie's at the cabin."

"You *left her* there?" Quinn yanked Cantrell forward just to slam the man against the truck again.

"I didn't want to," the guy growled. "But the rain had started, and I couldn't get the ATV up the mountains with all three of us. Jolie insisted on staying behind so I could get Kaylee out. She needs medical attention."

For the first time, Quinn realized the girl had removed her helmet, and he flinched at the sight of her bruises, too many memories of his past and childhood flooding at him at once. "You have a lot of people worried about you," he said to the girl.

She blinked and looked away. "I know."

"They're going to be really happy you're safe," he added.

Austin placed the helmets on the asphalt before lifting the one-shoed girl off the ATV.

"Open the door," Austin ordered.

Quinn frowned but opened the passenger-side door so Austin could deposit Kaylee gently inside.

"I'm taking her to the hospital. You going after Jolie?" the man asked.

"I'm not going to leave her there," Quinn said, furious that Jolie had insisted on staying behind and that Cantrell had actually done it.

Austin reached in and pulled a spare can of gas from behind the seat.

"Then fill it up and get going," Austin said. "And this time, don't be a jerk when she tries to talk to you."

Quinn lifted his head, surprised by the man's words. He hated surprises, and that was the second— no, third— one today. "She talked to you about me?"

Austin closed Kaylee's door and started around to the other side of the truck, but he paused to glare at Quinn and toss him a handheld GPS.

"She told me some things. Now I'll tell you something— You'd better treat her right, or you'll answer to me."

Quinn stared at the other man, wondering how it was possible for Jolie to rip him in two and put him back together when she wasn't even present.

"You should probably know I left my gun with her and basically told her to shoot anything that moves," Austin added, climbing into his truck. "Hope she doesn't get spooked."

A bullet would probably serve him right.

Quinn waited for Austin and Kaylee to leave before he hefted his gear and grabbed the gas can, taking Austin up on the offer to use it. Muddy trails or not, it would still be faster than on foot.

He had almost made it to the first turn off of park property and onto Jolie's grandfather's land when a tree toppled right next to him.

Limbs were popping all around him, crashing to the forest floor, and covering the trails. More than a few branches took a swipe at him as he rolled by, and some kind of barbed bush ripped through his jeans.

He slid more than rolled down the mountain toward a fast-moving creek. It was still shallow enough to get through, but on the other side he rolled to a stop, knowing there was no way around the tree that had fallen. He'd hoped to make it farther before having to hike, but this was the end of the trail for the ATV.

He got off the four-wheeler and hefted the backpack onto his shoulders, deciding to leave the helmet on considering the noise of crashing all around him. Jolie was up that mountain somewhere, and he couldn't let anything stop him until he found her.

J olie watched the storm roll over the mountain from within the safety of the cabin. The air outside nearly sizzled as the thunderclouds tumbled overhead. The trees whipped to and fro, and she recognized the loud cracks surrounding the cabin as limbs breaking from trunks and trees toppling, unable to withstand the fifty- to seventy-mile-an-hour gusts.

Please, God, don't let a tree fall on the cabin. Please keep us both safe.

Maybe it was selfish to pray for a piece of property, but the cabin was a tangible reminder of her grandparents, most especially her grandfather, and the love and tenderness they'd shown her when she'd needed it most.

She wasn't sure why she'd stayed away so long. Why she'd let life keep her away. Because now that she was here, all she could think of was how much it comforted her.

The old typewriter her grandfather had used when he'd worked was still on the desk in the corner, covered with cobwebs. A ream of paper was stacked in a drawer, yellowed with age and warped with dampness. The kitchenette held a water pump that drew fresh water from the mountain stream, and the cabinets had a few pots and pans for cooking over a potbelly stove. The back room was a tiny bedroom, and the last remodel of the cabin had included installing an old-fashioned bath and toilet because Gram said she was too old to brave an outhouse in the woods. Jolie tentatively flushed the toilet, pleased to see the system still worked.

She had a hard time believing everything was in such good shape after sitting unused for so long, but if any of the local hunters had made use of the cabin— and she believed they had— they had been careful enough and respectful enough to leave things the way they'd found them.

Jolie made her way back to the front room and paced, keeping a wary eye on the storm raging outside. Her grandmother had always feared one day the cabin would slide off into the lake below, much to her grandfather's amusement. But as the wind made the cabin creak and groan in complaint, Jolie wasn't so sure ending up in the lake was impossible, considering how the cabin was perched on the rock outcropping near the falls.

Pacing gave Jolie plenty of time to ponder her conversation with Austin as they'd made their way to the cabin.

Apparently there were multiple definitions of "safe," but truth be told, she did feel safe with Quinn. Safe in a heady, scary way.

Jolie stayed awake and moving as long as possible, but there came an I-love-him point when she simply couldn't take another step.

Quinn. Big, imposing, fierce, sweet, caring Quinn.

The cabin was stuffy so she left the door open and eventually curled up in the recliner to watch the storm. Her lashes grew heavier by the second as ideas of how to go about approaching Quinn took over her mind.

Smiling, she dreamed of Quinn, his fingers lightly tracing her throat, brushing her hair back from her face. For a moment, she felt weightless as Quinn picked her up and cradled her against him, and she sighed in pleasure when he settled her against his chest. She pressed her face into his neck and breathed him in, knowing as long as she lived she would never forget his scent or how safe she felt in his arms.

J olie opened her eyes with a start the next morning, unsure of what had awakened her or how long she'd been asleep. But in an instant, she knew something was very, very—

"Easy, sweetheart. It's me."

"*Quinn.*" She elbowed him in the stomach in her haste to sit up, only then realizing she was on his lap. *How on earth?* "You came after me? *In the storm?*"

"Do you really think I wouldn't?"

He said it so matter-of-factly that she blinked. "But... how did you get in here without me hearing you? How did you pick me up and—"

"The storm probably covered up my arrival, but you'd left the door open. You were so sound asleep you scared me. I actually checked you for a pulse."

Her dream. Her dream had been real; she'd just been too exhausted to realize it. "I was so tired. I stayed awake as long as I could to keep an eye on the storm but— I can't believe you came after me. You were so angry when you left."

"I still am," he murmured. "We have some things to discuss."

Quinn's eyes were closed, but his fingers brushed her knee in lazy strokes. Distracting, tantalizing strokes. She swallowed hard and shook her head to clear it. "Kaylee— Did Austin and Kaylee make it down all right? Quinn..."

He slid his hand under her hair at her nape and tugged her down against his chest.

"Yes. Last I saw, Austin had Kaylee in his truck, and they were on their way to the hospital."

"What about Damien?" she pressed. "Does Kaylee's father know she's okay? Did Emma get my message?"

"Easy," he said softly. "You're going to explode if you don't slow down."

She squirmed against him, rolling her head along his shoulder to better see him in the dim light. "Sorry."

Quinn squeezed her gently, looking completely exhausted himself.

"When I left this morning, Emma was planning on helping Tommy open the coffeehouse. Ian was going with her so they'd be off the mountain. Said they'd stay in town until things died down."

"I just hope everyone is safe," Jolie said, feeling guilty that she had even sent the message to Emma now. Given Kaylee's condition and the storm, who cared if the coffeehouse was open?

"Kaylee will be fine. I'd say her father and the police will be keeping her ex away, especially once they see what the guy did to her."

"Damien hurt her. Badly."

Quinn squeezed her shoulder.

"I know, sweetheart. But she's tough. She'll be okay."

She rested against him for a long moment, just enjoying the experience of being held. How had she ever *not* considered Quinn safe? "Is that how you knew to come here? You saw Austin and Kaylee?"

"Go back to sleep, love. We can talk later."

Quinn was tired. She was tired. But sleep was impossible now, and there was something about the way he'd said that that didn't sound quite right. "Quinn, how did you find me?"

His chest lifted and fell beneath her, his sigh blowing against her hair.

"I talked to Blake Parker."

"*What*?" she cried, lifting her head to stare at him in horror. "Quinn, no. Please tell me you didn't."

Quinn lifted his hand to her cheek and smoothed his knuckles along her jawline.

"I would talk to the devil himself if it meant keeping you safe. For what it's worth, Parker was ready to put a team together to come up the mountain to search for Kaylee. He seemed genuinely concerned about finding her."

She cringed, doubting Blake could be concerned about anyone but himself.

Jolie ran her fingers over Quinn's hand, frowning when she saw more than a few scrapes and bruises. "Your poor hands. Coming up here in the storm must've been hard."

"They're not all from the storm."

"What do you mean?"

"Parker and I had a talk."

She jerked upright and turned on his lap to stare down at him. "Quinn, he's a cop! You'll go to jail because of me."

She tried to scramble from his lap, but he caught her around the waist and held her in place.

"No charges. We made a... gentleman's agreement."

"I don't understand," she told him. What kind of agreement could they have made that would keep Blake from slapping Quinn with an assault charge? "Quinn, you can't trust him. Please tell me you don't."

"He said some things, Jolie. Things I think you should hear."

She gazed at Quinn, his expression, but didn't see what she wanted to see. Hurt and betrayal hit her hard, and this time when she shoved at Quinn, he let her go.

She had so much to tell him. So much they needed to discuss, but how could she broach the topic now or even think about being with Quinn after he'd just said he and the man who'd helped rape her had an *understanding*? Indicated that she needed to hear Blake out? "I need some air."

Jolie stalked toward the door and slammed it behind her.

Quinn wasn't the only one who could walk out.

Quinn debated the wisdom of going after Jolie. Then he remembered how he'd walked out on her during a very crucial moment and figured it served him right. They were both exhausted and on edge. And they still had a lot of baggage to sort through before they could get to wherever it was they were headed. He just thanked God he'd found her safe and sound.

He took a quick look out the window to make sure she wasn't in the storm and saw her sitting on the porch floor. The wind and rain were still going strong, the cabin's tin roof taking a pounding.

Quinn grabbed his gear and found the satellite phone he'd brought with him.

"About time," Ian said on the other end. "Emma's been going nuts with worry about you and Jolie."

"She's fine. Mad at the moment, but fine," Quinn said wryly. "How's the girl?"

"Broken nose, two cracked ribs, and severely sprained ankle. Might be broken, but the docs can't tell until the swelling goes down some. And before you ask, the Damien kid's bail has been revoked and he's sitting in lockup."

"How'd that happen?" Quinn asked, pleased by the news but surprised all the same.

"Not sure, but I think the new deputy had something to do with it," Ian said.

Interesting and more interesting, Quinn mused. But it also backed up what he'd learned about Parker during their "discussion."

"I'll let the deputy know you two are safe and staying put until the storm is over," Ian said. "The park service is reporting major tree loss and says the trails are already impassable. It's closed until further notice."

Given what he'd seen on his way to the cabin, that wasn't hard to believe. "Tell Emma to stop worrying. I'm going to turn the phone off to conserve the battery, but we're both fine. We'll see you when it's safe."

Quinn turned the device off and set it aside to dig into his pack, adding his food to that on the old desk. It wasn't a bad spread. He'd definitely had worse.

Last night, it had been too late and too dark to get a good look at the interior of the cabin, and he did so now, noting the beds and staring in genuine surprise at the bathroom. Impressive. He hadn't been expecting a bathroom way up here. There was even an old-fashioned tub and a system to pump water. He tested it, and the water ran clear and cold.

Quinn puttered around inside the cabin killing spiders and getting his bearings while giving Jolie time to cool off. When he got bored, he grabbed some water and granola bars and slowly opened the door. "You hungry?" he asked, stepping outside to join her.

Jolie got to her feet.

"Not anymore. Enjoy," she said, walking into the cabin and shutting the door behind her.

He lowered himself to the porch with a sigh. "This is why Emma prefers animals to people."

25

It rained the entire day, but by late afternoon, the worst of the storm had blown through, and things were calming down. Jolie stared at the damage to the trees and land around her, realizing her prayer had been answered because the cabin was not only still standing, it was intact. No water leaks, no major tree damage. Just a lot of clean-up work.

She glanced over her shoulder and through the open door, seeing Quinn standing in front of the potbelly stove her grandmother had used for cooking.

Quinn had kept busy all afternoon and ignored her silent treatment, seemingly willing to give her some space and time to sort things out in her head. Not that she'd been able to. What on earth could Blake have said to Quinn to make him take Blake's side? Nothing excused what Rick and Blake had done to her. Nothing.

"I have a surprise for you," Quinn said from behind her.

She turned and saw him in the doorway, thumbs tucked into the pockets of his worn jeans. One leg had a rip in it she hadn't noticed until now, with blood caked on the ragged edges. "What happened?"

His mouth curled up at the corners, and he shifted to empty the doorway to give her room.

"A hungry bush took a bite out of me on the way up. Come on, I've made a peace offering."

Jolie crossed her arms over her front but followed Quinn into the cabin. She looked toward the stove first, thinking he'd made them something to eat besides granola bars and trail mix, but the pan she'd seen him standing over earlier was gone.

Quinn stopped on the far side of the bathroom door and waited for her to look inside. As soon as she spotted the tub, her mouth opened in surprise. The tub was nearly full, and there were several candles lighting the room.

"I'm not taking his side or downplaying what they did to you. But I do think you need to hear him out. That's all."

Her pleasure at the thought of a long, hot soak diminished at Quinn's words. "What could he have possibly said to you to make you think I should give him one second of my time?"

Quinn held up his bruised hands.

"I don't understand."

"He never lifted a hand to protect himself. Not once. I pounded on him for his part in what they did to you, and he took it, without a word of complaint. Then when it was over, he called in some favors and told me how to find you."

She closed her eyes against the knowing awareness she saw in Quinn's gaze. "That just means he feels guilty because he *is* guilty."

"I'm not defending him, Jolie. I'm simply telling you what happened." Quinn stretched an arm out to pick up a gray T-shirt from a spot near one of the candles. "Take your bath. I can't do anything about the jeans, but I'd sure rather see you wear my shirt than Cantrell's."

Jolie stared at the material in Quinn's hand and slowly reached out to accept it. "Thanks for the hot water."

Quinn pulled the door closed, and she stood there a long minute, taking in the pretty sight of the candlelight and the claw-foot tub. Who knew truces could be made with candles and a bath?

Seconds later, she'd stripped and lowered herself into the soothing water, biting her lip to keep from releasing a loud and very unladylike groan of relief. She was sore in places she didn't even know she had.

Quinn moved about and acted like climbing mountains was nothing in a day's tasks, but she wondered how she would make the hike back to civilization sore as she was.

She lingered in the tub until the water turned uncomfortably cool and her skin pruned up and shriveled. Since she lacked a towel, she used Austin's shirt to dry off, grateful it was reasonably clean, and donned the undies she'd rinsed in the tub. Since there wasn't much to them, there wasn't much material to dry.

Jolie rearranged a few candles to better see herself in the tiny cracked mirror above the sink. Her makeup was long gone, hair a mess of tangles she finger-combed the best she could.

She left the bathroom, feeling inordinately exposed wearing Quinn's shirt even though it was a size larger than Austin's. "Quinn?"

"Out here."

She followed the tiny sliver of moonlight to the porch and found Quinn sitting outside on one of the wooden chairs from the kitchen, his feet propped up on the porch post by the steps.

She felt the heat of his gaze taking in her wet hair and squeaky-clean appearance.

"That shirt's never looked that good on me," he said softly.

She frowned at the compliment, wondering how she could feel so close to him and still not understand him the way she wanted to.

Jolie padded closer, and before Quinn could move, she lowered herself onto his lap and ignored his surprise. Now or never, she mused.

"Jolie—"

She placed her finger over his lips. "It's my turn to talk and your turn to listen."

He stared up at her, green eyes smoldering, but after a moment, he nodded.

"I don't know what Blake told you, and right now I don't care," she said, still holding her finger over Quinn's lips. "Maybe one day, I'll be able to hear him out, but it's too much for me right now, and I need you to understand that. I know I have to find forgiveness, and I'm working on it. I am. But seeing Blake makes me want to hurt myself. To hurt him. And I don't want to do either of those things."

She was able to see Quinn's gaze soften in understanding, and the sight gave her the courage to continue. She slipped her finger from his lips and lowered her head, resting her forehead against his. "When I said what I did to you— no, you have to listen," she ordered when she saw him wince and open his mouth to speak. "When I said what I did to you," she repeated, "I didn't tell you the complete truth. I want to feel safe and with you… "

"Go on," he murmured.

"But emotionally, you scare me. Because of how you make me feel. Physically, you scare me. Because when we k-kiss I feel… I enjoy it— *so much*— but I'm afraid. Not *of* you," she quickly added. "I'm afraid of how you make me feel and what might happen next and… I wonder if I could handle more. No one knows me the way you do. *No one* understands me or-or the way I think. Quinn… I don't know if you feel the same way or not but…"

Quinn tugged her closer and nuzzled her mouth with his.

"I do."

"You—you do?"

"Yeah, sweetheart, I do." He tugged her low so that her mouth brushed his. "Marry me, Jolie. I want to be with you, grow old with you. I've never wanted a home or family, but you've made me want it all with you because when I look at you… Baby, you're mine. I think I claimed you as mine the first time I laid eyes on you. I love you."

She blinked at him, her breath catching in her throat. She opened her mouth, but no sound emerged for several seconds. "I love you, too."

"So is that a yes?"

She smoothed her hands over his bulging arms, loving the feel of his soft skin over such impossible strength. Quinn was a beautiful example of how someone could overcome his upbringing. His past. How one could be better, kinder than one's family.

Quinn's past, his story, the way he understood her pain. God had chosen Quinn just for her. But until now she'd been too afraid to see it. "Yes."

EPILOGUE

Eight Months Later...

Jolie stared down at the sample wedding invitation and practically danced in place in front of the keyed mailboxes. She was going to be a July bride, and thanks to Quinn's hard work in clearing the area around the cabin, they were going to be married at the falls.

No trails had been made for the sake of preserving the hideaway and keeping strangers out of their private place, but Quinn had cleared a landing pad big enough for a helicopter so the small wedding party and few select guests wouldn't be required to hike to the cabin.

She couldn't wait to show the *Besties* the invitations and hurried out of the building— promptly running into the man walking through the second, outer door. Jolie dropped the box in the collision, and some of the invitations scattered across the concrete walk. "Oh, no!"

"I'll get them," the man said.

Blake. Jolie looked up from the ground only to find Blake Parker dressed in street clothes. He was squatted down and gathered the pieces of coffee-colored linen paper in his big hands, carefully adding them to those that remained in the box lying on the ground between them.

"I heard the news. Congratulations," he said.

"Thank you." Despite Quinn's insistence last October that she needed to hear Blake out and listen to whatever he had so say, she'd managed to put it off these many months and focus her attention on her relationship with Quinn, running her business, and going to therapy to be as healthy a bride as possible.

Blake had stopped coming to Cuppa Jo's, and she'd made a point to avoid him whenever and wherever possible, even if it meant walking in the opposite direction. But if she truly wanted a new start with Quinn, a new life... "I'll take those. Thanks," she said, making a grab for the box.

"Jolene—"

"I can't." She shook her head firmly. "I'm grateful you helped Kaylee and her father prosecute Damien, but you have nothing to say that I want to hear. I can't pretend it never happened a-and just be *friends.* Please, just leave me alone." She turned to escape, grateful the small-town post office wasn't busy this time of day and there were no witnesses to their conversation.

"I let go," Blake called after her. "I know you think you got loose, but the truth is, I let go."

Jolie stopped in her tracks, the box clutched to her chest. Her heart pounded against her ribs, and she felt dizzy and sick, images from that night bombarding her and erasing her happy mood from minutes ago. "What?"

"I became a cop because of you, Jolene," Blake said from behind her. "Because of what happened."

She squeezed her eyes tight and shook her head. "No."

"It's true. I have a wife and a baby girl. I can't stand the thought—Jolene, my hand on a Bible, I swear I didn't know what Rick was doing to you. It was dark; you were in the water. I was *ten years old*. I thought you two were playing a game."

"*No.*"

"I thought he was wrestling with you," Blake insisted. "When I realized he— When I realized it wasn't a game, I let go."

She whirled around, her whole body shaking. "Fine. Whatever you say. Am I supposed to be thankful now?"

"No. But if you want to be thankful for something," he said, lowering his voice when a truck drove by on the street with its windows down, "you can thank me for not stopping you when you grabbed the rock. I could've. You wouldn't have been able to stop me. I was bigger than you even then. But even I couldn't believe what he'd done to you. So I sat there, and I *let you* hit him, punish him for hurting you."

Jolie stared at Blake in disbelief. Quinn had told her repeatedly that Blake had something worth listening to, but this— She would never have believed he'd say *this*.

"You're not the only one to blame for Rick's injury. I could have stopped you, but I didn't because he'd hurt you. I told my mama and daddy that too. I told them that every single time they tried to say Rick had been wronged by you, and I reminded them that I could've stopped you, but I let you defend yourself instead. Jolene, I swear to God I didn't know when it happened, but I swore that night I heard our parents make that deal that I'd never be like them. I left home the day I turned eighteen, and I've never gone back."

Jolie swayed on her feet. She didn't know what to do. What to say. What to believe.

"Everything okay?" Quinn asked from behind them.

He'd stayed in the truck to take a call while she'd run into the building to get the package. So much time had passed he must've come to see what was keeping her.

"Jolene...."

She didn't respond. Couldn't. All she could do was stand there and stare into Blake Parker's eyes and go through that night second by horrifying second. Parts of it were such a blur. Screaming. Fighting. Shock. But her mind froze on a flash of Blake's ten-year-old face when she'd scrambled out from under Rick *with* Blake's help and seen the boy staring at her, big, fat tears rolling down his cheeks.

"I'll leave you be," Blake said. "But I'm happy for you, Jolene. I'm glad you've overcome it. And for what little it's worth, I *am* sorry."

Jolie let Quinn guide her back to the truck and help her inside. He got them moving, but instead of going back to Cuppa Jo's, he drove her home. To what would be their home very soon.

Tucker had been Mad Dog Security's first graduate and now resided with a fourteen-year-old blind girl whose mother was running for political office. The program was going well, with Bentley and a handful of other dogs to be sent out into the world next as canine protectors.

"You going to say anything?" Quinn asked as he stopped the truck.

Ever since their time in the woods, she'd kept her record of not cutting. She'd even bought herself some expensive designer jeans with bling on the rear pockets, the dressy kind of jeans she could wear to work and still feel professional. "I was okay with believing Rick was capable of rape, but the thought of Blake participating a- and watching. Of him being here now— I couldn't understand. I couldn't accept it. I *hated* it! I tried to ignore what he was saying, but... images kept coming. Memories. Details I didn't remember. Not until... now."

"So, it is true? What he said?"

"I don't know what he told his parents but— Yeah? I think so? I mean, all this time, I remembered Blake holding me down until I got loose. But today, I remembered Blake sitting there in the mud, crying, looking scared out of his mind— horrified. I mean, I used to *babysit* him sometimes, and he really was a big goof. He was a boy. Just a little boy."

"Which is why he thought it was a game at first," Quinn said.

She nodded, realizing in her heart it was true.

"Sounds like he was still the kid you thought he was and not what his brother tried to make him."

"I've been wrong all this time. I was so messed up afterward. I-I thought..."

"You were a kid, too, Jolie. It's understandable."

Quinn leaned over the expanse of the truck and tugged her to him for a kiss, one that healed the tattered edges of her heart even more. She kept her eyes open on his, drawn in by the love and protectiveness she saw in the depths.

He was right. Timing was everything and in this case... the timing wasn't right— until now.

But after all of these years she'd finally made it through the valley to the other side.

WANT MORE OF STONE RIVER? READ ON BELOW FOR A SNEAK PEEK AT DUNCAN'S STORY IN TO PROTECT HER (FORMERLY LEAD ME NOT):

Redemption 220 miles.

Duncan MacGregor sat on the idling Harley and stared at the road sign. If only redemption were that easy to find in reality.

The sight of his next destination's name, should this one not work out, left his gut tight, because the name the small Georgia town bore was a smack in his face, one heavy-fisted with the guilt he'd carry for the rest of his life.

He gunned the 1948 Panhead and swallowed the lump in his throat, wishing for the millionth time he could turn back the clock.

Owen Redd was dead. It was the only explanation for his disappearance.

Duncan had spent the last week attempting to track Owen's cell phone, his credit cards, computer, all dead ends. His best friend and vice-president had seemingly fallen off the face of the earth.

In their line of work as security experts— bodyguards, drivers, personal security trainers, high-level corporate protection services providing a wide range of skills— enemies were easy to make. Especially when protecting the other person meant becoming the target yourself. Had Owen run into someone from the past?

Duncan gunned the Harley again, the tires spitting loose gravel as he made his way back onto the highway, past the exit sign leading to Redemption. He continued traveling, making his way to what had once been Owen's temporary boyhood home.

If Owen was holed up anywhere and laying low, injured, or

unable to communicate, it had to be at the farm Owen claimed as his saving grace during his rebellious teen years.

But if Owen wasn't here...

Duncan followed the twisting Blue Ridge Mountain roadway until he saw the mile marker Owen had once described. After six more miles, Duncan spotted the house-sized, forked boulder off to the left of the road. Getting close, he slowed and turned his attention to the right, seeing the narrow opening of a once-gated entrance.

Crossroads—A Home for Boys.

The gate was long gone, but large trees had been downed across the road to deter trespassers.

It took some doing, but he managed to maneuver around the logs to the other side of the driveway. He wanted to rush but couldn't, given the road condition, and wound up playing dodge-em with the mass of ruts and mud holes marking the distance.

Finally, Duncan rolled up near the paint-chipped porch steps of the large, Edwardian-style farmhouse and cut the motor, silently issuing a final prayer.

"Freeze," a low voice called.

Duncan slowly lifted his hands to remove the old-school black helmet, his gaze scanning the porch, house, and windows for a sign of the person. "I'm not here for trouble. Just looking for a friend."

"You're trespassing on private property. Leave or I'll shoot."

Female. The voice was female, edged with fear, and followed by the distinct sound of a shotgun being set to fire. Duncan's gut knotted. Fear plus gun equaled unpredictable.

He carefully placed the helmet aside and lifted his hands back into the air. "Like I said, I'm looking for a friend by the name of Owen Redd. Thought I might find him here."

Silence followed his words. The wind rustled through the trees, rattling the dried fall leaves like a skeleton's bones.

"Who are you?"

Ah, now they were getting somewhere. "I like to see who I'm talking to."

"I like to target practice."

He almost smiled at her snarky rebuttal but wasn't sure just yet that she *wouldn't* practice her shooting skills on him. "My name's Duncan MacGregor."

"MacGreg— Owen's boss?"

The woman's tone reflected her surprise. Movement caught his attention, and he turned his head, watched, as the woman stepped out from behind a shed near the rear of the house.

He almost swallowed his tongue. The beautiful stranger wore a long-sleeved, white button-down rolled at the cuffs and cut-off denim shorts with ragged threads that drew attention to the tanned flesh of her long legs. Her brown hair had a markedly reddish cast to it and was pulled back in a simple ponytail, and her mouth curved down in a ferocious frown.

She was dark-complected for a sun-kissed redhead, a trait he attributed to the massive amount of freckles covering every inch of bare skin he could lay eyes on, even from the distance separating them. Still, with the gun in her hands, she looked like the perfect cover model for the NRA. "Yeah, I'm Owen's boss. Who are you?"

She didn't lower the gun.

Duncan nodded his head toward the weapon. "You mind pointing that somewhere else?"

It took her several seconds to decide, but in the end, she lowered the shotgun enough to give him some breathing room.

"You've come to see Owen?" she asked. "Does that mean you've talked to him?"

The knot in his gut tightened even more at her words and the worried expression pinching her eyebrows together. "No," he said simply. "But Owen told me once that if he were ever in trouble and I couldn't find him, I might try this place."

The woman wet her lips and blinked, and he wondered if she fought off tears.

"So he hasn't checked in with you— or me— which means…"

Duncan swung his leg over the Harley and stood, aware that her words trailed off with a low hitch of her breath. "It means he isn't able to check in," he told her, surprising himself by taking a positive stance on Owen's disappearance instead of the negative one that had plagued his mind for the last week.

Every day that passed meant a colder trail to follow— not that Duncan had any leads since Owen had taken a few weeks off before he'd gone off the grid. Not knowing who Owen's "friend" was, Duncan couldn't come right out and say what was on his mind. Not to a total stranger. "Long ride from Atlanta. Something to drink would be much appreciated."

He didn't move closer, not wanting to scare her and have her swinging that shotgun up in defense.

"Let's see some I.D."

Duncan dug his license out of his wallet along with a business card, slowly walking them to where she stood. He also added a picture his sister-in-law, Emma, had taken at a recent barbecue of him and his brother, Ian, along with Owen, Nathan Quinn, and Emma's stepbrother, Zack, mainly because he'd stuck it into his wallet for safekeeping at the time because he hadn't known quite what to do with it.

The woman snatched the items from the tree stump where he left them and backed up a few steps while she looked them over. He stood still, keeping a close eye on the barrel of her gun. "You got a name?"

"Bethany."

Her name seemed familiar, but Duncan couldn't place her. "Nice to meet you, Bethany. When did you last see Owen?"

"A week ago when he brought me here."

Bethany returned the items to him, lowering the gun to rest at her side with comfortable ease. The gun was old, probably something Owen kept on hand in the house for visitors who came calling in the middle of the night. But that didn't explain who she was or why she had it.

Who was she to Owen? Friend— or lover? Because if she was the latter, Tasha, Owen's girlfriend back in Stone River, was bound to find out. "Mind if I ask what you're doing here?" He tucked the items back into the leather. "Are you and Owen...?" He let his words trail off suggestively and nearly laughed aloud when an expression of horror crossed her face.

"Ew, no. He's my *brother*."

Her brother. For reasons Duncan refused to consider, relief poured through him. "Ah, I remember now."

And he did. Owen referred to his sister as Monkey or Monkey Wrench, rarely Beth. But now that Duncan had moved closer to her and knew the genetic link, he spotted visual likenesses between the woman and his good friend. Namely the abundance of freckles and the slight dimple in the middle of her chin.

"What about you? When did you talk to Owen last?"

"About three weeks ago," Duncan told her, not disclosing the details of Owen's last voice mail because of the way she'd worded her question. "Owen called to tell me he was taking time off."

"For me," she said with a nod. "Owen came to Redemption to stay with me after my ex-boyfriend's death. You know, attend the memorial, make sure I was okay. While Owen was there, someone broke into my apartment."

"Any idea who?" Duncan asked, his mind zeroing in on that bit of information.

"No. I thought it was random. Redemption is a small town, and everyone knew I'd be at the service. But Owen... He insisted there was something strange about it and that he was going to look into Charlie's death. A few days later, Owen told me he'd decided to hang around a while longer."

Duncan's suspicions grew, as well as his dread. "He didn't say why?"

"No." Her tone revealed her irritation. "He asked me to come with him to visit this place because he hadn't been here for a while. Two or three days at most," she stressed, making a face. "It wasn't until after we got here that I realized he'd planned to leave me behind while he did his thing. He said he'd come back to get me. Only... he hasn't come back."

Exactly the news Duncan didn't want to hear. "What happened to your ex that Owen found strange?"

"It's complicated." She lifted and lowered one shoulder in a shrug. "Charlie... left town about eight weeks ago. He said he wanted space and a new start. So he moved to Virginia Beach, but a couple of weeks after that, the Coast Guard found Charlie's rental floating at sea— with a suicide note at the helm."

Duncan stared down at Bethany Redd, hating the question he had to ask. "Was Charlie the type to do something like that?"

"I don't know. I would say no, but before he left... Charlie started acting really weird. Not at all like himself."

"Did Charlie ever do drugs?"

"No. Charlie wasn't that kind of guy. But Owen said he was going to dig into Charlie's background, just to be safe."

That would have been his first move, too. Something definitely wasn't adding up.

But it also meant Owen had not only had suspicions about his sister's ex but he'd *found* something, prompting Owen's call for help.

A call Duncan had ignored, due to a business matter requiring his attention at the time, and returned too late.

Duncan turned away from Bethany, sick to his stomach because he'd let his friend down in the worst possible way. Worry ate at him, angered him.

"Duncan?"

The guilt over not answering Owen's call threatened to smother Duncan. "Yeah?"

"Something's wrong, isn't it? Really wrong. That's why you're here looking for Owen— isn't it?"

I hope you have enjoyed the teaser for TO PROTECT HER (FORMERLY LEAD ME NOT). Listed below are links to the rest of the books in the series so you can continue reading about Duncan and Bethany and all of their friends.

Word of mouth and reviews are the two best ways an author has to gain attention for their books. While you're browsing the titles, please consider taking a moment to leave a short review of this book.

Thank you,

Kay

The Stone River Novels

WORTH THE WAIT
NOT BY SIGHT
MORE THAN LOVE
TO PROTECT HER
CHRISTMAS AT HOLLY WOOD
THEIR CHRISTMAS MIRACLE
SECOND CHANCES

Want a sneak peek at my most current series? Keep reading for a snippet from BABY BE MINE book one in my BLACKWELL BROTHERS SERIES.

Alec Blackwell opened the door to his townhouse to leave for work, but stopped abruptly when he spotted the woman standing on his tiny porch. "No soliciting."

"Oh, I'm not here to— I'm not selling anything. " The woman sounded nervous, her voice wobbling a bit as she spoke.

His grip tightened on his keys, and he searched the area behind her to make sure no one else was around. He'd recently watched a news story about women going up to doors pretending to need help while their armed cohorts waited for their moment to strike. Crime like that wasn't a thing on the relatively peaceful island or in Carolina Cove, but he supposed there was always the possibility. "What do you want?"

The woman opened her mouth and then closed it, her chest lifting as she took a shaky breath. She seemed to have some kind of mental debate going on while staring up at him from behind her cheap sunglasses.

The neighbor across from him watered his shrubs and side-eyed them, but Alec ignored the man. When he turned his attention back to the woman, he noted she'd removed the glasses to reveal wary, blue-green eyes.

"Are you Alec Blackwell?"

If she had to ask, she wasn't an islander.

Due to his family's gas and convenience store and generational residence on the island, those who knew, knew. "Depends. What do you want?"

"I'd like to talk to him—uh, you. It's important."

"Okay, so say whatever you have to say, but hurry it up. I have somewhere to be."

"It's not something I can just—" She broke off and paused a moment before lifting her chin. "Mr. Blackwell, I have something to tell you—give you—but before I do, I have...questions. Important ones."

He narrowed his gaze on the woman and took stock of her. About five –feet six, she had light-brown hair and lightly tanned skin with a dash of freckles across her nose, cheeks, and shoulders. She wore a faded red sundress and flip-flops and looked to be around thirty. "Look, this isn't a good time. If you have something to deliver, just give it to me so I can get to work."

Her mouth pinched, and she looked upset at his words, but with a shake of her head and flattening of her full lips, she stepped forward and lifted a baby carrier that had been set off to the side, one he hadn't noticed in his preoccupation with her and the fact it blended in with his one and only porch rocker.

Alec glanced at his watch just as his phone pinged. Head down, he checked the message from Brooks, the younger brother closest to him in age.

Allie's in labor. Ky said you're on your way. Get here NOW.

"Look, lady, I *really* have to go." He employed some great people, but either he or one of his brothers tried to be onsite during regular working hours. No one cared about a business as much as an owner did, but with Brooks out for baby delivery, and their younger brothers otherwise occupied with their regular jobs, he couldn't let the ball drop.

Alec glanced up just as the woman lowered the baby carrier to the ground at his feet.

"Your delivery," she said in a flat tone.

Alec didn't blink. "Excuse me?" Unadulterated shock rolled through him.

The woman pointed, and for the first time, Alec saw a note tucked into the carrier seat by the kid's leg.

Thank God. For a second there he'd thought—

"This isn't how I wanted to tell you, but you leave me little choice. She's yours. And so long as you're a decent human being, it means we need to discuss coparenting."

Coparenting? "Now wait a minute," he said, the panic he'd felt moments ago rocketing through him for a second time. "I don't know you, and I know for a fact we didn't have a kid together."

"Meggie Flannery," the woman said simply, tightly, with a lift of her stubborn-looking chin.

Alec stilled when he heard Meggie's name, but he quickly shook off the unease churning in his stomach. "What about her?"

THE BLACKWELL BROTHERS SERIES:

- BABY BE MINE
- SECOND CHANCE WEDDING
- THE GETAWAY GUY
- OFF-LIMITS LOVE
- FLIRTING WITH FOREVER

BABY BE MINE is available for pre-order! Grab it on my store October 23, 2023!

Or, get it November 6, 2023 everywhere else!

SIGN UP FOR KAY'S NEWSLETTER AND RECEIVE FREE BOOKS, UPDATES ON NEW RELEASES, CONTESTS, PRE-RELEASE BOOK INFORMATION, EXCLUSIVES AND MORE!

Your folks must be glad to see you.

KAY LYONS BOOKS

MONTANA SECRETS SERIES:

- HEALING HER COWBOY
- IT HAD TO BE YOU
- HERS TO KEEP
- MILLION DOLLAR STANDOFF
- HIS CHRISTMAS WISH
- THEIR SECRET SON

THE SEASIDE SISTERS SERIES:

- THE LAST GOODBYE
- LATTES AND LULLABYES
- MAP OF DREAMS
- WORTH THE RISK
- LOST LOVE FOUND

TAMING THE TULANES SERIES:

- SMALL TOWN SCANDAL

- THEIR SECRET BARGAIN
- CROSSING THE LINE
- THE NANNY'S SECRET
- SOMEONE TO TRUST

The Stone River Novels

- WORTH THE WAIT
- NOT BY SIGHT
- MORE THAN LOVE (FORMERLY THROUGH THE VALLEY)
- TO PROTECT HER (FORMERLY LEAD ME NOT)
- CHRISTMAS AT HOLLY WOOD
- THEIR CHRISTMAS MIRACLE
- SECOND CHANCES

SMALL TOWN SCANDALS SERIES:

- BRODY'S REDEMPTION
- FALLING FOR HER BOSS
- WITH THIS MAN

SECRET SANTA SERIES:

- SECRET SANTA
- SECRET SANTA II: A CHRISTMAS TO REMEMBER

MAKE ME A MATCH SERIES:

- ROMANCE RESET
- RULES OF ENGAGEMENT
- THE MATCHMAKER'S SECRET
- PERFECTLY MISMATCHED
- BY THE BOOK

**COMING SOON: (LINKS WILL BE UPDATED ASAP)
THE BLACKWELL BROTHERS SERIES:**

- BABY BE MINE
- SECOND CHANCE WEDDING
- THE GETAWAY GUY
- OFF-LIMITS LOVE
- FLIRTING WITH FOREVER

AUTHOR BIO

Kay Lyons always wanted to be a writer, ever since the age of seven or eight when she copied the pictures out of a Charlie Brown book and rewrote the story because she didn't like the plot. Through the years her stories have changed but one characteristic stayed true— they were all romances. Each and every one of her manuscripts included a love story.

Published in 2005 with Harlequin Enterprises, Kay's first release was a national bestseller. Kay has also been a HOLT Medallion, Book Buyers Best and RITA Award nominee. Look for her most recent novels with Kindred Spirits Publishing.

For more information regarding her work, please visit Kay at the following:

www.kaylyonsauthor.com

@KayLyonsAuthor (Twitter)

Kay Lyons Author (Facebook)

Author_Kay_Lyons (Instagram)

Kay Lyons, Author (Pinterest)

SIGN UP FOR KAY'S NEWSLETTER AND RECEIVE FREE

BOOKS, UPDATES ON NEW RELEASES, CONTESTS, PRE-RELEASE BOOK INFORMATION, EXCLUSIVES AND MORE!